BELOW THE BARREL

SALTWATER SPRINGS SERIES BOOK 2

TANISHA HEADLEY

This one is for anyone who has been given a second chance and for those who are still waiting for theirs.

CONTENT WARNINGS

Some details of the professional surfing world have been altered for your reading enjoyment.

To check content warnings for this book, scan the QR code above or visit tanishaheadley.com/content-warnings

PLAYLIST + QR CODE

Away From You – MC4D, zachy
We can't be friends (wait for your love) – Ariana Grande
Loved By You – Justin Biever, Burna Boy
Can We Pretend That We're Good? – Daniel Seavey
Locksmith – Sadie Jean
Ocean Eyes (Instrumental) – John Adams
My tears ricochet – Taylor Swift
Everywhere, Everything – Noah Kahan, Gracie Abrams
You're Losing Me (From The Vault) – Taylor Swift
BLEED – The Kid LAROI
The grudge – Olivia Rodrigo
Never knew a heart could break itself – Zach Hood
I wish you cheated – Alexander Stewart
Something to remember – Matt Hansen
Friction – Avery Lynch, Gatton
It's alright – Motel 7
Better off without me – Matt Hansen
Cherry – Harry Styles
No Mercy – Austin Giorgio
Ghost Town – Benson Boone

Useless information – Avery Lynch
It Only Cost Everything – Victor Ray
Friend – Gracie Abrams
Hollow – Victor Ray
Slow summer – Zachary Knowles
I miss you, I'm sorry – Gracie Abrams
NIGHTS LIKE THESE – Benson Boone
Before You – Benson Boone
I think you loved me – Noah Henderson
Hello Love – Benson Boone
Why me – Zevia
Love Of Mine – Benson Boone
1000 reasons – Caleb Hearn
Stargazing – Myles Smith
Klonopin – Caleb Hearn
Pretender – Thomas Day
Forget I Exist – Sam MacPherson
ROOM FOR 2 – Benson Boone
Two Places at Once – Haley Joelle
The Hardest Part – Olivia Dean, Leon Bridges
Love Me For The Both Of Us – CJ Fam
Fall into You – Daniel Seavey
Nothing Compares To You – Daniel Seavey
Dive – Olivia Dean
She Calls Me Back – Noah Kahan

WORLD SURF ASSOCIATION CHAMPIONSHIP TOUR INVITATION

We are thrilled to officially invite you to compete in the 2024 World Surf Association Championship Tour! This prestigious event brings together the world's most talented surfers, showcasing their skills on some of the most iconic and challenging waves across the globe. Your performance in recent competitions has earned you a coveted spot on the tour, and we are excited to watch you ride the waves to victory.

The 2024 Championship Tour will take you on an exhilarating journey through 10 spectacular locations, each offering its own unique and powerful surf. Below are the official tour stops for this season:

Lower Trestles - San Clemente, California, USA
Bells Beach - Victoria, Australia
Margaret River - Western Australia, Australia
Cloudbreak - Tavarua, Fiji
Saquarema - Rio de Janeiro, Brazil
Punta Roca - La Libertad, El Salvador
Teahupo'o - Tahiti, French Polynesia
Supertubos - Peniche, Portugal
Sunset Beach - Oahu, Hawaii
Banzai Pipeline - Oahu, Hawaii

As a competitor, you will not only test your abilities against the fiercest waves on the planet but also be part of a global community of surfers, all vying for the prestigious title of World Champion. This year's competition is sure to be one of the most thrilling and closely followed yet, with live coverage across major networks and streaming platforms.

We look forward to seeing you on the water and wish you the best of luck as you prepare for this incredible journey.

ONE

MALIAH | SALTWATER SPRINGS

THE SOUND of my heartbeat pounds in my ears, erratic and loud, echoing the chaos swirling through my mind. Tomorrow, I leave for the World Surf Championship Tour, and I couldn't be any less excited. I've looked forward to this moment my whole life, allowing the dream of making it here be the fuel that pushed me to work my ass off and earn this spot. Yet, as I sit across from Koa, my ex-boyfriend, teammate, and now tour-mate, I'm dreading what's to come.

Staring at him feels like someone has shoved my head underwater and is holding me under, preventing oxygen from getting into my lungs. I stupidly never considered the possi-bility that we would both earn a spot on the Championship Tour together, but that's exactly what's happened. I am going on tour with the one person who I can't bear to be around, the one person who I loved with everything in my being, the one person who ripped my heart out in a matter of seconds.

The world fades into a distant buzz, and Gabriel's voice becomes muffled as he talks about the surfing techniques we should focus on this year to push us through to the finals. But instead of listening and taking mental notes, a thousand thoughts race through my mind at once. Each thought clamouring for attention, yet not even one making any coherent sense as I stare at Koa.

He leans back in his chair, muscular arms crossed over his broad chest, stretching the fabric of his black long sleeve shirt. Dark strands of hair curtain his forehead as his grey eyes track Gabriel. He's sun kissed from our countless hours training in the sun, and he's put on more muscle since our split just over a year ago.

His eyes slide away from Gabriel and land on mine, causing my heart to painfully thud in my chest. My eyes widen momentarily, feeling both hyper-aware and strangely numb under his gaze. As I stare into his eyes, I'm caught between the desire to run away and the stubborn instinct to confront this uncomfortable situation head-on, but as I move to open my mouth, my words get stuck in my throat.

Tightness forms in my chest as he studies me, my breathing becoming shallow and even more erratic. I can't talk to him, not when my feelings are still so conflicted. Sure, I might have loved him once, but he broke my heart, and I can't forget that.

I can't forgive it either.

I've never cried over anyone in my life as much as I did for Koa after our breakup, and I refuse to let anyone else have the power to make me feel that way again. So instead, I do what I've done for the last year. I channel my sadness into anger and give him the dirtiest look that I can muster, before rolling my eyes and returning my attention to Gabriel.

It's best to keep Koa at a distance, for my own sake.

"I'll be flying in for most competitions, and we can jump on a video call for training sessions on the days I can't make it there," Gabriel says.

Gabriel is the coach for The Saltwater Shredders, the professional surf team that I've been a part of since my teen years. Despite Koa and I going on tour together for the next year, Gabriel can't join us for the whole tour because he still needs to train with the rest of the team here, in Saltwater Springs, and try to get them into qualifiers for next year's tour.

"How does the pairing situation work?" Koa asks, his deep voice vibrating through me and causing the hairs on my arm to stand.

"Every surfer will start off with a solo competition in California, and based on the results of that surf, you'll be paired with another surfer of similar skill level."

"So, what happens if we get paired with two other surfers, how will you coach us then?"

"You won't be paired with other surfers," Gabriel says simply, leaning against his oak desk and crossing his legs at the ankles.

His piercing blue eyes find mine and my hands start to tremble from my pent-up anger. I slide them under my thighs to try and hide my emotions.

"So, what you're saying then, is that no matter how many points we score or don't score, Koa and I will inevitably be paired together at the end of the day?" I muster enough courage to ask.

Gabriel grins. "Exactly. Think of this as an opportunity for you two to put whatever bullshit happened last year to rest. It's time you two learned how to work as a team again."

"And what happens if we can't?" I challenge.

"Then there won't be a spot for either of you on the team when you return from the tour."

My blood runs cold, and my eyes slide back to Koa who's eyeing Gabriel. I can't tell what he's thinking, his features schooled into a mask of indifference, but I, on the other hand, feel a tidal wave of emotions.

"You're going to kick us off the team because we won't be friends? Are you serious right now, Gabriel?" I ask, my voice shaking as I begin losing control of my emotions.

"Deadly," he says as his grin fades away and he meets my eyes with a warning look. "I'm not asking for you two to become friends. I'm asking for you both to figure out how to move past your shit and learn to work as a team again. That means no more ignoring each other, or getting upset when you're paired together during practice, or fighting."

I open my mouth to argue, but I'm cut off by Koa. "That shouldn't be too hard," he says, turning to look at me. "It's not like we haven't done it before."

I dig my fingers into my palm as I hold Koa's gaze.

That was before you obliterated my heart.

"Good," Gabriel says, slipping that forced grin back in place. "Have fun at your going away party tonight, and I'll see you both in the living room bright and early tomorrow morning."

Gabriel pushes himself from his desk and walks out of the meeting room without a word or second glance, leaving Koa and I alone. I keep my eyes fixed on the floor, refusing to meet his gaze, silently hoping he'll leave too.

I should know by now that hope is a useless thing to have.

Koa stands from his chair, shoving his hands into his shorts' pockets, and walks towards me. He comes to a stop when our shoes are mere centimetres apart, as his cologne causes my head to spin. He still wears the same cologne I bought for him all those years ago, the one that smells like lavender and rosemary blended with cedar wood and patchouli that creates an intoxicatingly addicting scent.

"What?" I grind out, raising my eyes to his.

His eyes sparkle with mischief as he stares down at me. "Are you excited?"

"Ecstatic," I reply dryly, crossing my arms over my chest.

"Oh, come on Maliah, you can do better than that," he says in a low voice.

My heart betrays me once again with its erratic thudding as

I stare up at him. The fact that his voice alone has this effect on me is enough proof that I'm totally screwed. How is it possible to still be so damn affected by him after everything he's done? And how do I survive the next year, fighting our attraction while spending almost every waking moment together?

"Oh, believe me, I'm well aware that I can do better." I look him up and down with a bored expression before standing up and confidently leaving him behind in the meeting room.

For a brief moment I feel strong and powerful, as if my words cut him as deeply as his actions cut me, but it doesn't take long for the doubt to creep back in. I told him I could do better, but do I believe that?

Deep down I know that I deserve better. I deserve someone who respects me, who cherishes me, who doesn't betray my trust. So why can't I let him go? Am I doomed to a lifetime of reliving the memory of what Koa and I once were, before it all went to shit?

I clench my jaw as I stomp my way up the stairs and into my room, slamming the door behind me, and throwing myself onto my bed next to my half-packed suitcase. He ruined love for me, and now it feels like he's going to ruin surfing for me too.

He ruins everything.

"YOU HAVE TO TEXT US EVERY DAY," KAIRI, MY BEST FRIEND AND teammate, says.

Her naturally tanned complexion glows under the bar lights at our local beach bar, The Kooky Coconut, while her hair stops just past her shoulders, curls framing her face. Her hazel eyes track my every move, my every expression. I've learned that if anyone is going to know that I'm hurting, it's her. She is too attentive for her own good.

"And a video call at least once a week," Eliana adds.

Eliana is the social media manager for The Saltwater Shredders and my best friend. She joined our team about four months ago and although she had a rocky start with Griffin, previous surfer turned youth team coach, they quickly warmed up to each other and are now exclusively dating.

Her brown hair falls past her shoulders in thick waves and her ivory complexion, along with her freckles, make her green eyes pop. She's drop dead gorgeous, and I'd be lying if I said I never worried about Koa taking an interest in her because of how perfect she is, but I quickly learned she only had eyes for Griffin.

I laugh as I wrap my hand around my glass, swallowing past the building emotion.

"I'll try my best," I say. "I don't know how busy this tour will make us, but I'll try to text you guys at least once a day."

Eliana gasps before reaching out and gripping onto Kairi's arm with wide eyes. "She said *us*. I'm not imagining it, right? She said *us* to refer to her and Koa."

I roll my eyes and bring the paper straw of my strawberry daiquiri to my lips and take a long sip while her and Kairi giggle together like children.

"Is there an *us* when it comes to you and Koa?" Kairi asks.

"There was, once upon a time, but not anymore," I mumble with the straw in my mouth.

They both release an exaggerated huff. "I'll never understand why you guys don't just give your relationship another go. It's obvious that you two still love each other," Kairi says.

I lower my glass back to the table and turn to face them both.

"It's more complicated than that. Too much has happened between us to be able to move past it and try again."

"Like what?" Eliana pushes.

Silence descends upon our table as I stare at them both with my lips pressed together. I haven't shared the details with anyone about why Koa and I broke up. Experiencing that pain once was more than enough for me and I refuse to experience the emotions again just to explain the situation to somebody.

"It doesn't matter, it won't change anything." I turn towards Kairi. "Plus, you're wrong. He doesn't still love me."

She lifts an eyebrow. "Is that so?"

I roll my lips and close my eyes while I nod. "I'm afraid so."

"Then can you explain why his eyes haven't left you all night?" She juts her chin out, signalling that I look over my shoulder.

I blink at her once before turning my head and glancing behind me, my eyes instantly finding Koa's. He sits at the bar with the rest of the guys, but instead of joining in on their conversation, he has his back to the bar as he faces me.

He's wearing a black dress shirt and pants. Ever since we broke up, he's purged his closet of colour, choosing to wear black as if every day were a funeral. Going for a moody bad boy vibe, I assume.

I meet his gaze for a few seconds before turning back to face the girls, my cheeks growing warmer with each second. Avoiding their questioning eyes, I shrug and take another sip of my drink. I've caught Koa staring at me probably as many times as he's caught me, but I don't let myself think anything of it. It's hard enough living together and surfing on the same team, I don't need to fill my head with pointless theories over his staring.

So quit the team and move out.

It's a thought that's bounced around my mind for nearly a year. If I hadn't been with The Saltwater Shredders since I was seventeen, I would've quit months ago, but the team has become a family to me and the thought of leaving and never seeing them again, all because of a stupid guy, has always stopped me from acting on that thought.

Sure, every time I see Koa, or breathe his cologne in, or hear his voice, I feel like somebody has thrown a handful of daggers at my chest. But seeing Kairi, Eliana, and the rest of the team has made that pain bearable.

"I really thought you two were back on speaking terms after The Cove party," Kairi says, busying herself with the wrapper of her straw.

A few months ago, Gabriel left us for the weekend to go visit Zalea. She's the older sister of our teammate, Zale, and also in a situationship with Gabriel. Zalea used to be part of The Saltwater Shredders but decided to leave the team and go solo a few years back.

In Gabriel's absence, we may have thrown a beach bonfire party at our local private beach, The Cove. It was such a great party up until Griffin's criminal ex-girlfriend showed up and sprinkled her bad luck all over the place. Eliana and one of my teammates, Colton, were thrown into the freezing ocean when the old boat dock broke apart beneath them.

Not only did they almost drown, but Colton needed CPR. The events from that whole night freaked me out too much to sleep, so I'd gone to the kitchen sometime around two in the morning to get a glass of warm milk in hopes that it would put me to sleep. I hadn't expected to run into Koa already pouring himself a glass. One look at me and he was pulling out a second one from the cupboard, pouring the steaming milk into it and then sliding the glass towards me.

We'd sat in silence, side by side at the kitchen island, for thirty minutes while we drank from our glasses. It reminded me of when we were still together, staying up late and being each other's comfort.

When the exhaustion had started to hit, I'd stood up and walked toward the stairs only to find that Koa was right behind me, also heading up. When I stopped in front of my room door, I glanced over my shoulder to find him watching me. His eyes spoke volumes, more than words ever could, but I couldn't handle it. I quickly hurled myself into my bedroom and slammed the door shut behind me.

"Well, you thought wrong."

I bring the straw back to my lips and chug the rest of my drink, ignoring the blinding pain of brain freeze, before slamming it down on the table and sliding out of our booth. I turn to face Kairi and Eliana, both watching me with rounded eyes.

"Enough about that," I say, forcing a smile, "let's go throw darts. I finally got my hands on the mug shots of Eli's stalkers."

Eliana perks up in her chair, eyebrows raised. "Alex and Meghan?"

Alex is Eliana's ex-childhood friend who was currently serving time in prison for blackmailing her. Meghan, on the other hand, is Griffin's ex girlfriend. She kind of lost her mind and almost killed the guy, then tried to ruin Eliana's life. She's in a psych ward getting the treatment she desperately needs.

"Yup!"

"How did you get your hands on those?" Kairi asks, suspicion coating her features.

I look at my nails innocently. "It doesn't matter, let's go."

"I can't," Kairi stares at her glass with a pinched expression.

"What?" I whine. "Why not?"

Eliana clears her throat and nods toward the dart board. I glance in the same direction only to find Zale and Colton in a heated game of darts. They both look about ready to rip each other's heads off.

When Colton returned to The Saltwater Shredders a month ago, after ditching us for The Rip Raiders one town over, we didn't exactly give him the warmest welcome. But most of us have forgiven him for leaving, except Zale. Though I feel like his hatred toward Colton is more to do with Kairi than anything. They're both into her but too afraid to actually pursue anything.

I groan as I look back at the girls. "Okay, we're clearly too sober for this. I'm going to get us shots."

"Please, no tequila," Eliana cries out when I turn my back to the table.

I snort as I walk towards the bar and do my absolute best to ignore the way my body reacts when I come to stand next to Koa, whose eyes haven't left me this entire time. I order our vodka shots and impatiently tap my fingers on the bar top as I wait, but when Koa silently turns to face me in his stool, I feel my body tense up.

"What?" I grunt, refusing to look at him.

"Are you still afraid of heights?"

I turn to look at him and all the oxygen in my lungs disappears as I realize how close we are to each other. He sits at the edge of his bar stool, leaning closer to me with one hand propped on the bar, holding his glass of water.

It should be illegal to look as good as he does. I'm convinced he could wear a garbage bag and I'd still be turned on.

"Yes, why?" I squint my eyes at him.

"Because in less than twelve hours we'll be on Gabriel's private plane," Koa says, his eyes slowly burning a path down my body. "When was the last time you were on a plane?"

I gulp as I watch his eyes continue their tortuous journey down my body, a smirk forming on his face when his eyes pause on my hard nipples poking through my tight T-shirt. Of all days to not wear a bra, it had to be tonight. I mentally kick myself.

"It's been a few years, but I'm sure I'll be fine."

"Might be a good idea for you to buy Gravol before we leave tomorrow. It'll help put you to sleep for most of the flight."

I scoff before returning my attention to the bartender, who walks over with a small tray holding three full shot glasses.

"If I wanted your advice," I say, as I pick up the tray, "I would have asked."

I pin him with a cold stare, my heart thudding painfully as I watch the smirk fade from his face. I hate being mean to him, but it's the only way to make sure I don't cave and give him another chance. I turn around, my long blonde hair swishing behind me as I walk back to the girls.

I DRAPE MY ARM OVER MY EYES, FOCUSED ON DEEP BREATHING AS the plane hits turbulence for the third time in the last thirty minutes. Each time it happens, I get an irrational fear that the plane blew its motor, or another crucial part broke and we're about to nosedive straight into oblivion.

"You doing okay over there?" Gabriel asks from the seat next to mine, separated by the narrow aisle.

"Yup," I mumble, "couldn't be better."

"Right, well, I'm going to go check on the pilot and find out how much longer we have until we arrive in California."

I hear the leather of his seat groan as he stands up, his heavy footsteps fading as he moves toward the cockpit.

When we hit another bout of turbulence five minutes later, I'm certain that I'll puke from sheer fear. I stand up on wobbly legs, glancing at Koa who faces me in his seat fast asleep. He's wearing all black, as usual, with his hood on and hands in his pocket while he sleeps peacefully.

Must be nice to sleep through this anxiety-inducing plane ride.

I take a deep breath and make my way to the plane's restroom, gently closing the folding door behind me. I turn to face myself in the mirror and note my pale sweaty appearance.

Great.

Not only do I feel like absolute shit, but I also look like it too while on the plane with the hottest guy on the planet.

Not that I care what he thinks of me.

I splash some water on my face and then dry away the moisture with a paper towel. I should've listened to Koa last night and made sure I bought myself a pack of Gravol before flying today. It would've been so much easier if I could just sleep through this whole flight like he is. With a deep sigh, I exit the tiny room and make my way back to my seat.

Before I sit down, a small bottle on my food tray catches my attention. It wasn't there when I left to go to the restroom. I pick it up and read the label as I sit down.

Gravol.

My eyes slide towards Koa who is in the same position as how I left him, hands tucked into his hoodie pocket as he sleeps. I study him, trying to find any sign that he's awake, but his consistent slow breathing convinces me that he's asleep. Gabriel's flight attendant must have dropped it off.

When the turbulence hits once more I don't think twice about taking the Gravol. I sit back and recline my chair to get comfortable. Within minutes, my eyelids grow heavy, and the last thing I see before everything goes black are grey eyes staring back at me.

TWO

KOA | SAN CLEMENTE, CALIFORNIA, USA

"I KNOW you probably don't see a point in trying your hardest in today's individual surf, but the points still count towards the championship title, so make sure you're putting one hundred percent into how you surf today," Gabriel says as our driver pulls into Trestles Beach.

The Lower Trestles is our first wave on the World Surf Championship Tour and one of the easiest and safest surf spots on the itinerary. In today's competition, surfers will be paired based on their overall points, aside from Maliah and I. Regardless of how we score today, Gabriel has already pulled strings to ensure we're paired together. It's all part of his master plan to get Maliah and I back onto speaking terms.

"Whatever," Maliah grumbles from beside me.

She's looking a lot better than she did on the plane ride here. The Gravol I gave her knocked her out almost instantly, and she was able to sleep through the rest of the flight without a care in the world about the constant turbulence.

I, on the other hand, refused to sleep the whole flight down. I'm positive the pilot was new because I've never been on a flight that had me fearing for my life, until now. I had to make sure I was awake in case the plane nosedived, and I had to be the one to save Maliah from drowning in her sleep.

"I'm serious. A single point can be the difference between a World Champion and a loser." Gabriel runs a nervous hand through his hair, his brows pulled together as he stares at Maliah.

"Don't worry, Gabriel." She frowns at him as she sinks into her seat with crossed arms. "I didn't come this far just to lose."

"Good." He sits back in his seat with a satisfied smile and looks out the window as the driver parks the car and opens our doors.

After climbing out, I hold my hand to help Maliah exit the car, but she swats my hand away and climbs out on her own, brushing past me wordlessly. I stare at her back as she walks away and feel a familiar ache grow in my chest.

Maliah and I are from two different worlds.

Where she grew up in a high-class, wealthy family, I grew up in a low-class, low income one. I knew from the very first day that I didn't deserve her. That someone with my upbringing could never be good enough to keep a girl like her in my life.

I join her and Gabriel on the sand as we stare at the Surf-Flix camera crew setting up. Not only are we competing for first place in every competition, but each of us will also be followed by a camera crew, recording everything that happens behind the scenes.

"Do you have any tips to share for Lower Trestles, Gabriel?" I ask, turning to face him.

"Lower Trestles makes the perfect wave, it almost looks fake, but it's an easy wave to break and should be a piece of cake for you both to surf."

"Perfect," Maliah says quietly.

We continue to watch the camera crew set up until a producer approaches us. Her dark hair is tied back in a ponytail and loops through her baseball cap. She chews her gum obnoxiously as she looks down at her clipboard.

"Name?" she asks, tapping her pen on the paper.

"Koa."

"Do you have a last name, Koa?"

"Foster."

I watch as she checks off my name on her list and shuffles over to Maliah, asking her similar questions until she finds her name and checks her off.

"Follow me."

We both glance at Gabriel who just shrugs and follows the producer towards the camera crew. I follow his lead and shake the hands of everyone there, Maliah following suit.

"This is your assigned camera crew. They'll split up into teams of five and follow you individually whenever you're not together," the producer says, her Bronx accent more noticeable now.

"Thanks, Jackie," a tall, slender man with sandy blond hair and brown eyes says as he smiles at her. "My name is David, I'm the headman for this team. If you have any feedback you want to share with me about the team over the next year, I'm your guy. How about we get started filming your intros?"

"Sure," I reply cooly, not missing how his eyes roam over Maliah with too much interest.

Within seconds, we're split up into our separate crews, shaking hands with each person and posing for B-Roll shots with the ocean behind us.

"You should smile, girls love a guy with a nice smile," Vincent, the cameraman, says.

He's a short Italian man with a staring problem. I roll my eyes and force a half smile while he circles around me. I'm not a fan of the idea that we'll be recorded for the next year, but it was either that or drop out of the tour, and I wasn't going to leave Maliah to do this without me.

I stare past my team to where Maliah stands with David, twirling her golden hair around her finger as she laughs halfheartedly. My fist clenches as I watch, recognizing that she always plays with her hair when a guy makes her uncomfortable. As much as I want to run over there and tell him to fuck off, I know that will only piss her off. Maliah can handle herself in this situation, so I bite my tongue and continue with the rest of the shoot, but by the end of it, I'm quieter than usual as I stew in my annoyance.

"I will never get used to this." Maliah groans as we rejoin Gabriel, who's been on his phone for most of the time.

"Well, you better learn because it's only going to get worse from here."

He's always been the blunt, tell it how it is, type of guy and I respect him for it. Maliah rolls her eyes before glancing at me.

"You're awfully quiet."

"Is that satire?" I smirk as I look down at her.

"Quieter than normal," she corrects.

I hold her gaze as my smirk fades away. I wish I could tell her how seeing her put into situations where she has no choice but to speak to people who make her uncomfortable makes me angry. It's one of the reasons I fought so hard last season to make sure I'd be here with her.

But I don't tell her that. I don't, because I know it'll just push her further away from me. We broke up because I'm not good enough for her. I can't drag her back in, she deserves someone better. Someone who makes her happier than I ever could. Someone who can take care of her better than I ever would.

Maliah deserves the best, but that isn't me.

I tear my gaze from her eyes and watch as the other surfers, who are leaving their introduction filming, begin introducing themselves to one another.

"I think we should go say hi," I say.

"You didn't answer my question."

"I don't believe you asked a question, Maliah."

I begin walking towards the slowly growing group of surfers, leaving her standing in the sand behind me. The last thing I want to do is leave her side, but I don't want to lie to her either, the worst thing I could do for us both is telling her how much I still love her.

"Well, look-y here. If it isn't the famous Koa Foster," a blond guy around my age says. "My name is Charles."

He holds his hand out for me to shake and I begrudgingly do, forcing a smile to rival his own.

"Nice to meet you, Charles. Is that a French accent you've got?"

"Oui," he replies, his lips curling into a smirk.

"Koa, I saw your qualifying surf, and man, I was so impressed," a slim, dark-haired guy with an Australian accent says from beside Charles. "I'm Reese."

"Nice to meet you, Reese," I say, shaking his hand, "and thanks."

He smiles kindly before his eyes catch on something, or someone, behind me. I let go of his hand and glance over my shoulder only to find Maliah approaching the group.

"Back in my country, we'd call her a *magnifique femme*," Charles says breathlessly.

I don't blame him. Maliah has this special charm about her that attracts everybody. It's not just her looks, though her blue eyes and golden hair are breathtaking, it's how she carries herself too. Her elegance and confidence exude from her, and anyone within a twenty-foot radius of her can't help but watch in awe.

Me included.

"Hi," she says with a quick wave as she studies each person here.

"Bonjour," Charles says, pushing past me until he comes to

a stop in front of her and begins to lower his lips to the back of her hand.

It takes one look at her uncomfortable smile for my resolve to break. I take a step so that I'm standing next to Charles and causing Maliah to look up at me.

"Hey, babe," I say in a dangerously low voice.

Charles freezes with his lips inches from her skin before rearing back as if she slapped him. He looks between me and her as I pick up the hand he dropped and bring it to my lips, placing a gentle kiss on her soft skin as I stare into her eyes.

The rich blue colour reminds me of the ocean and the blue sky. Deep and endless. The flecks of light and dark shades of blue add depth to her eyes and completely captivate me. Her eyes have always had a way of drawing me in, making me feel like I'm the only person in the world under her gaze, like it doesn't matter where I come from or who my parents are.

Staring into her eyes makes me feel like I'm enough.

Even though I'm not.

Her lips part slightly, and I let my eyes drop down to them as I gently pull away from her hand. The pink plumpness drawing me in almost as much as her eyes. What I would do to be able to feel them against mine one more time.

I look down at our hands, my eyes snagging on her arms covered in goosebumps. I lift my eyes back to hers and see the moment she realizes she's been staring too long. Her back snaps straight before she walks past me and introduces herself to everyone else in the group.

"She's your girl?" Charles asks.

I clench my jaw before turning to face him with a forced smirk.

"Wouldn't you like to know." I wink before walking towards the others and introducing myself after Maliah.

"THE RESULTS OF THIS COMPETITION WILL DETERMINE YOUR partner for the remainder of your time here. So, if I were you, I'd surf with absolutely everything I have," the Surf Sports Official shouts over the sound of the roaring waves.

I stand in between Charles and Reese as we face the ocean. It's been a long day of waiting for my turn but it's finally here. I plan to surf the best I can today, even though I know I'll be assigned to Maliah regardless, to put some fear into Charles.

I just met the guy, but I don't like him. He's more invested in the girls here than he is about the tour itself. The Official holds a small BB gun into the air and begins to count down, so I position myself better and wait for the sound of the gunshot before I sprint towards the ocean, surfboard tucked under my arm.

The coolness of the water sends a chill up my spine, but as soon as the water reaches my knees, I throw down my board and hop on, using all my strength to paddle further out. I reach the lineup first and face the horizon, waiting for the perfect wave to swell, and it doesn't take long for me to spot one.

I turn my board, facing the shore, and begin paddling again so that I'm just ahead of the breaking lip, but Charles has the same idea as he begins to desperately paddle beside me. I don't let him distract me.

We both stand on our boards just as the wave lifts us up and shoots us forward, allowing us to drop in with the nose of our boards facing downwards at an angle. To my surprise, the wave splits right in between Charles and I, and he takes off in the opposite direction. I return my focus to my own wave and bend my knees so that I can get more momentum as I begin to carve through it.

Once I've reached the right amount of speed, I complete a bottom turn at the base of the wave to begin executing as many maneuvers as I'm able to, before jumping off next to my board as the wave falls away.

"Dude," Reese exclaims, his eyes wide and his hands holding his head as he stares at me, "that was crazy. I've never seen anyone do that much in a single wave."

I chuckle to myself as I come up next to him on the lineup just as another wave begins to swell.

"You should catch that if you want a decent partner." I nod in the wave's direction.

"Fingers crossed it's Maliah." He winks at me playfully before paddling off to surf his wave.

"That little shit," I mumble to myself as I watch him pull off a decent aerial.

I glance toward the beach and search with my eyes until I find Maliah next to Gabriel. She's stretching with her headset on, intently watching each surfer's performance as if she's taking mental notes.

She probably is.

I've never met anyone as dedicated to winning as Maliah is, and that dedication comes paired with an obsession to learn her opponents' weaknesses and strengths from the inside and out. Her eyes move to mine and she holds my gaze momentarily, my heart ricocheting in my chest, before she turns to Gabriel to say something.

This year I plan to win her back, even if it's just as a friend. I can't imagine a life without Maliah in it, in any capacity, and because of that I know that if we both get kicked off The Saltwater Shredders team, she'll disappear for good.

I catch a few more waves before our heat finishes, and I paddle back to the shore with the rest of the surfers. We were the last group to surf for the males and now the last female group is next, Maliah's group.

When the water is shallow enough, I slide from my board and walk the rest of the way, tucking it under my arm. When my feet touch dry sand, I shake out my wet hair before sliding a hand through it and slicking it backward.

A chorus of wistful sighs catches my attention, and I look up to find a large group of the female surfers watching me with glazed eyes. I swear one of the girls is even drooling. Just behind them I spot my camera crew recording the girls and my reaction and I can't help but roll my eyes and make my way to where Maliah and Gabriel stand.

"Looks like you've got yourself a fan club," Maliah says, holding my towel out for me to take.

I smirk and lean forward so that we're eye level, watching as her eyes slowly peruse my face and pause on my lips before rising back to my eyes.

"Jealous?" My smirk grows into a grin when she rolls her eyes instead of answering me.

Is she jealous?

It doesn't matter, you're not enough.

My voice of reason extinguishes any flame of hope her reaction gave me and I find myself standing up straight and taking the towel from her.

"Thanks," I mutter before throwing it over my head and rub my hair dry.

"What was that?"

I lift the towel from one of my eyes to peek at her and confirm she's talking to me, her ocean eyes piercing right through mine.

"What was what?"

She lifts her finger and waves it in my face in a circular motion. "That look. You went from a goofy smile to suddenly straight faced. What were you thinking about?"

For the second time today, I find myself staring into her eyes with the truth sitting at the tip of my tongue, but as usual, I swallow my words and drop the towel back over my face so that I can continue drying my hair.

"The fact that there are cameras recording my every expression right now." It's not necessarily a lie; I'm uncomfortably aware of their presence following me.

"Right." She doesn't sound convinced, but she also knows now isn't the time to push for answers.

I slide the towel so that it drapes over my shoulders behind my neck, and I watch as she picks up her freshly waxed bright pink surfboard. She recently had it custom made by our team board shaper, after some green haired goblin of a woman tripped her at a competition a few months ago, and caused her to break her favourite board.

She checks her ankle strap twice, takes a deep breath, and straightens her back as she walks towards the remaining surfers lined up by the Surf Sports Official. Within minutes, the BB gun is shot into the air and the girls are sprinting into the ocean, Maliah leading the way. As she furiously paddles towards the lineup spot, I turn to face Gabriel.

"Did you actually rig it so that we'd be paired together, despite our rating?"

He turns to look at me with calculated eyes. I watch as he contemplates his answer before he returns his attention to Maliah.

"No," he says, sliding his hands into his pants pockets. "I was just trying to take some of the pressure off you guys. I remember how nerve-wracking the first competition on tour can be."

His answer shouldn't surprise me, it's a typical thing for Gabriel to do, but it leaves my blood running cold because that means Maliah might actually end up paired with someone other than me. I whip my head up to the scoreboard and see that I currently hold the highest ranking for the men, which means I'll be paired with the highest-ranked woman.

I push my way to the front of the crowded beach and search until I find her paddling after a wave, while another girl paddles closely behind, chasing the same wave. I cup my hands around my mouth and do something I will probably regret later.

"Give it your best, Maliah," I shout.

She raises her head when she hears me, and I watch as her brows raise slightly before she refocuses herself and drops into the wave first at the perfect moment. She cuts through the face of the wave and absolutely crushes the maneuvers. That wave alone is most definitely worth enough points to have her ranked highest for the females, but I refuse to get my hopes up so instead I continue to cheer her on as she surfs her final wave.

When she handles that one perfectly, I'm satisfied enough to return to Gabriel who is smirking as he watches me approach.

"That was cute," he says.

"Shut up, no one else here can surf as well as she can, and I intend to win," I say defensively.

"Mhm," he mumbles with an annoyingly smug smirk as he watches her paddle to the shore along with the rest of the women from her heat.

When she reaches us, I hold out her towel for her and she wordlessly takes it and wraps her hair up before I pass her another towel for her body. Within minutes, we hear music play as images on the digital scoreboard begin to fly around the screen until a picture of my face lights up the screen for first place male ranking, followed by a picture of Maliah's for women's first place ranking. The words *Team One* float above our pictures and I feel a warmth spread in my chest.

That warmth quickly turns ice cold as Maliah turns to look at Gabriel and I over her shoulder, pinning us with frosty eyes that cause the hairs on my arms and the back of my neck to rise. Without a word, she picks up her board and marches over to the car that will take us to our hotel. I watch as the driver takes her surfboard and opens the door for her before securing the board to the top of the car.

Gabriel whistles beside me. "Looks like you've got your work cut out for you, bud," he says before walking towards the car.

I mumble a few choice words for him under my breath before I pick up my board and follow him. He's not wrong. She isn't going to make this year easy for me one bit, but I refuse to give up this time.

THE COOL AIR FROM MY AIR-CONDITIONED HOTEL ROOM FEELS amazing after being out in the hot sun for most of the day. In five minutes, I'll have to go back out there to join Gabriel and Maliah along with the rest of the tour attendees for a welcome dinner.

I stand in front of the mirror, staring at my all-black outfit: black dress pants, a black dress shirt, and an uncomfortably tight black bow tie. I've been wearing black for over a year now, ever since Maliah broke up with me. Every time I attempt to wear colour, I'm overwhelmed with memories of her, and I can't bear the pain. Black is the only colour I can handle wearing, because it's the only colour she hates and the only colour I never wore while we were dating. It reminds her of her mother's funeral, and it's been off-limits for her since day one.

With a sigh, I walk over to my queen-sized bed and fall back onto it so that I can stare up at the smooth ceiling. Maliah always loved that I still had both of my parents in my life. She always told me I had no idea how lucky I was. But even that wasn't enough to keep her by my side.

A knock at my door has me bolting upright and readjusting my bowtie before grabbing my hotel key card off the dresser and walking out into the hallway where Gabriel waits. He's wearing a white dress shirt and navy dress pants.

"At least one of you is ready on time," Gabriel mutters as he looks me up and down and then glares at the door across from mine.

We wait five more minutes before Gabriel's impatience wins, and he knocks on Maliah's hotel room door again, more aggressively. I hear her curse on the other end before the door swings open and she steps out.

My breath is sucked right out of my lungs as I take her in. She's wearing a fiery red dress that hugs her body in all the right places. Her blonde hair is curled and pinned to one side of her head, falling over her shoulder. She's painted her lips with a red lipstick to match her dress, and her eyes are lined with a black liner, causing her blue eyes to stand out even more. My eyes trail down her body once more, unable to look away.

She clears her throat, and my eyes snap back up to hers only to find her watching me with a knowing smirk.

Fuck. This girl is going to be the death of me.

She raises her chin high and walks past me, her ass swishing side to side as she goes, my eyes hypnotized by the sight. It's only until Gabriel smacks my chest that I begin breathing again and tear my eyes away from her.

"You've got it bad." Gabriel snickers before making his way after Maliah towards the elevator.

I swallow back the drool that had pooled in my mouth and follow him, keeping my eyes glued to the floor the whole elevator ride down. When the doors open, our camera crew is waiting for us, and the cameramen quickly start their cameras and begin following behind us, as we make our way toward the outdoor terrace where the welcome dinner is being held.

Low background music can be heard as we enter the space, and all eyes turn toward us as we enter. The female surfers give Maliah a once over before their predatory gazes find me and I physically feel the energy in the room shift. The male surfers don't even spare a glance my way as their eyes track Maliah's every move, and I can't blame them. Of all the women here tonight, she's the most beautiful. Though I'm certain she could wear anything, and I'd still stand by that statement.

We make our way to the last three available seats at the long rectangular table and Gabriel grabs the first seat, leaving the last two chairs for Maliah and me, forcing us to sit side by side for the first time in months. She freezes and stares at the chairs, curling her hand into a fist, before begrudgingly taking the middle seat between Gabriel and me.

I lower myself into my seat and spare her a sideways glance as she lifts her wine glass to her lips and drinks the whole glass in one go. A nearby waiter quickly walks over and tops up her glass, which she brings to her lips again.

"Woah there," I hear Gabriel mumble to her as he places a finger to the rim of her glass and forces her to lower it back down to the table. "Let's try to avoid getting shit faced on the first night."

The minute he turns his head away from her, she picks up the glass and chugs its contents again. I watch as the waiter returns and refills it. The night carries on this way until the end of dinner, and while Gabriel decides to retire to his room shortly after, I'm stuck at the table, keeping an eye on a very tipsy Maliah.

"So, mon chéri, how long have you and Koa been together?" I hear Charles ask.

I lift my gaze from my plate to find that he's taken Gabriel's spot next to her at the table. Maliah barks out a laugh as she shoots me a displeased look over her shoulder before returning her attention back to Charles.

"Koa? I barely know him."

Her words cut deep, as usual, but I force the ache down and snake my hand up her thigh. She gasps at the contact and turns to look at me when I gently squeeze. Her eyes are lust-filled but the frown she's pasted on her face shows me just how mixed her emotions are. I lean towards her, stopping when my lips are right next to her ear.

"Really?" I purr. "I thought we knew each other very well at one point."

I watch as goosebumps crawl their way down her arms, and she visibly shivers. I pull away, just far enough to look her in her eyes with a knowing smirk. Even though I know she wants nothing to do with me, seeing how responsive her body still is fills me with a stupid amount of happiness.

I watch as she swallows before plastering the fakest smile on her face and placing her hand atop mine on her thigh.

"I think we can both agree that we're both very different from the people that we once were."

With that, she tightens her grip around my hand, yanks her thigh out of my grasp, and throws my arm back at me before turning her attention back to Charles with a flirtatious giggle. I stare at the back of her head for a moment, the rejection stinging, before I clear my throat and return my focus to my half empty plate. Any plans I had on finishing my dinner tonight are gone as I shove it away, a bitter taste in my mouth.

THREE

MALIAH | VICTORIA, AUSTRALIA

THE LONG PLANE ride to Australia was enough to convince me that I never need to come back to this country ever again. I had taken a Gravol at the start of the flight, but it had already worn off by the time I woke up. With eight hours left in the flight, and Koa in the way of my carry-on, I decided to bear through it. It probably wasn't the smartest idea, given how sick to my stomach I feel right now, but I refuse to speak to him.

Being around him for the next year is already going to be hard enough for me, but hearing the confirmation that we're paired together, all because of Gabriel, is the final straw. I've done my best to avoid him as much as I can over the last year; to push him away and hope the love I still feel towards him follows suit. But the way he looked at me at our welcome dinner the other night, and the way his hand felt against my thigh caused my heart to beat harder than ever before.

It was proof enough that I still love him and that makes me even angrier to have to be around him when I'm trying so hard to move on.

"Looks like this is your room," the hotel property owner of

our temporary accommodations in Victoria says as he passes me my key card.

"Thank you," I reply, taking it from him.

"And this," he says, turning toward the door across from mine, "is your room."

I watch in horror as he gives Koa his key card and drops our suitcases to the ground before leaving us in the hallway alone.

"Great." I huff, snatching my suitcase away from his vicinity. "Another place where I'm forced to see you."

I see the flash of hurt cross his face as he stares back at me, but I don't allow the guilt to creep in as I swipe my key card against my door and barrel into my room, slamming the door behind me. I press my back against the door and close my eyes, steadying my breathing until I hear his door close too.

I don't enjoy hurting him. I know that he still has feelings for me, despite the fact that he broke up with me, but it's the only way to keep that barrier up between us. I'm scared that if I'm nice, I'll open the door on our relationship and let him back in. I promised myself during one of my pity party cry fest nights that I would never let him back in.

The vibration of my phone pulls me out of my thoughts. I push myself from the door and search for it in my purse, pulling it out to see Gabriel's name written across the screen.

GABRIEL:

Meet me in the lobby. Training starts today.

I groan as I stare at the text, letting my head fall back so that I'm staring up at the ceiling. After a nearly twenty-four-hour flight, all I want to do is take a quick shower and sleep away the rest of the day.

MALIAH:

I think I'm going to skip today's training. I feel
a bit sick from the flight.

GABRIEL:

> There are no sick days on tour. See you in five minutes.

I clench my jaw as I stare down at his message. I have no idea how Zalea puts up with Gabriel's tough guy façade, it pisses me off. If he wasn't such a good coach, I would have been long gone.

Tossing my suitcase down, I zip it open and begin digging through my clothes until I find one of my workout sets. I quickly strip down and throw on the olive-green leggings and matching sports bra, before sliding my feet into my gym shoes and tying my hair back into a low bun. I grab my phone, key card, and water bottle before exiting my room only to find Koa leaving his room in his own workout clothing.

"I'm guessing Gabriel texted you too?" he mumbles.

I let out another frustrated sigh and, without a word, stomp down the hall towards the lobby, Koa in tow. When we reach the lobby, Gabriel is pacing around with a scowl on his face and his phone pressed to his ear. When he spots us, he hangs up and approaches us.

"I might get an important call during training that will require me to leave early, so let's try to get as much done as we can in the meantime," he grumbles.

Koa and I follow him down the hall and towards the empty onsite gym. He swipes his key card and unlocks the door to let us in. The hotel's gym is impressive with its high ceilings and large windows that flood the room with bright sunlight. It doesn't smell like a gym either, instead a fresh scent of eucalyptus subtly floats in the air.

I make my way inside, Koa following closely behind, and find a bench to toss my belongings on. The modern machines are organized impeccably around the room, practically glistening, and many of the machines have large screens with virtual workout options on display.

"Wow," I whisper as I slowly turn in a circle, my eyes bouncing from the machines to the free weights, and separate rooms for yoga and spinning.

"It's a bit of an upgrade from Saltwater Springs' gym." Gabriel smirks.

"That's an understatement," Koa says, dropping his things next to mine on the bench.

"Alright," Gabriel clears his throat, "we only have an hour, so let's get started."

Over the next forty-five minutes, Gabriel has us doing deadlifts, bench presses, and weighted bar squats. Normally, this would be a piece of cake for me, except for the fact that he has Koa and I spotting each other.

I nearly drop the weighted bar when I accidentally rub against him during a squat. My eyes snap up to his and although his eyes are focused on the back of my head, I see the clench in his jaw and the pinch between his brows.

Great, he probably thinks you did that on purpose.

I could kick myself.

I'm careful to avoid his body as I rise back up, barely able to get the bar back on the rack. Koa reaches past me and helps me secure it in place before I step out from under it and walk towards the plethora of face towels at a nearby wall, without thanking him. I can't thank him, even if I wanted to. My throat feels like it's completely sealed shut after the electric currents I felt from the quick contact.

"Alright, for the last fifteen minutes, let's go over Bells Beach and what to expect from the waves," Gabriel says, as he wipes down the equipment we used.

"Bells Beach has a long and explosive right-hander that will really test your rail game skills, so stay focused," he says, eyeing me. "It's not a great wave for aerials so don't bother with those, just focus on carving."

Koa nods, his arms crossed over his chest as he studies Gabriel. My eyes roam down his body, the veins in his arms more visible after Gabriel's tough workout. I drag my eyes back up to his and butterflies explode in my stomach when I find him looking back at me with a knowing look.

For fuck's sake, woman. Stop drooling over the guy.

I whip my head towards Gabriel with a frown. "Anything else we should look out for?"

"The rip currents can get a bit trippy out there so it's best to stay triangulated to avoid getting swept away to the sharks."

"We should get a practice session in before the actual competition," Koa says, though I refuse to look at him again.

Gabriel nods. "Not a bad idea, I'll plan something over the next few days."

All three of our phones notify us of an incoming message. I quickly walk across the room to the bench where my phone lays as Gabriel takes his out from his pocket and curses.

ELIANA:

Have you guys seen this article?

LINK SHARED

I open the link to the article, and my heart drops to my stomach as I read the headline.

MISSING: SURF PRODIGY, ZALEA EVANS

I look up at Gabriel, who is glaring down at his phone while the team group chat explodes with messages from the others.

ZALE:

Gabriel, do you know anything about this? Her phone goes straight to voicemail. Where is my sister?

KAIRI:

Zale, relax, I'm sure she's fine.

ZALE:

I wasn't talking to you.

GABRIEL:

Enough.

ZALE:

Where. Is. She.

Gabriel lets out a frustrated growl from across the room, his hand running over his short hair. I glance up at Koa with a concerned expression as he watches Gabriel.

GABRIEL:

I don't know. I've had my people looking for her all morning.

ZALE:

You knew she was missing from this morning, and you didn't think to fucking tell me? Are you out of your mind?

GRIFFIN:

Enough, Zale.

ELIANA:

I don't know if this is much help, but she had mentioned to me once on a VERY drunken night something about running away to Italy if all else fails.

Gabriel is on a call almost instantly, relaying Eliana's information to whoever is on the other end of the line. Worry lines run across his forehead as he paces, deep in conversation.

"You found her?" he exclaims. "At the airport? Where in Italy was she flying to?"

He stops pacing as he turns to look at Koa and me.

"Rome?" he asks with barely restrained frustration. "Tell the pilot to get ready, I'll be at the tarmac in thirty."

He hangs up and looks at us apologetically.

"I have to go," he says, his voice defeated. "I'll video call you two every day to make sure you're keeping up with training and getting along. I'm not sure when I'll be back, but I'll send my pilot back here once I reach Italy, so he can take you two to the next competitions."

"Understood, Gabriel," Koa says, his brows furrowed. "We'll be fine."

Gabriel eyes us both skeptically so Koa bumps my shoulder playfully, a smirk pulling at his lips as he glances down at my frowning face. He winks at me and butterflies explode inside of my stomach, my frown fading.

"Y-yeah," I stutter, "we'll be fine."

I've never felt more like a liar than I do right now, as I stare into the eyes that destroyed my world.

FOUR

KOA | VICTORIA, AUSTRALIA

OUR DRIVER STOPS the car next to twelve identical SUVs parked on an expansive hill in the middle of nowhere. I glance at Maliah who sits beside me, and I notice the worry etched along her features as she stares at the large hot air balloons in the distance. She's never liked heights, but she's also never had to face her fear out in the open like this, in front of people she doesn't know and a camera crew, to top it off.

I open my mouth to share some comforting words, but she's out of the car before I can get a single word in. That's how she was this morning during our virtual training session with Gabriel. She only spoke to me when she needed a spotter, and even then, she avoided eye contact at all costs.

With a deep sigh, I open my door and climb out of the vehicle, not surprised to find a camera shoved in my face within seconds.

Not this shit again.

I raise a brow at the cameraman, a short blond guy. He backs away and glances over his lens at me, his face flushed.

"Sorry. First day on the job," he says with a shaky voice. "My name is Matt."

I ignore him as I glance over his head to see Maliah with her back to us, as she stares at the balloons in the distance timidly.

"Oh, right," Matt says as he digs in his bag. "I was told you two need to wear these."

He pulls out mini-Bluetooth microphones that are meant to clip onto our tops. Maliah slowly walks over and takes hers from him, clipping it onto her bubble-gum pink shirt. Matt does a sound check of her mic before giving her the thumbs up and turning towards me. He holds out the mic as I stare down at it.

I hate the idea of being watched and listened to at any moment. I've seen the narratives that reality TV pushes about people, and I don't like the idea of that happening to me, or worse, to Maliah.

"Please," Matt says, moving the mic closer to me. "I really can't afford to get fired."

With a glare that causes him to shrink away, I take the mic and clip it onto my black T-shirt. I let him do his sound check and then set off toward the hot air balloons where the other surfers and production crews are gathered, Maliah following quietly behind me.

"Look who finally decided to show up," Charles calls out with a sneer as he stares at me.

I watch as he realizes Maliah is behind me and his whole demeanour changes. His sneer melts from his lips, replaced with soft vulnerability. His eyes, narrowed at me only seconds ago, now hold a warmth instead as he studies her. I recognize that look—it's the same way I look at her when she walks into a room.

Jealousy twists in my chest like a knife, quickly replaced by fear. He's seeing her the same way I always have. What if she sees something in him, too? The thought makes me feel sick and helpless.

"Bonjour, Maliah," he purrs.

I glance over my shoulder to see with my own eyes how she reacts, expecting her to ditch me for him the way she did at our welcome dinner the other night. Instead, she surprises me by giving him a small smile that doesn't reach her eyes before walking up to stand next to me, her shoulder brushing against my arm.

Charles stares at our touching arms before glancing up at me with narrowed eyes filled with venom. I can't hold back my smirk as he meets my gaze, winking before I turn my attention toward the hot air balloon instructor.

"Okay, now that we're all here, eyes to the front please," an elderly gentleman says, clapping his hands together to attract everyone's attention.

For the next twenty minutes he goes over safety and operational instructions for the balloons. I cling onto every word because there's no way I'll be putting Maliah's safety, or mine, into anyone else's hands. I know that a pilot's license is required for this, but somehow SurfFlix was able to bypass that requirement for this activity. I glance at her from the corner of my eye when the instructor pauses to take a sip of water. She's staring down at her intertwined fingers, twiddling her thumbs distractedly.

I hate that she's forced to do this event despite her discomfort just because SurfFlix needs content for this ridiculous show, and because she'll be kicked out of the whole tour if she doesn't do as they say.

"Alright, it looks like everyone is in groups of four except for your team," the instructor says as he limps over to me, Maliah, and Matt.

I nod. "Our coach has a personal emergency to attend to," I share, curtly.

He nods in understanding before handing me a walkie talkie and pointing to the last available balloon on the field.

"That one is yours."

I thank him before walking towards it, Maliah sticking close by my side as Matt follows us.

"Why do we have to do this?" Maliah whispers, as if her mic won't hear her if she keeps her voice low.

"Apparently, it's part of the new team building activities of the tour," I say before glancing behind us to the camera. "Though I'm sure it's more for entertaining television."

"I don't think you're supposed to say stuff like that when we have the mics on," she chastises.

I snort. "Was I supposed to whisper it instead?" Her cheeks flush. "Besides, I'll say whatever I want to. I'm sure their editors will cut it all out of the final versions anyway."

Matt jogs ahead of us, jumping into the hot air balloon basket and turning to face us for a better camera angle. I wish I could just float him and his ridiculous camera away from us, I'm sick of it all.

I help Maliah get in before following behind and locking the basket door behind us. She rushes to one side of the basket while Matt positions himself on the opposite side with his camera focused on her.

"Everybody ready?" the instructor's voice comes through the walkie talkie.

"Yes sir," I reply.

"Alright, you're clear to depart."

I ignite the burner in the centre of the balloon, waiting as the warm air begins to lift us off the ground. I crank the heat higher so that we reach the same height as the other team, then lower the heat to stabilize us at that height, before I glance at Maliah.

She has a vice grip on the basket railing, eyes squeezed shut and a slight tremble racking her body.

Go comfort her.

Absolutely not. I shake my head to get the words out of my

mind. If we were on better terms, then maybe, but if I try to do that now, she might just push me off this balloon. Plus, comforting her in front of the camera will just give them a fake storyline to run with that could cause more damage for her reputation than good.

"Crap," Matt says, lowering his camera with furrowed brows.

"Everything okay over there?" I ask.

"Yeah, just a weird camera glitch. I'll need a few minutes to fix it."

I watch as he slides to the floor and begins playing around with his camera, tongue jutted out of his mouth as he concentrates on whatever it is he's doing.

Now's your chance.

I glance at Maliah and before I can change my mind, I walk over to her and bump her shoulder with mine.

"How are you hangin' in there?"

"Shut up," she says through clenched teeth, eyes still squeezed shut.

I take a deep breath and try again. "It's probably scarier than it has to be because you're closing your eyes."

"Shut. Up."

"You probably think we're minutes away from space."

"I hate you," she mutters.

Hearing her say that out loud hurts more than it should. It doesn't surprise me, though; she's treated me like her worst enemy ever since I broke up with her.

"Yeah, you've made that very obvious over the last year," I say, trying to sound lighthearted but failing miserably when she opens her eyes and turns to study me.

I swallow past the lump in my throat as her ocean blue eyes hold mine. I feel like I could drown in their depth. She tears her gaze away from me, opting to focus on my shirt instead.

"I'm not your problem anymore, Koa. You don't have to try and comfort me when I get scared."

She turns her gaze to the view, and I watch as her eyes go round before she jumps toward me, gripping my shirt with trembling fingers. I mentally kick myself for feeling as happy as I do with the fact that she ran to me for safety, as if I'm still her safe space.

I instinctively wrap my arms around her, pulling her in closer, and rest my chin on top of her head.

"I want you to be my problem, Mal," I mumble, ignoring how she stiffens in my arms.

After nearly a whole minute, I feel her wrap her arms around my waist in return, causing my heart to pick up at a rapid pace in my chest.

"I don't remember you being such a cuddler," I lie. She used to love cuddling at every opportunity she could get—in the morning, evenings, and between the sheets.

I hear her scoff, but she doesn't say anything more as we stand embracing each other as if nothing ever changed.

"I fixed it," Matt shouts, jumping to his feet and pointing the camera in our direction.

Maliah releases me and pulls out of my hold in an instant, returning to facing the views with a face flushed red. I glare at Matt before turning my back to him and standing shoulder to shoulder next to her.

"We never speak of that moment, ever. Got it?" she hisses.

And just like that, my bubble of happiness and obliviousness bursts and reality sets in like a tidal wave.

"I wouldn't dream of it," I reply, not bothering to hide the disappointment from my voice as I turn around and walk back to the burner after noticing the other balloons beginning to descend.

I use the burner and the venting system to release some of the hot air from the balloon and steady our descent to the landing site, trying my best not to frown as Matt turns the camera toward me.

GRIFFIN:

Wait, she hugged you back?

I SIGH AS I STARE AT MY PHONE SCREEN. I'LL PROBABLY REGRET telling him about what happened between Maliah and I on the hot air balloon earlier today, but staring at the ceiling from my bed with my thoughts raging wild wasn't doing me any favours either. So, I turned to the only person I knew who could keep a secret.

ME:

Yeah, but like I said, as soon as the camera was on us, she was gone from my arms and telling me that the moment never happened.

I've replayed the interaction in my head on repeat and I can't make sense of it. Does she hate me or not? Does she still have feelings for me?

GRIFFIN:

Do you know what this means?

I tap my finger on the edge of my phone as my scowl deepens. I mean, what else could it mean? She's obviously embarrassed to be seen anywhere near me. Once a poor kid, always a poor kid—as her father put it. But I don't tell Griffin that.

ME:

What?

GRIFFIN:

> She's not over you, bud. I think it's time you pull out all the stops. Remind her why she fell in love with you in the first place. Remind her she's still in love with you.

And how the hell am I going to do that?

I let out a groan as I re-read his text. He makes everything sound so much easier than it really is. How does anyone convince Maliah Cooper to do anything? I've known her for the better half of my life, and I've never been able to do that. Not even when we were together.

So instead, I do something I absolutely know I'll regret. Something utterly stupid. I exit my conversation with Griffin and click on Maliah's name instead.

ME:

> Sweet dreams.

I wait until my message switches from delivered to read. Another five minutes of waiting, but she still hasn't replied. Regret crashes over me like a boulder when I realize she's not going to reply. I curse under my breath, turn my phone off for the night, and toss it onto my nightstand harder than I meant to. Rolling over, I squeeze my eyes shut, letting the calm nothingness of sleep take over.

MALIAH | VICTORIA, AUSTRALIA
KOA:

KOA:

Sweet dreams.

MY HEART STARTS to pound in my chest as I stare at those two words, reading them in his voice in my head. When we were together, there was never a night he didn't text me those two words, even if we were right beside each other. It was a nightly ritual.

I feel my body become hot as memories of him whispering those words in my ear start to swirl around my mind. He'd lean over, his lips brushing against my ear as I'd start to fade into sleep after a night of crazy sex, and he'd say those two words before gently kissing a trail from my ear to my collar bone.

I quickly lock my phone when I realize I'm panting, and an unbearable heat is building between my thighs. I squeeze my eyes shut, trying to tame my breathing and think of anything but Koa, but it doesn't work as the need grows stronger and I shoot out of my bed and run straight for the shower, turning the water on the coldest setting before stripping out of my pyjamas and jumping in.

I refuse to let Koa Foster weasel his way back into my heart. *As if he ever left.*

MY EYELIDS FEEL HEAVY TODAY AS WE TOUR AROUND THE BUSHLAND Wildlife Animal Sanctuary in Victoria. It's another excursion, as Koa put it, for entertaining television. I probably would have enjoyed this one a lot more than the hot air balloons yesterday if I wasn't so exhausted. I follow the group towards the Crested Cockatoos enclosure which has a handful of colourful birds.

"What did you think about the hot air balloons yesterday?" Charles asks.

He's been glued to my side ever since Koa and I arrived with the rest of our production crew, and I didn't miss the scowl on Koa's face as he watched us before wandering off to talk to a group of other surfers. I was partly relieved to see him go, but also partly sad.

Relieved because after the mind game he tried to play with me last night with his stupid text message, keeping me up until nearly three in the morning, I don't want to be anywhere near him until I can sort out my thoughts. But sad because as much as the distance helps me think more clearly, a part of me just wants to be close to him. That same part of me is the reason I couldn't leave the Shredders after we broke up.

"Maliah," Charles sings my name, "are you with me?"

I glance at Charles, remembering he asked me a question.

"Oh, sorry, I'm just a bit tired. The hot air balloons were... interesting. It was my first time on one."

"Really? Well, when you visit me in France one day maybe we can go again, just the two of us."

I give him a forced smile before my eyes begin searching for Koa. Charles is nice, but he's not my type. Do I even have a type?

Koa's my type.

I bite my lip as punishment for even thinking that, for letting Koa sneak his way back into my thoughts. My eyes find him, surrounded by the rest of the female surfers who are twirling strands of their hair while they look up at him flirtatiously. I frown at them, annoyed that they even think they have a chance with him.

Koa has higher standards than that.

I look up at Koa to see if he's enjoying the attention, but I never expected to find his eyes staring back at me. Chills rack through my body as I hold his gaze, my face and chest growing warm. Why is he still able to get this physical reaction out of me?

"Are you cold? You have, how do you say, chicken skin?"

I turn to look at Charles with a confused expression.

"Pardon?"

"In France, we call it *chair de poule*. I think that translates to chicken skin." He grabs onto my arm and points at my goosebumps. "It's bumpy, like a plucked chicken's skin."

I stare at him, blink twice, and gently pull my arm out of his grip.

"I'm fine. I'm going to go get a closer look at some of these animals, I'll see you at the winery for dinner."

I give him a small wave, ignoring the confusion on his face, as I walk away from the group and toward the wooded Brushtail Possum enclosure. I squint as I peer into the enclosure trying to find one, but all I see is dense foliage and large tree hollows. I let out a sigh as I rest my forehead against the fence, my mind replaying two words on repeat.

Sweet dreams.

"Did you know that brushtail possums can rotate their back feet nearly one hundred eighty degrees?"

I glance up and it feels like the world freezes when my eyes meet Koa's. He's smiling down at me mischievously before looking back toward the Possum enclosure.

"So fascinating," he whispers to himself.

I swallow nervously before forcing myself to look back toward the deserted area.

"I didn't know you were so knowledgeable about possums," I mutter.

He chuckles before pointing at an information sign in front of me that states interesting facts about the species, including how their back feet rotate. I roll my eyes before shooting him a glare which only causes his smile to grow. I stare at his smile, dazzled by it. It's rare to see Koa smile and I hadn't realized how much I missed it.

You're digging your own grave, Maliah.

I tear my eyes away, focusing on where the possums should be, but a slight movement in the branches above catches my attention. I watch, fascinated, as a creature with thick, grey fur makes its way down a tree trunk, back feet rotated, and bushy tail trailing behind it. It slowly and carefully makes its way to a feeding station and gently picks up fresh fruit with its small paws.

"Well, would you look at that," Koa says gently, his eyes tracking the possums' movements.

"Why are you here, Koa?"

He looks at me again, shrugging. "Same reason as you; it's required of me."

"No," I shake my head, "why are you here, next to me, instead of with the rest of the group?"

Instead of with the other girls, is what I really want to say, but I bite back the words.

It's not my place to get jealous anymore.

"I could ask you the same," he says, glancing over his shoulder as he eyes Charles who is standing apart from the rest of the group and watching us with an expression full of envy.

"I just needed some space to think," I mutter, returning my attention to the hungry possum.

"About?"

"You," I say before I can stop myself.

He shifts on his feet, turning to face me as he leans his shoulder against the fence.

"You're thinking about me?" Koa asks in a flattered tone.

I roll my eyes before I mirror his pose, crossing my arms over my chest.

"Why did you text me *that* last night?"

"Text you what?" he asks, brows furrowed. "Sweet dreams?"

Hearing him say those two words out loud sends a bolt of electricity through my body, and I'm left feeling both turned on and pathetic. He studies me, as if he can read my mind, before he reaches across, closing the distance between us, and tucks a loose strand of my hair behind my ear.

"Did it keep you awake, princess?"

I close my eyes at the sound of my nickname. He's the only person who's ever called me that and the sound of it breaks my heart all over again.

"Don't call me that," I whisper.

"Okay," he says, simply.

I open my eyes and find that he's still studying my expressions, head tilted to the side. He turns to look at the possums before that mischievous smile creeps its way back onto his lips.

"Maybe I should call you possum instead," he says, nodding in their direction.

I turn my head to look at the hungry possum only to see it's now puffed up, nearly twice its size, as its back arches like it's about to pounce. I notice another possum nearby, inching closer to the feeding station.

The first possum opens its mouth, revealing its sharp, pointed teeth as a low, chilling hiss escapes from its mouth. It begins to growl and hiss as the other possum nears closer. I watch as its bushy tail begins to flick aggressively behind it, a clear sign of its agitation.

"Yup, I think possum is a much better nickname for you," Koa says, nodding as he continues to watch the face-off. "You look just like that when you're angry."

I clench my teeth, my lips pulling back, as I turn to glare at him. He glances at me from the corner of his eye before snorting.

"Basically twins. Nearly identical."

He turns his back to me and walks away, joining the rest of the group, as I seethe behind him.

ORCHARD AND OAK IS THE MOST UPSCALE WINERY I'VE EVER BEEN to. The floors are polished oak while the walls are a beautiful, pale stone. With exposed beams, the open concept of the place feels timeless. I sit at the large bar at the back of the room, near the exit doors, on the world's most comfortable plush bar stools.

"Another top up, miss?" The bartender offers as I place my empty wine glass down on the bar.

"Go for it," I say, trying my best to sound sober.

He smiles obliviously as he refills my glass for the third time tonight. I glance over my shoulder, watching Koa have the time of his life at his dining table surrounded by the other female surfers. He smiles politely at them as they talk, almost every girl twirling a strand of their hair between their fingers.

It makes me sick.

I grab my glass off the bar and stumble upright as I hop off the barstool. Without another glance his way, to spare my own feelings, I clumsily make my way toward the outdoor seating area. Taking a seat on the wooden bench just outside the dining hall doors, I bring the glass back to my lips for another sip as I admire the carefully manicured gardens of the estate. The neatly trimmed hedges and vibrant coloured flower beds remind me of my father's home in Portugal. It's been years since I last visited him there.

I push thoughts of him out of my mind, not wanting him to deflate the small buzz I have going on tonight, as I spot a small pond with a rustic wooden bridge in the distance.

The perfect place for a peaceful stroll, I decide.

I've been searching for a quiet moment alone all day.

I stand up, and begin walking toward the charming pond, noticing the subtle fragrance of blooming flowers and fresh grass surrounding me on my way. I'm grateful that the cameras have been put away for the night and the microphones removed from my clothing. It would have been so embarrassing to have myself recorded in this state.

I don't know why two simple words have me so rattled, but I need to figure it out before tomorrow's competition, or I'm screwed. I need to stay focused for the waves ahead, but I can't do that with thoughts of Koa running wild in my head.

I make it to the bridge, the wood creaking softly beneath me as I walk to the centre of it. Glancing down at the pond, I notice the water lilies floating around the waters that reflect the surrounding trees. It's so peaceful and I finally feel like I can think.

Closing my eyes, I focus on the sounds around me. The gentle ripples of the water, the rustling of leaves, and the soft buzzing of insects in the surrounding grass. A feeling of calm finally washing over me, that is until I feel a hand rest over mine and the wine glass is taken from me.

My eyes fly open as I look over at the wine thief, ready to give them a piece of my mind, but the words get stuck in my throat as my eyes land on Koa. I watch as he brings my glass to his lips and drinks the rest of my wine in one gulp, his eyes never leaving mine, before he places the glass on the edge of the bridge railing.

"You and I both know you shouldn't be this drunk the night before a competition," he says disapprovingly. He holds out a water bottle for me to take, but I muster up the angriest look I can as I stare back at him.

"Take it," he says sternly, "and drink it, or so help me God, Maliah."

"Or. What," I challenge.

He doesn't say anything at first as we continue our stare-off, the tensions between us crackling. In one swift movement, he has me thrown over his shoulder, and we're on the move, walking past the dining hall and toward the cars.

"Put me down," I shout, smacking his back.

It earns me a slap on my ass that has heat rising to my face and my tongue silenced.

"You're being very bad tonight, princess."

I squeeze my eyes shut, my heart pounding in my chest as I feel the heat spread from my face, down my chest, and in between my thighs. His hands gripping the back of my legs feels like fire against my skin and I almost can't take it.

He opens a car door and gently lowers me into the passenger's side before he reaches across and buckles me in, his hand brushing along my thigh, leaving a fire trail beneath my skin.

"I'm fully capable of buckling my own seatbelt, Koa."

He smirks before shutting the car door and walking around the front to the driver's side. He slides in effortlessly, adjusting the seat to suit his long legs better before he pulls out of the pebbly parking lot and onto the dark country roads. It's a twenty-minute drive back to the hotel, and I have no idea how I'm going to survive it.

I tighten both of my hands into a fist, my nails digging in my palms, as I try to mentally distract myself with anything other than Koa for the rest of the drive, but I'm overly aware of his presence and constant glances my way. I'm certain when I get out of this car, I'll be leaving a puddle in my wake.

Twenty minutes feels more like an hour by the time we reach the hotel, and it's not until I'm stomping down the hall-way, Koa in tow, that I realize I left my bag at the winery. I freeze, mid step, Koa narrowly avoiding crashing into me.

"What's wrong?" he asks, eyeing me as his brows pull together in concern.

"My key card is in my bag," I say, sounding on the verge of tears.

"Okay, where's your bag? Did you leave it in the car?"

I shake my head, meeting his gaze. "I left it at the winery."

Understanding flashes across his face as he stares at me before glancing at his watch.

"The front desk is closed for the night," he says, raising his eyes back up to mine. "No one will be back to get you a spare key until the morning."

My throat tightens as panic begins to set in. Normally, I wouldn't be this concerned, I'd probably suggest driving back to get my bag or calling someone there to bring it back with them, but right now I'm drunk and I'm not thinking straight. Especially around Koa.

"Sleep in my room tonight," he suggests.

"Excuse me?" I shout. "Is this your sneaky way of trying to get me into the same bed as you, Koa Foster?"

He sighs before rolling his eyes. "I can sleep on the floor, Maliah. Let's go, it's already late and we both need at least some sleep before tomorrow."

He walks to his door, swiping his key card and holding the

door open for me. I bite my lip nervously before finally giving in and brushing past him on my way into his room. I stand by his bed awkwardly and silently as he tosses his jacket and card onto a chair before heading to his suitcase and pulling out an oversized T-shirt which he hands to me.

"There's mouthwash in the bathroom," he says, turning his back to me as he begins to strip out of his clothes.

I'm tempted to watch, but I know that images of Koa's body will only keep me awake longer than I hope to be. So, instead, I turn my back to him and head to his bathroom to change out of my clothes and into his large T-shirt, gargling mouthwash as I stare at my reflection.

I hate that this shirt smells like him. Everything in this room smells like him. I can't even pretend to be in my own room even if I tried. He's everywhere here. I spit out the mouthwash and make my way back to the room, finding him shirtless and in grey sweatpants.

Not the grey sweatpants.

I practically whimper as I try my best to look anywhere but at him as I climb into his bed, hiding myself under the sheets as he heads to the bathroom to brush his own teeth. Tonight is going to be pure torture.

Five minutes later he walks out of the bathroom and turns off the light, darkness swallowing my vision. I hear him trying to find a comfortable spot on the floor and I say something I'm sure I'll regret later.

"I'm not going to have you sleep on the floor the day before our competition, Koa. Get in bed."

He doesn't answer at first, the room filling with silence aside from our breathing, but after a few seconds I hear him get up and the bed dips as he crawls under the sheets beside me. I try to stay as far to the edge of my side as I can to make sure no part of us touches.

"I can hear your heart pounding in your chest," he whispers after nearly three minutes.

"You frustrate me incredibly," I mumble back, trying to play off the erratic beating as anger.

"It's not like we've never slept next to each other before, princess. Get comfortable, I won't touch you. Don't worry."

He turns around, his back now facing mine, making it easier for me to move closer. But his words keep playing on repeat in my mind.

I won't touch you. Don't worry.

But what if I want him to touch me?

It's the last thing I think about as I fall asleep.

SIX

KOA | VICTORIA, AUSTRALIA

THE FAMILIAR AND comforting scent of vanilla drags me out of my sleep. I slowly open my eyes, staring at my ceiling as I blink away the sleepiness. Turning my head towards the clock across the hotel room, I notice it's eight in the morning. Surely that's a mistake, I haven't been able to sleep past four in the morning in nearly a year.

Something moves on my chest and that's when I notice the weight there. I glance down and my heart begins to sprint in my chest. Blonde hair cascades across my body, the scent of vanilla finding me again. I hear her soft, rhythmic breathing and feel each exhale softly brush against my skin.

The urge to wrap my arms around Maliah and hold her close, never letting her go again, is almost overwhelming. But my words from last night stop me as I remember my promise to not touch her, so instead I lay there and watch her quietly, savouring this moment for as long as she'll allow it. Her long lashes rest softly against her cheeks and minutes later they begin to flutter open as she slowly begins to wake up.

The peaceful expression she had just moments ago gives way to confusion before her eyes widen with the realization that she's on top of me. She scrambles off, falling out of the bed with a loud thump.

"Ow," I hear Maliah groan quietly.

I press my lips together to stifle the chuckle as she slowly rises from the floor, her blonde hair now a wild mess around her face. Her cheeks are flushed as her eyes meet mine, and in an instant, she's glaring at me, as usual. I roll my eyes as I sit up, resting my back against the headboard and bunching the sheets at my waist to try and hide my morning problem.

"Is there a reason you were touching me?" she hisses.

"You know," I start, trying to hide my amusement from my voice, "you're the one who was cuddling me, not the other way around."

I watch, fascinated, as her cheeks turn an even deeper shade of red. It's enough proof that she still has feelings for me, despite how she treats me in public. I can see her trying to muster up a retort, but I spare her the embarrassment as I lean over and pick up my hotel phone, dialling reception.

"Good morning, mister Foster, how can I help you today?" a raspy voice says from the other end.

"Good morning," I reply. "My teammate in room two twenty-two forgot her keycard at an event last night. Is there any way you can bring a spare to my bedroom along with your breakfast special for two?"

"Absolutely, sir. I'll send someone up shortly."

"Thank you."

I hang up the phone and turn to look back at Maliah. Her face still flushed as she avoids eye contact. Well, this is new, I'm not sure I've ever seen this expression on her before.

"I'm sorry," she mumbles.

I arch a brow. "Sorry for what?"

"Cuddling up to you. I didn't knowingly do it or anything."

I let out a breathy chuckle. "I wasn't complaining about it, Maliah."

Her blush deepens and she shoots me a quick, embarrassed look. "Stop saying it like that."

I tilt my head curiously. "Saying what, like what?"

"My name," she huffs. "The way you say it."

Her reaction is intriguing, it's a side of Mal I don't think I've seen in a very long time. I scoot closer to her, leaning forwards as she watches me with nervous eyes.

"Maliah," I repeat, drawing out her name teasingly.

My eyes dart to her thighs, noticing how she squeezes them together before she lets out a shaky exhale.

Interesting.

"Mal—"

"Koa, I swear to God," she says exasperated. "Stop saying my name like that."

I raise an eyebrow, playing along. "Like how?"

"Like you...like you want to...I don't know! Like *that*!"

I don't miss the look of embarrassment and longing in her eyes, and I can't hold back my smile with how flustered she's becoming.

This could be fun.

I lean even closer to her, my eyes catching on her perfect lips, before I force myself to look into her eyes.

"Maliah," I say again.

"Shut up," she snaps, her voice a mixture of annoyance and something softer.

Something vulnerable.

"Make me," I challenge, my gaze locked onto her.

I'm so close to her that I feel the warmth of her shaky breathing tickle my nose. The tension is palpable, almost like a crackling energy electrifying the air around us. Her eyes trail down to my lips, and I watch in anticipation as she fights to hide the lust from her expression.

She wants me to kiss her.

And I almost do, but a knock at the door shatters the

connection and she leaps backward in an instant, her back thudding against the wall behind her as her panicked eyes fly up to mine. I hold her gaze, struggling to mask my disappointment while also trying to absorb the realization that this moment has irrevocably changed everything between us.

Her frantic reaction confirms that as much as she likes to pretend that she hates me, she still feels something for me beneath the surface. Whether it's genuine affection or just physical attraction, I'm not sure, but I know that regardless, it gives me a chance to fix things between us.

This is the turning point I've been patiently waiting for.

With a deep, resigned sigh, I swing my legs over the side of the bed and head toward the door. I spot a hotel staff member pushing a breakfast cart, holding Maliah's extra key card in his hand.

Maliah darts past me, snatching the key card from him in a hurry, and running out into the hall.

"I'll take my breakfast in my room," she says swiftly, barely concealing her urgency to get away from me.

Without waiting for a response or offering another glance my way, she bolts into her room. I notice she's still wearing my oversized T-shirt and I glance back into my room, spotting the outfit she had worn the night before folded neatly on a chair.

Turning back to the staff member, I offer him a polite smile before taking my food tray and closing the door behind me. The soft click of the latch echoes in my now quiet room, but I still feel the tension from earlier coiled within me. I place the tray on the edge of my bed and lift the cover, revealing a protein packed plate of eggs, sausages, and bacon. The aroma of the food does nothing to mask the scent of Maliah in my room, reminding me she was here only moments ago.

I lower myself onto the bed and try to focus on eating, knowing I'll need every ounce of energy to get through today's surf competition, my stomach growling in anticipation. But my mind isn't on the food, it's on Maliah and the memory of our earlier moment—an intense, electric connection that is still buzzing beneath my skin. I can still feel the warmth of her body and it sends a shiver down my spine.

With a frustrated sigh, I set the tray aside, abandoning the idea of breakfast altogether. Pushing myself off the bed, I head toward the bathroom in hopes that a cold shower will be enough to cool down both my body and my thoughts.

I strip down to nothing and step into the frigid water, letting it cascade over me, but it does little to quench the heat raging beneath my skin. The memory of her is relentless, torturous, and as my pulse quickens, I know that there's only one way to find relief in this moment.

I let the cool water mix with the heat she's left behind, as I wrap my rough hand around my hard cock. My hand, slick with water, moves with a mind of its own as I begin pumping slowly. Closing my eyes, my mind replays the curve of her perfect lips, the feel of her soft skin against mine, and the way her breath hitched when our eyes locked.

I imagine her here with me again, her hands replacing mine, and her body pressed against me in a way that sends a bolt of desire straight through me. With a grunt I lean forward, my wet hair waterfalling around me as I use my free hand to hold myself up against the wall.

I pump my cock faster as the tension builds, coiling tighter with each passing second, each flicker of memory. The little breaths and moans she used to let out when we'd fuck swirling through my mind on an endless loop. I can't stop myself from picturing how her wet body would fit against mine again, or the way her hands would glide over my slick skin, or how her angelic voice would sound while whispering my name.

The pressure inside me reaches its breaking point as my breathy moans turn into a deep growl. My muscles tense, and with one final pump, I come all over the shower wall, the tension finally releasing.

For a moment, the world is silent, the only sound is the steady patter of the water against the tiles, my breathless breathing, and my heartbeat pounding in my ears. Even now, with the heat sated, the thought of Maliah still lingers—almost stronger than before. It's not something that can be washed away.

After rinsing the shower wall, I turn off the water on a sigh, grabbing a towel and drying myself off, deciding to return to my breakfast and preparations for today's competition. I know another moment like today is bound to happen again with Maliah, and when it does, I won't be able to ignore my urges.

MALIAH WAS OFF IN TODAY'S COMPETITION. I NOTICED IT FROM the moment she started to paddle out into the lineup at Bells Beach, her movements not as fluid as normal and her focus completely shifted. The waves were formidable today, rolling in with a power that can either make or break a surfer's run. Bells Beach is known worldwide as a legendary spot, but it's also unforgiving. The way that the tides shift, and the swell refracts off the reef can turn any solid wave into a nightmare if the surfer isn't fully focused.

This would normally be a piece of cake for Maliah, she thrives in conditions like this—carving through the waves with exact precision and confidence. But not today. Today her take-offs were hesitant, and she struggled with positioning, getting caught too deep or too far out on the shoulder every single time. On a critical wave, she had scared me half to death when she pulled back from a drop at the last second, causing the lip of the wave to crash down on her and send her tumbling underwater in a brutal wipeout.

My heart was in my throat as I watched from the beach, waiting for her to resurface, and when she did, her eyes were filled with frustration as she glanced toward my direction. The rest of the heat hadn't gone much better, and by the time it had ended, it was clear that she hadn't done enough to keep us in the lead. We'd gone from first to sixth in a matter of minutes.

I can tell it's eating her up inside as she sits beside me quietly on the beach, her face a mask of disappointment. I can feel the weight of her self-reproach hanging in the air between us.

"What happened out there?" I ask, trying to figure out how to explain this to Gabriel.

"Koa, stay out of my business," she snaps, her eyes not meeting mine.

My phone vibrates in my hand. "He's calling," I say as I hold up my phone to show an incoming video call from Gabriel.

She stares at it for a moment before nodding. "Answer it."

So, I do, and I regret it instantly as Gabriel's furious face comes into view.

"Are you guys fucking kidding me?" he yells, running a frustrated hand through his disheveled hair. "From first to sixth? That must be a record place drop."

Maliah tenses beside me, her fidgeting fingers now still as she grips onto her knees so tightly that her knuckles turn white.

"The waves were really tough today, Gabriel," I say, trying to calm him down.

"Don't give me that bullshit," he shouts again. "I watched Maliah miss key sections in waves which could have been a huge opportunity to rack up points with a solid maneuver. She even lost her balance during a crucial cutback; she threw the whole thing."

I hear her breathing grow shallow and quick beside me, and when I glance over, I notice her blinking rapidly, her lashes wet with unshed tears, her body completely curled into itself.

"I don't know why you tried so hard to make it into this championship tour if you're just going to throw it away like it doesn't matter," he spits.

"It does matter," she shouts back, her voice cracking on the last word.

She bites down on her lower lip, the pressure turning it pale as she struggles to keep her composure. But the first tear finally escapes and slides down her cheek, Maliah quickly wiping it away with the back of her hand, but more tears follow.

"It does matter," she repeats quieter, her voice trembling with emotion.

The sight of her crying brings me back to the day I broke her heart, and it slices right through me to see her like this again. I turn back to Gabriel who silently watches, a shocked expression on his face. He's never seen her cry before, no one has, except for me.

"We'll talk later," I say abruptly before ending the call.

"Why did you do that?" she shouts, her voice trembling with emotion.

"Because he shouldn't be talking to you like that," I say calmly.

"Yes, he should. He's my coach and he was right, I screwed up. I deserved to get shit for it," she continues yelling. "You shouldn't have involved yourself in that. You just made it worse for me. Stop involving yourself in my business, I'm tired of it."

Her shouts are so loud they echo in my head as she stares at me with so much rage that I flinch.

"No one deserves to be yelled at like that, Maliah. If it bothers you that I stopped him from continuing, then I'm sorry, but I won't ever let anyone speak to you like that when I'm around. I don't care who they are."

She stares at me with a shocked and confused expression as tears continue streaming down her face, but before I can say anything, she stands up and storms toward our car. I watch as a nearby cameraman runs behind her, filming her breakdown as she climbs into the backseat of the car. I had forgotten about the camera crew and as I look around, I notice them surrounding us at a distance, cameras pointed at me and the car that Maliah sits in. Her whole breakdown is going to be broadcast to the world on SurfFlix, and I know that will hurt her worse than anything Gabriel could ever say.

I need to fix this.

SEVEN

MALIAH | WESTERN AUSTRALIA, AUSTRALIA

THE SUN IS HIGH TODAY, its rays glistening on the surface of the turquoise water as the boat gently rocks beneath my feet. The warm salty air blows my hair around as the other surfers on the boat talk with an excitement I don't share. It's hard to be excited when my heart feels this guilty. It's been gnawing at me ever since Bells Beach two days ago.

I haven't spoken to Koa or Gabriel since then, training on my own in the early mornings and ignoring both of their texts. I know it wasn't fair, the way I'd lashed out at Koa for hanging up on Gabriel, but deep down I know he was just trying to protect me in the moment.

The ocean at Bells had been fierce the day of our competition, but it wasn't the waves that had thrown me off. I couldn't stop thinking about Koa the whole time—how he made me feel that morning, the intensity of our connection, and how much I had wanted him to kiss me at that moment when we were face to face in his room. He was all I could think about, and it had completely shattered my focus and performance out in the water when it mattered most.

Every single time I had tried to set myself up for a wave, his face would flash through my mind, making my heart race in a way that had nothing to do with surfing. Instead of reading the waves like I should have been, I was replaying our moments together and trying to decipher my feelings. I couldn't shake him, and it cost me. It cost us. We went from first place to sixth, all because I couldn't get him out of my head.

The boat slows to a stop as the captain calls out to us that we're in the perfect spot to see the whale sharks on the Ningaloo Reef. Another stupid excursion meant for entertainment. The surfers around me start whispering excitedly as the production crews set up their cameras to get every angle of the boat. I watch as some people pull on their snorkels and fins, but I hesitate, looking over my shoulder instead.

Koa is on the other side of the boat with a few of the male surfers, his broad shoulders and familiar stance standing out among the group. I watch entranced as he laughs at something one of the other guys says and the sound of his voice makes my heart ache. I want to walk over there and apologize to him, but the words get caught in my throat every time I try to form them.

I replay the moment on the beach, the way I'd yelled at him, the hurt in his eyes as I stormed off, and to top it all off the stupid cameras filmed the whole thing. He didn't deserve any of it.

I take a steadying breath as I look away from him and towards my snorkel gear. I need something to quiet my thoughts, even if just for a moment. Pulling on my gear, I glance at the others who are already out in the water, their laughter and shouts filling the air as the first whale shark glides below them. I want to lose myself in the wonder of these gentle giants too, anything to shake the heaviness inside of me.

As I slide into the water, the coolness surrounding me, I feel a moment of peace. The world above fades away, replaced by the sound of my breathing through the snorkel and the vast blueness stretching out beneath me. I get goosebumps as I look around, a reminder that the ocean is huge and unpredictable and I'm small and insignificant in its grandness. I spot a whale shark in the distance, its massive body moving with a slow and powerful grace that takes my breath away, and in that moment, I forget everything—Koa, the competition, the guilt—and just float there, mesmerized.

But the peace doesn't last as the female surfers swim up to me, their excited voices cutting through the tranquil bubble I'd found. I rise to the surface and pull my snorkel gear off so I can see and breathe normally.

"So," Vanessa, one of the redheads on tour, starts, "are you with Koa?"

I hesitate, the question catching me off guard. "No, I'm not," I finally reply, trying to sound casual.

As soon as those three words leave my mouth, they start to gush excitedly over him.

"Oh my god, he's so hot," another girl says, her eyes widening as she glances back toward the boat where Koa stands.

"If you don't want him," a third girl adds with a wink directed at me, "we'll gladly take him off your hands."

I force a smile, trying to match their enthusiasm, but it feels hollow. They don't know the whole story, or how tangled up my emotions are right now, how complicated everything has become for me. The thought of them eyeing Koa, wanting him, *taking* him, makes something ugly twist inside me—something I wasn't ready to face yet.

Jealousy.

I glance back at the boat and my heart skips a beat when I notice Koa is watching me with a steady, unreadable gaze. Our eyes are locked together, and the world seems to shrink to just the two of us.

What is he thinking? Does he know how much I regret the way things had gone at Bells Beach? The girls' laughter and chatter fade into the background, and all I can focus on is the intensity of Koa's stare and the feelings that I can't quite put into words.

I break eye contact first, feeling a flush rise to my cheeks even in the cool water. I hastily put my snorkel gear back on and plunge my head under the water to get away from his gaze, but no matter how much I try to escape it, Koa is always there, in the back of my mind, just out of reach.

It doesn't matter though, does it? I remind myself.

He was the one that told me he didn't love me anymore. He broke up with me, shattering my heart, and walking away. Those words, the way he looked at me when he had said them...they still echo in my mind, sharp and painful. I can't deny the pull he still has on me, the way he makes me feel alive, even though my every instinct screams at me to protect myself, to keep my distance from him. But the memory of his words and the cold finality of our breakup always rushes back as a painful reminder that I'm not enough for him.

And yet, here I am, wanting him just the same.

– THE BREAKUP –

I walk toward the pier, my heart bursting out of my chest as excitement bubbles up inside me like never before. This is it—I know it. Koa's been acting strange all week, distant and a little off, but I know it's just pre-proposal nerves. He texted me last night, asking me to meet him on the pier at sunset today. It's the perfect moment. Everything about this feels right.

I spent the whole day getting ready. My nails and toes are freshly done in a classy French tip, perfect for engagement photos, and my hair has been re-highlighted so that it catches the light just right. I'm even wearing my favorite blue summer dress, the one that Koa always loves, the one that makes me feel beautiful and confident. I even practiced my surprised expressions in the mirror for hours, imagining how I'll react when he gets down on one knee and asks me to be his forever.

Today is going to be perfect.

I reach the wooden pier and notice him standing there, his back to me, hands in his pockets, staring out at the ocean. My heart skips a beat at the sight of him, and an uncontrollable smile spreads across my face.

Thoughts of all the reasons I love him swirl through my mind:

his kindness, humbleness, his strength, the way he makes me feel like the most special person in the world. By the time I'm close enough to touch him, it feels like I've already said yes a thousand times in my heart.

I tap his shoulder, my smile widening as I prepare myself for this once in a lifetime moment that I've dreamt about ever since we started dating all those years ago. But when Koa turns around, something isn't right. His face is still, his eyes cold and empty. The warmth and love that I've always seen in his eyes are gone. The change in him is so stark that I instinctively take a step back, my smile faltering as confusion grips me. It's like I'm staring at a completely different person.

This isn't my Koa.

"Koa?" I whisper, unable to stop my voice from trembling as I search his face for any sign of the man I love.

He stares at me for what feels like an eternity, his eyes scanning my face as if he's trying to memorize every detail. The silence between us is heavy, suffocating, and I don't understand why. He finally speaks, his voice flat and devoid of the affection that I'm so used to hearing from him.

"I want to break up."

Those words hit me like a punch to the gut, knocking the air out of my lungs. My breath catches in my throat, and my entire body goes numb. I can't believe what I'm hearing. My vision blurs as tears instantly well up in my eyes, and my legs feel like they might give out at any moment.

A cold chill sweeps through me, making it feel like the ground is disappearing beneath my feet. I open my mouth to speak, but no sound comes out. My mind is reeling, trying to make sense of the words that just shattered everything I thought I knew. This has to be a sick joke. It has to be.

"W-why?" I finally manage to choke out, my voice small and broken, barely audible over the roar of the ocean behind us.

Koa doesn't meet my eyes, looking out at the ocean instead, as if this conversation is nothing more than a tedious chore.

"I don't love you anymore, Maliah," he says, his tone cold and detached, slicing through me like a knife. "Let's not waste each other's time."

The world around me starts spinning as my chest tightens painfully, and a sharp, stabbing ache radiates through my heart. The tears I've been holding back spill over, blurring my vision until all I can see is the distorted outline of the man I thought I was going to spend my life with.

He doesn't wait for a response, turning and walking away, his footsteps echoing hollowly on the wooden planks of the pier. I watch him walk away, frozen in place, my mind screaming at me to do something, to say something, but I can't move. The agony in my chest spreads like wildfire, consuming me from the inside out until I can barely breathe.

My legs finally give out as I collapse to my knees on the deserted pier, the rough wood digging into my skin. The physical pain is nothing compared to the devastation tearing me apart inside. Sobs wrack my body, each one more painful than the last, as I bury my face in my hands, letting the heartbreak consume me completely.

All the dreams I cherished, the future I imagined with him, shattered into a million pieces, leaving me with nothing but the unbearable pain.

He doesn't love me anymore.

I'm not enough.

EIGHT

KOA | WESTERN AUSTRALIA, AUSTRALIA

THE MORNING AIR is warm as the sun begins to rise, casting a golden hue over the coastline. The production team is setting up cameras and equipment for today's shoot. SurfFlix has planned a helicopter ride for all the surfers to capture breathtaking aerial shots of the coastline from above. I glance at Maliah, and I can tell she's not thrilled.

She stands a few feet away from me, listening to the crew explain the plan, but I notice the way her eyes widen just a fraction along with the subtle tension in her shoulders, the thought of getting into a helicopter is clearly freaking her out.

When the crew finishes explaining, I walk over to Jackie.

"Hi." She turns to face me, brow arched.

"Hello, Koa," she replies.

I look over my shoulder at Maliah who looks to be doing her best to keep her face neutral, not wanting to show any sign of weakness, as usual.

"We want to opt out of this one," I say.

"We need this shot," she says, looking directly at Maliah over my shoulder. "It's already paid for, and it's going to look incredible. Everyone has to go. No exceptions."

I bite back the angry words that sit at the tip of my tongue. "It's going to be a shitty shot if we both look miserable up there."

Jackie frowns. "Is that a threat?"

I take a moment to reply, knowing that if I piss her off she'll give us the worst edit in television history.

"How about this," I say, glancing at Maliah once more before turning to look at Jackie. "I'll do what I have to do to make sure Mal isn't scared shitless up there, I'll even give you guys some great content to work with to build the storyline, on one condition."

Her growing smile falters slightly before she narrows her eyes, waiting for me to continue.

"Cut the scene of Maliah yelling and crying at the end of the Bells Beach competition. We don't want that aired."

Jackie thinks about it for a moment, tapping her chin thoughtfully before holding her hand out to me.

"Deal."

I shake it with an appreciative smile before I return to Maliah.

"Ready?" I ask, stepping in front of her to block her view of the helicopter.

She nods, forcing a small smile, but I can see the fear in her eyes. She's not fine, no matter how hard she's trying to pretend otherwise. I know her too well—know that she's feeling trapped, like she doesn't have a choice but to go along with it. But I also know it's more than just the helicopter ride. It's Gabriel.

Ever since her performance at Bells Beach, she's been avoiding Gabriel. I've seen the way it's been getting to her, how she's been carrying the weight of it all, trying to make up for that one bad day. She goes to the gym before I even wake up, leaving just as I get there, and then goes back again at the end of the night. She's pushing herself to her limits to make sure that it never happens again.

Now, with this helicopter ride, I can tell she doesn't want to risk getting in shit with him again, even if it means confronting one of her biggest fears. I step closer to her, wanting to say something, to tell her everything will be okay. But before I can speak up, she turns to me with that same forced smile, her eyes betraying the anxiety she's trying so hard to hide.

"I'll be fine," she says with a slight tremor to her voice. "It's just a helicopter ride, right? I did the hot air balloon ride, so I can do this."

I nod, but inside, I'm uneasy. I realize this is another heights excursion and the production team is aware of how Maliah feels about heights. It's almost as if they're doing this on purpose. I hate seeing her like this, but I know Maliah, once she's set her mind to something, there's no talking her out of it.

I help her step up to the helicopter, watching as her free hand grips the doorframe a little too tightly. She buckles herself in while I take a seat across from her, buckling myself in too. We wait for the cameraman to join us before the helicopter's rotors begin spinning to life, cutting through the silence with a deafening roar. As the helicopter lifts off the ground, I watch her grip onto her shoulder straps and squeeze her eyes shut.

Within seconds, the helicopter is airborne, slicing through the clear blue sky of Western Australia. Maliah's gripping the straps so tightly that her knuckles have turned white as she forces herself to look out the window, her eyes wide and filled with fear. I lean in closer, trying to catch her attention.

"Remember that time when you convinced me to climb that massive tree at the back of The Shredder House?" I start, keeping my voice light and casual.

Maliah glances at me, her grip loosening just a fraction as she nods, a faint smile tugging at the corner of her lips. "Yeah, I remember. I was trying to see if we could spot the Kooky Coconut from up there."

I chuckle, the memory vivid in my mind. "You were so focused on getting to the top, but halfway through, you lost your footing and fell. I've never seen you move so fast in my life."

She laughs softly, the sound easing some of the tension in the air. "I was trying to grab onto that stupid branch, but it just snapped under me. I ended up with a nasty cut down my hip. You were so freaked out."

"I thought you were going to break every bone in your body," I admit, shaking my head with a small smile. "You scared the hell out of me."

Her smile grows wider and the fear in her eyes softens. "You carried me all the way back to my room. I'm pretty sure you were more scared than I was."

I grin, the memory warming my chest. "I probably was," I nod, "but I'm pretty sure that's when you started to hate heights."

She nods and I watch as the tension completely drains from her shoulders. "Yeah, I think you're right."

We share a quiet laugh, and I notice the cameras filming us, capturing this moment. But for once, I don't care about them or the footage. I'm just happy to see her relax, even if it's just for a little while.

As the helicopter lands, her grip on her shoulder straps finally loosens completely, the colour returning to her knuckles, and I watch as she breathes a sigh of relief. The cameramen jump out first and when they do, she turns to me, her expression soft and grateful.

"I know what you were doing with that story," she says. "Thank you, Koa."

I smile and nod but notice that she hasn't moved yet. "Is everything okay?"

She shakes her head, looking down at her lap as she fidgets with her fingers. "I wanted to apologize for yelling at you at Bells."

I whistle and sit back in my seat. "Is *the* Malia Cooper apologizing to me right now? Today must be my lucky day."

"Oh shut up," she says, pinning me with a frown. "This is why I don't apologize."

She huffs and gets up, grabbing onto the doorframe of the helicopter to get out, but I stand and grab her arm, tugging her toward me gently. She turns to face me, our bodies almost touching.

"You don't need to apologize to me, princess. I know you were just caught up in the moment."

"It doesn't make it okay, so I'm sorry."

Her eyes wander my face, pausing on my lips a few times before she finds my eyes again.

"Okay, I forgive you. Will you go back to doing training with me in the mornings instead of avoiding me now?"

She scoffs and rolls her eyes. "I wasn't avoiding you."

I smirk, seeing right past her white lie. "Oh, no, of course you weren't."

I walk past her, unable to hide the smirk as I step off the helicopter and extend my hand for her to take. She hesitates for a moment, before sliding her small, soft hand into mine and letting me help her out.

Progress.

THE NEXT MORNING, THE ENERGY IS ELECTRIC AS WE PREPARE FOR the competition at Margaret River. The break here is legendary, powerful and unpredictable. Gabriel told us the waves here can reach up to fifteen feet on a good day.

The men are competing first today. I paddle out, the swell already building and the waves rolling with a demanding force. The water here is colder than I'm used to, and the sharp reef below is at the back of mind as I position myself for the right set. The moment the first wave rises, I'm on it, dropping down the face with speed and precision. It's massive, curling over my head into a barrel. I can feel every shift, every surge, and I move along with it, carving sharp turns and cutting through the spray.

The ride is exhilarating, the kind that makes your heart race and your senses sharpen. It reminds me of Maliah. I finish strong, riding the wave all the way to the inside, feeling the adrenaline coursing through my veins as I kick out. The rest of the men's round goes like this for me, and I'm not surprised when I see that I've ranked highest.

As I finish paddling back to the shore and find a spot to sit on the beach, I turn my attention to Maliah watching as she prepares to paddle out. Her eyes are focused and determined today, and I'm confident she'll give it her all.

She paddles out confidently and waits quietly to catch a wave, and when she does, I watch as she pops up on her board smoothly, her movements fluid as she navigates the wave with precision. She's in control, completely in sync with the water, and it's clear she's in her element. She carves through the face of the wave with ease, her turns sharp and controlled. There's no hesitation, no second guessing—just pure focus. She finishes with a smooth cutback, the spray of the water catching the light as she rides it out, and as she paddles back out to the lineup to continue, I can see the hint of a smile on her face.

Her eyes meet mine for a brief moment and I can't hold back the pride from my smile as I clap. There's a glint of satisfaction in her gaze, a quiet acknowledgement that today, she's back to her confident and fearless self.

By the end of the day, we've both done our best, and when the scores come in, we've managed to climb from sixth place up to third. She turns to look at me with a happy smile, one I can't help but return.

"We should be able to get back to first place in the next competition," I say as we turn to walk towards the car, "as long as we both perform like that again."

She nods in determination before we hop in and head back to the hotel.

NINE

MALIAH | WESTERN AUSTRALIA, AUSTRALIA

"OKAY, screw movie night, we need details," Eliana says the moment she jumps into the group video chat.

I feel like a deer caught in headlights as I stare at hers and Kairi's curious gazes through the screen.

"Details on what?"

"You and Koa, obviously," Kairi says, rolling her eyes.

"Yeah, he's been talking to the boys, but Fin refuses to give me details." Eliana pouts, crossing her arms over her chest.

He's been talking to the boys about me?

With a deep sigh, I spend the next hour filling them in on everything that's happened so far, including the night I spent in his room. By the end of it, Eliana's jaw has dropped to the floor and Kairi is squealing while she covers the blush creeping onto her cheeks.

"So...okay, wait. Let me get this straight," Eliana starts. "You discovered that you still have feelings for him, and he *very* clearly has feelings for you—"

"I don't know that," I cut in.

"What's there to know? He's being extremely obvious about it, Mal."

I want to believe her, with all my heart I want to, but I can't. I thought he had feelings for me before too, only to find out he had somehow fallen out of love with me in a matter of days.

"I think he just sees me more as a comfort while on tour. Someone he knows and is familiar with, that's why he seems affectionate," I theorize.

"You and I both know damn well that if I were on the tour with him instead of you, he would not be trying any of that with me," Kairi says, suddenly becoming very serious.

"Yeah, but it's just because we have a history together, It's a different type of comfort," I say in defence.

"He's a guy, he can find comfort with any girl there." Eliana's words reignite the ugly jealousy inside of me and I ball my hand into a fist on my lap. "But he's choosing you. I don't think you should write him off so easily."

That's easy to say when you don't know the full story.

If they knew how Koa and I ended, how he broke my heart, they wouldn't be trying to convince me to give him a chance right now.

"Anyway," I say, trying to change the subject. "Today has been emotionally exhausting, helicopter ride and all, I think I'm going to call it an early night and go to bed."

They both give me disappointed looks but neither of them fight me on it. We say our goodbyes and I quickly hang up before climbing out of bed and pacing around my room. Eliana was right about one thing, he can find comfort with any girl here.

I snatch my phone from the nightstand, my thumb hovering over his name before I finally press it, typing out a quick message.

ME:

What are you doing?

He doesn't answer right away, the seconds ticking by, and

after ten agonizing minutes of waiting for his reply, I find myself snatching my key card from my dresser and storming out of my room, crossing the hall to his door and banging my fist on it without a second thought, the sound echoing down the empty hallway.

I hear a muffled commotion behind the door—footsteps, something being knocked over—and finally, the door cracks open. Koa stands there, shirtless, a towel slung low around his hips, droplets of water glistening on his chest and dripping from the ends of his damp hair. His frown deepens as he looks down at me, confusion etched in his features.

"Maliah? Is everything okay?" he asks, stepping aside to let me in, his voice laced with concern.

But all the words I was ready to say vanish the moment I take in the sight of him—his broad shoulders, the defined lines of his abs, the way his wet hair clings to his forehead. My throat tightens and my mouth goes dry.

"I...I uh..." I stammer, unable to think of a single coherent thought.

He studies me for a moment, his gaze intense, before he reaches out and gently takes my hand. The warmth of his touch sends a jolt through me as he pulls me into his hotel room, the door clicking shut behind us. He leads me further inside, stopping at the foot of his bed before releasing my hand. I watch as he walks over to a chair, picking up a neatly folded pile of clothing and bringing it back to me.

"You left this the last time you were here," he says softly, holding the clothes out to me.

I look down and recognize the outfit I wore to the winery—the night I spent in this room with him. Memories of that evening flood my mind as I think back to the warmth of his body next to mine, the way I'd woken up on top of him. I remember how close I'd come to kissing him, the tension between us thick.

But I don't take the clothes. Instead, I raise my eyes to his, then let them drift to his lips. What would it have felt like that morning, to close the gap between us, to finally give in?

Before I can fully process the thought, the clothes slip from his hands, forgotten, and in an instant, he's on me. I'm pressed against the wall, his body molding to mine as his hands cup my face, his touch both gentle and possessive. His breath is warm against my skin as he leans in, his voice low and rough.

"I told myself I wouldn't hold back the next time you looked at me like that," he murmurs, his words sending a shiver down my spine.

My heart races, pounding so hard in my chest that I'm sure he can feel it. I look up into his eyes, seeing the desire that mirrors my own. It's clear he wants this as much as I do, the intensity between us growing with every passing second.

"Kiss me," I whisper, the words barely escaping my lips.

Koa doesn't hesitate. His mouth crashes into mine, and the world around us disappears. His kiss is demanding and hungry, but there's also a tenderness beneath it. The feel of his lips on mine ignites a fire deep within me, and I melt into him, my hands sliding up his chest, feeling the firm muscles beneath his skin.

Our bodies press together, every inch of him burning against me, and I can feel his heart beating just as wildly as mine. His hands move from my face, sliding down my neck. He leaves one hand to rest there while the either continues to slide down my shoulder, until he's gripping my waist and pulling me closer.

Koa deepens the kiss, as if he's afraid to let go, afraid to let this moment slip away. I respond by tangling my fingers in his hair as I tilt my head to give him better access. His tongue sweeps against mine, and I moan softly into his mouth, the sound vibrating through both of us.

The intensity of this moment threatens to overwhelm me,

and I find myself breaking the kiss. Koa rests his forehead against mine as we both gasp for air. His eyes are dark with lust, his breath ragged.

"Maliah," he breathes, his voice thick with emotion.

My heart twists painfully at the sound of his voice, filled with a longing I've missed for so long. But, instead of pulling him back in, instead of giving in to the overwhelming desire that's been building inside of me, I shake my head and gently place my hands on his chest to push him away. The warmth of his skin beneath my fingers feels like a cruel reminder now of everything I've lost.

I look down, avoiding his eyes as I try to steady my racing heart.

He's the one who broke up with me, I remind myself, the memory flashing through my mind.

He's the one who said he didn't love me anymore. The words echo in my head, cold and cutting, pulling me back to reality.

I finally look up at him and I know he can see the hesitation and hurt in my eyes, so I force a small smile, but it doesn't reach my eyes.

"I should go," I say, my voice barely above a whisper, scared that if I speak any louder I'll burst into tears. "I have to pack for the camping excursion tomorrow."

Confusion and hurt flicker in Koa's eyes for just a moment before he hides them behind a mask of calm. He silently watches as I bend down to pick up the clothes he'd handed me earlier, my hands trembling slightly as I gather them in my arms.

I avoid his gaze as I turn to the door, afraid that if I look at him again, I'll lose the strength to walk away. Every step feels like I'm leaving a part of myself behind, the room growing colder, emptier with each one. When I reach the door, I hesitate, my hand hovering over the handle. A part of me wants to turn back and run into his arms and forget everything that's happened between us, but I don't think I can. I close my eyes for a moment, trying to steady the storm of thoughts swirling around in my head.

It feels like I'm constantly here, on the brink of giving in, only to remember why I can't let that happen. With a deep breath, I force myself to turn the handle and open the door, but before I can step out, his hand connects with the wood, gently pushing it closed again. My heart skips a beat as I feel the warmth of his body behind me, so close I can almost feel his breath on my neck.

"Don't go," he says softly, his voice a mix of pleading and determination.

I swallow hard, my fingers tightening around the door handle as I fight to hold my ground. I can't let myself give in to him, not now. But the raw intensity in his voice, the way he's pleading for me to stay, leaves me frozen—unable to move, unable to think. I can't bring myself to look at him, afraid that I'll cave from a single glance.

"Maliah," he continues, his voice low, "please, just wait a moment. I know things are...complicated between us. Our past...it doesn't make things easy, but can we just focus on right now? On how we feel about each other in this moment?"

I shake my head slightly, my eyes still fixed on the door in front of me. "I don't know if I can do that," I whisper, my voice trembling with the weight of my emotions. "You hurt me, Koa."

"I know," he says, his voice thick with regret. "I know I hurt you, and I wish I could change what I did, what I said, but I can't. But this, what I feel for you right now and what you feel for me...it's real, Maliah. It's right here, this moment. Can't we just see where that takes us? Just for one day?"

His words hang in the air between us, and for a moment, I feel a flicker of hope. What if he's right? What if I could let go of the past, just for a day, and only focus on what we have now?

I'm torn between the safety of holding onto my pain and the possibility of something I've always wanted.

I finally turn to face him, my eyes meeting his. The sincerity in his gaze and the raw emotion that he's not even bothering to hide, makes my heart ache in a way I can't ignore anymore. Maybe I *can* try, just for a day, to see what happens if I let myself feel what I'm feeling without the burden of what happened in our past.

"I don't know if I can just forget," I admit. "But maybe I can try. Just for one day."

A look of relief and hope washes over his face, and he nods, stepping back slightly to give me space.

"That's all I'm asking for," he says with gratitude. "We can take it at our pace. No pressure, no expectations. Just us."

I give him a small, tentative smile, then turn back to the door. Opening it, I step out into the hallway, but instead of leaving, I pause, the door still slightly ajar. I glance back at him one last time, catching the hopeful expression on his face.

"Goodnight, Koa," I say softly.

"Sweet dreams," he replies, sending bolts of electricity through my body.

I close the door behind me and cross the hall back to my room. As soon as I close my door, I lean my back against the cool wood, clutching the clothes he'd returned to me earlier against my chest. My thoughts are a whirlwind, my heart still racing from what just happened. I don't know if this is the right choice, if I'm making a mistake by letting him back in, even for a day. But there's a part of me that wants to believe it's possible —to believe that maybe we can find our way back to each other.

I hug the clothes tighter, letting out a shaky breath as I close my eyes. Tomorrow, I'll try. I'll pretend the past didn't happen, just for the day. And maybe I'll find out if there's still something worth fighting for between us.

TEN

MALIAH | WESTERN AUSTRALIA, AUSTRALIA

I WAKE up feeling refreshed this morning, like a weight has been lifted from my shoulders. I jump in the shower, remembering the kiss I had with Koa last night, along with the conversation. I'm nervous but I'm more excited than anything to see how this goes. After my shower, I quickly do my hair, tying it up into a ponytail before changing into comfortable clothing.

I grab the duffle bag that I packed last night and leave my room, not expecting to find Koa waiting for me in the hallway. He smiles softly at me, studying my expression to see if I've maybe changed my mind since last night. I smile at him reassuringly, and he pushes himself off the wall to approach me.

"Good morning, princess," he says, taking my duffel from me and throwing it onto his own shoulder.

Ever the gentleman.

We make our way to the lobby, meeting the rest of the surfers just as the transportation bus arrives. Today we're going to the Pinnacles Desert to sandboard, before setting up tents to stargaze for the night. For once, it's an excursion I'm looking forward to. The idea of sandboarding across the dunes sounds like a much-needed escape from the intensity of our competitions.

Koa leaves my side to drop our duffel bags in the pile of bags for the bus operator to load, before returning to me and taking my hand in his. I don't miss the curious glances of nearby girls, or the annoyed expression on Charles' face as he watches us from a distance.

As we load onto the bus, Koa finds us a seat near the middle and slides in with me, our shoulders brushing as I settle.

"Did you have a good sleep?" he asks, the corner of his mouth turning up.

I nod. "One of the best sleeps I've had since coming on this tour," I admit, feeling my cheeks warm.

"It didn't top waking up with you on me, but it was definitely close."

My eyes go round before I whirl my head in every direction making sure no one heard him. He lets out a boyish chuckle before chewing on his bottom lip to try and hide the amusement. The bus rumbles to life and we fall into a silence that feels different now—softer, less strained.

By the time we arrive at the Pinnacles Desert, the sun is high, casting long shadows across the strange limestone formations that jut out from the sand. The landscape is surreal, almost otherworldly, with its golden dunes.

Everyone piles out of the bus, the excitement in the air palpable as everyone heads toward the sandboards lined up nearby. I watch as Koa grabs a sandboard, effortlessly balancing it under his arm like a surfboard before turning to me with a grin.

"You ready, princess?"

"Ready as I'll ever be," I reply, trying to match his enthusiasm even though my stomach is doing somersaults.

We make our way to the top of one of the dunes along with our production team, the sand warm beneath my feet as we climb. When we reach the peak, Koa sets his board down, motioning for me to do the same. I follow his lead, my heart racing as anticipation builds. He glances over at me, a playful gleam dancing in his eyes.

"Race you to the bottom?"

I can't help but laugh, the sound surprising me. Seeing him like this reminds me of when we were still getting to know each other and doing risky things to see how far the other would go, like climbing that ancient tree when we were younger.

"You're on," I reply.

We both push off at the same time, the boards slipping down the slope with a rush of speed that sends my heart soaring excitedly. The wind whips through my blonde hair, and for a few amazing moments, I'm free—free from the weight of the past and the expectations of the future. It's just the two of us, racing through the desert like we're the only people in the world. It reminds me of how surfing makes me feel, the freedom is addicting.

When we reach the bottom, breathless and laughing, Koa's hands find mine. He pulls me close, the laughter still lingering in his eyes.

"You almost had me," he mumbles.

"Almost," I tease back, feeling lighter than I have in months.

We spend the rest of the day racing each other down the dunes, taking turns on who wins, but as the sun begins to set we decide to take a break.

"Come with me," Koa says, his voice soft.

Curious, I follow him as he leads us away from the others. We walk in comfortable silence, the sound of our footsteps muffled by the soft sand beneath us. As we crest a smaller dune, Koa points ahead and my breath catches in my throat.

A small group of wild koalas lounge lazily in the low branches of a nearby eucalyptus tree, their round bodies and fluffy ears making them look unreal. I can't hold back my smile as I watch them, their slow movements and peaceful demeanour making me feel strangely calm.

"I noticed them on the bus ride in," he says, from behind me.

"They're incredible," I whisper.

"You're incredible," he says.

I glance up at him and realize he's watching me instead of the koalas. My heart flutters and I look away, pretending to focus on the koalas, but the warmth in my chest spreads through my whole body.

We stand there for a few more moments, soaking in the beauty of the scene, before heading back to the campsite. The sky has already begun to deepen into twilight, so we quickly set up our tent together, our hands brushing occasionally as we work. Each touch sends a spark through me, and I can tell he feels it too in the way he hesitates.

Most of the teammates were given their own tents, but some, including Koa and I, were given one larger tent to share. I try not to overthink it as we put our duffle bags inside of the tent before joining the others around a small fire. Only a small group of cameramen remain to film us, while the rest of them are setting up their cameras pointing toward the sky and surrounding landscape for filler shots.

I ignore the lens as I take a can of flavoured malt liquor from Koa. We both open our cans and take a sip, feeling refreshed after a day in the heat. I try to listen to the stories being shared around the campfire, but all I can focus on is the way his leg presses against mine, the way his shoulder brushes mine.

A burst of gasps has me jumping back to the present as I follow everyone's gaze to the sky, and my jaw drops at the sight of The Milky Way arching above us like a river of stars that seem almost close enough to touch. There are shooting stars streaking across the sky, their trail of light fading into the night.

It's beautiful and I feel overwhelmed with gratitude for being able to experience something so magical.

When the fire begins to die down and others start heading to their separate tents, Koa and I share a look before we both rise and slip away from the remaining people in the group into the privacy of our tent.

Inside the tent, the air feels charged, thick with unspoken tension as Koa pulls the tent flap closed behind us, sealing us in our own little world. We both change out of our sandy clothes and into the nightwear that we packed.

Koa wears a black T-shirt and a pair of light grey sweat-pants, slipping them over his boxers, before turning to look at me, resting his arm on his knee. I pull my top off, revealing my naked top half to him before I slip on an oversized pink T-shirt. I don't miss the way his Adam's apple bobs in his throat. I don't feel embarrassed showing him my bare body, he's seen it before. I slowly slip off my thong before throwing on a pair of pyjama shorts.

We sit and stare at one another for a moment in charged silence, and I'm not sure who moves first, but suddenly we're wrapped in each other, his hands on my waist and mine tangled in his hair. Our lips meet in a rush of heat, the kiss hungry and desperate, as if we've been holding back for far too long.

The dim light from the lantern we'd placed in the corner of the tent casts a soft glow over our features as he lowers me onto my back on the tent mattress. His body presses against mine, solid and warm, and I can feel the tension in his muscles as he pulls me closer, deepening the kiss.

His hands roam over my body, exploring, memorizing, while my fingers trace the lines of his back, the hard planes of his chest. His mouth moves from mine, finding the sensitive spot on my neck just under my ear and I let out a low moan as he gently sucks the spot. He continues his descent, kissing my collar bone just as his hand slips under my shirt. He finds my pebbled nipple and pinches it gently, causing me to jolt, a chuckle escaping from his mouth.

He lifts my shirt and stares at me appreciatively before lowering his lips to my nipple. Just as his lips close around the sensitive skin, a sudden, playful scream pierces the night, startling us both. We pull apart, panting, and he brings himself back up resting his forehead against mine as we catch our breath. Outside we can hear the others laughing, the sound of someone chasing after whoever screamed.

We both laugh softly, the moment broken but not lost. Koa brushes a stray lock of hair behind my ear, his earlier urgency giving way to something gentler, more tender.

"Maybe it's a sign," he murmurs, his voice low and rough.

"Maybe," I whisper back, my heart still pounding. But instead of moving away, I lean into him, resting my head against his chest. His arms wrap around me, holding me close, and for the first time in a long time, I feel as if everything is exactly where it's meant to be.

We settle down, the warmth of his body against mine lulling me into a peaceful haze until I drift off to sleep with a feeling of contentment I haven't felt in a very long time.

ELEVEN

KOA | TAVARUA, FIJI

"IT'S SHAPED LIKE A HEART," Maliah says quietly, more to herself.

Although her hands are in fists, knuckles white, she's bravely looking out of the plane's window down at the island we'll be staying on for the next two weeks. I glance out the window to see what she means, spotting the small heart-shaped island instantly. It's surrounded by vibrant hues of turquoise water, and I can see the massive waves from up here.

"Prepare for landing at the Nadi International Airport in 15 minutes," the pilot's voice sounds over the intercom.

Maliah jerks back in her seat, gripping her arm rests as an anxious expression takes over. Still afraid of heights, but she's getting better.

"Relax, we'll be fine," I say encouragingly, but I'm met with a fake smile and an eye roll.

I'm not sure why I thought things would be different after waking up from our night camping in the Pinnacles Desert. I guess I had hoped it would change something, maybe show her how easy it would be to go back to how we were when things were good between us. Instead, I woke up to an empty tent, she'd even taken her duffel bag with her. The bus ride back to our hotel was almost completely silent because she pretended to sleep the whole way, and we've barely spoken in the two days since.

I release an exaggerated sigh and close my eyes for the remainder of our flight. When we land in Nadi, I'm not surprised to find someone from our production team waiting for us with a private vehicle after we climb off the plane. We toss our bags into the trunk and hop into the backseats, small cameras fixed all over the interior point directly at our faces.

Forty-five minutes later, we're reunited with the rest of the surfers and production teams on a boat transfer to Tavarua Island. Maliah wanders off to stand with a group of female surfers for the thirty-minute boat ride, and I'm left wondering if I pushed her too far.

"So, are you two a thing now, or what?"

I glance to my left to see that Reese has joined me as I stare out at the crystal-clear water. I look over his shoulder and spot Charles close enough to listen in on us. His eyes find mine before he quickly looks away pretending to be focused on something else. I roll my eyes and return to staring at the ocean.

"I never said we weren't a thing," I reply.

"Does Maliah know that?" Reese asks.

I force a chuckle. "Did Charles send you to do his dirty work?"

He looks over his shoulder at Charles who is now staring up at the clouds as if they're the most fascinating thing he's ever seen.

"Nah," Reese replies. "I just noticed she's been a bit hot and cold with you on this tour."

I nod in agreement. "We have a history," I explain, "but Maliah knows we're more than friends, even if she tries to pretend like it's not true."

"That's how you know she's got it bad for you."

Reese closes his eyes and relaxes as the wind blows through his brown hair, sending it swirling in front of him for the rest of the boat ride. At some point, Charles had relocated next to Maliah, and I watch with a bitter taste in my mouth as he makes her laugh.

When we finally reach the island, I'm one of the first to get off the damn boat. I can't stand watching him put a smile on her face when it should be me doing that.

I study the island and feel a bang in my chest as I take in the white sand, swaying palm trees, and dense greenery. It reminds me of Hawaii. It reminds me of *home.*

Unlike the others on The Saltwater Shredders team, I wasn't born and raised in Saltwater Springs. My parents used up almost every cent they had to fly me out from our small community in Hawaii when I was seventeen. Gabriel had an opening on the youth team that included food and boarding, and after seeing a few recordings of me at local Hawaiian surf competitions, he had reached out and offered me the spot, as long as I would be able to cover my own flight expenses. I haven't been back since, but I miss it more than anything.

"All right, surfers, please stand next to your partner," Jackie calls out to us from further up the beach.

I watch as everyone shuffles around and seconds later Maliah finds her spot next to me. I force myself not to look down at her, even when I feel the heat of her gaze roaming over me.

"The accommodations here are going to be a bit different," Jackie starts. "Because of the high cost to stay on the island resort, you'll be sharing a beachfront villa with your partner for the next two weeks."

My jaw nearly hits the ground, and Maliah stiffens beside me as groans and giggles ripple through the surrounding surfers. I slowly close my mouth, composing myself as the cameramen hover around trying to capture everyone's reactions. I swallow past the nervous lump in my throat and allow myself a quick glance at Maliah, only to find her already looking up at me with flared nostrils.

Staying in a hotel room across the hall from her for a few days was hard enough. How am I going to share a whole villa with just her for two whole weeks?

"David here is the resort manager." A short round man with dark skin and grey hair beams at us before he steps forward with room keys. "He'll come around to each of you to hand you your room key. There is only one key per room so learn to share with your partner."

When David reaches Maliah and I, I watch as she extends her hand out for the key, but I quickly snatch it from his hand instead.

"She has a history of losing keys," I explain when he raises his brow to me. "It's better if I'm the one that holds onto it."

"It was one time," she argues, turning to glare at me with her hands on her hips.

"One is more than enough," I say, giving her a fake smile before turning back to David. "Don't you agree?"

He looks between us several times, the nervousness evident in his expression before he plasters on a polite smile.

"Whatever works best for you both," he says before hurriedly moving onto the next group.

"Great," Maliah mutters, "now I have to worry about you locking me out of our villa."

"I would never do that." I roll my eyes and turn to face her. "You, on the other hand, wouldn't think twice to do that to me. Another reason why I'll be holding onto these for the next two weeks."

I wave the keys between us, high enough for her not to be able to reach them in case she tries.

"Whatever." She crosses her arms over her chest. "Let's go."

I look around and notice that groups are leaving towards their villas with a staff member. A grumpy man approaches us with an army of younger guys, surely not even eighteen yet, each holding onto our bags.

"Please follow me," he says, turning towards the villas.

We follow him right up to a large villa with the number twenty-two hanging over the glass sliding door. The whole villa is made from timber and woven bamboo, with a thatched Fijian-style roof.

He turns to me and gestures that I unlock the door, which I do, letting myself and Maliah in first. It's an open concept villa, which makes it look extremely spacious especially with the high ceilings and large windows. All of the furniture is made from wood, and I notice paintings and wall art are the only hint of colour in this neutral toned home, but it all blends together nicely.

The boys that carry our luggage pass us and head towards a room. We follow them and come face to face with a king-sized bed, draped with a mosquito net.

"Where's the second room?" I ask, turning to look at the grumpy man.

"This villa only has one room," he states.

I feel all the blood rush out of my limbs and straight to my cock. I'm going to have to share a bed with Maliah for two weeks?

"Absolutely not," she argues, pushing past us to storm around the rest of the villa.

"So, everyone has to share a bed with their partner?" I ask the man, confused on how that will go down with the partners that have not been on the best of terms in the tour.

He shakes his head. "Only you two."

"Why is that?" I ask, my heart pounding loudly.

He looks down at his clipboard. "We ran out of double bed

villas and someone by the name of Gabriel Matthews confirmed that a single bed villa would be fine for you two.”

“I’m sorry,” Maliah says almost hysterically as she barges back into the bedroom. “Did you just say Gabriel Matthews approved this?”

She swings her arms around wildly, gesturing to the room. He stares at her expressionless.

“Correct,” he says, before turning back to me. “Now, do you mind signing this luggage delivery confirmation so that me and my team can leave?”

I take the pen from him and quickly sign my name before him and the young men leave, sliding the glass door shut behind them.

“I’m going to kill Gabriel.” Maliah seethes. I can almost see the steam floating out of her ears as she turns tomato red.

“Relax.” I sigh, walking over to my luggage. “I’ll sleep on the couch if sleeping next to me again is that big of a deal.”

I feel pathetic saying it, but it’s true. You would think our past years of sleeping next to each other, not to mention the tent two days ago, would make sharing a bed easier on her, but it’s almost like it’s made it worse.

She watches silently as I wheel out my suitcase and duffle bag to the living room next to the couch. I lay my suitcase down and rummage through it until I find my swimming trunks. I pull off my pants and shirt, throwing the trunks over my boxers, before walking out of the villa without a word and making my way into the ocean for a swim to clear my mind.

“How was the plane ride?” Gabriel asks over a video call later that night.

Maliah doesn't say a word as she glares at the camera. I glance at her with a raised eyebrow before turning back to look at Gabriel.

"It was comfortable. Thanks for letting us use your plane for the tour."

He nods, pleased, but I can tell he's a ball of stress. He looks like he's lost weight and there are bags under his eyes now.

"Any luck finding Zalea?" I ask, positive she's the reason for this version of Gabriel.

"We know she's in Italy, but I'm still having a hard time tracking her down myself," he says, running a hand through his usually perfect hair which is now pointing in every which way. "But I'm sure I'm getting close."

I nod and glance at Maliah once more, the glare hasn't left her face and I'm not even sure if she's blinked yet. I clear my throat and turn back to the camera, noticing that Gabriel is completely oblivious to her.

"Okay, so for this competition you'll be surfing Cloud-break," he says, propping his phone up against something as he uses his hands to explain. "It's a very tricky wave."

"Why's that?" I press.

"There are multiple sections so you'll both need to nego-tiate yourselves to escape the wave's thick lip."

"Sounds like the ideal wave for us," I say, smirking. "How do you suggest we tackle it, Coach?"

Gabriel chuckles as he nods in agreement. "There will be a lot of tube riding opportunities with this wave so take advan-tage of that. It's also got a great shoulder for carving, round-house outbacks, and plenty of power surfing maneuvers. This is the wave that you should really show off what makes you both the amazing surfers that you are."

"Got it," I say, making mental notes for us both since I know Maliah is not paying attention right now.

"Just remember, there are three points to this wave to keep

an eye on. The point, which is the top, is where you'll find the bigger waves perfect for top-to-bottom surfing. You'll be able to show off the maneuvers we've practiced here, like cutbacks, and bottom-turns. The middle point of the wave is where you'll find the tube time, but it's fast so don't let your guard down or you'll wipe out. And lastly is the inside, also known as Shish Kebabs, the wave speeds up here while also becoming extremely hollow so stay sure-footed or you'll get swallowed in an instant."

I nod, already starting to plan how I want to ride this wave.

"But Koa," Gabriel says in a warning voice, "plenty of surfers have risked their lives barreling this wave. Keep an eye on the razor-sharp reef or that could be you, too."

"Got it, Coach." I nod again.

"Maliah," he says, finally turning his eyes towards her with his brow raised. "Why the hell have you been staring at me like you're going to kill me?"

"I think the better question is why the hell you put us into a villa that only has one bed?"

Gabriel frowns at her, composing himself before answering.

"I'm sorry, did I miss something?" he asks, crossing his arms as he leans back in his seat. "Were you two not sharing a bed, in my house, for years? Or even sharing a tent two days ago?"

Her face turns crimson as she continues to glare at him. "You should have asked if we were okay with it before you made that decision."

"You really can't manage to share a bed with your teammate for two weeks? I'm not asking you two to fuck, though I find it hard to believe you two haven't already done that on this tour yet, it's just for sleeping on, Maliah."

"Oh my god," she exclaims, throwing her hands into the air, "you are such an impossible person, Gabriel. No wonder Zalea ran off."

Gabriel is silent as his eyes narrow on her, I know whatever he plans to say next will be catastrophic.

"Let's call it a night, I'm tired after all the traveling," I say, butting in.

"You're right," he says, turning his attention back to me. "It's been a long day for all three of us so let's reconnect after the competition. I trust you two can handle the practice without me for the next few days."

And with that, the call drops, and Gabriel is gone. I let out an exhausted sigh before turning to Maliah who is frowning at the floor, her cheeks still red.

"Are you hungry?" I ask, pushing myself up to my feet before holding my hand out to help her up.

She stares at my hand for a minute before slowly reaching out and taking it, allowing me to help her to her feet.

"A bit," she admits, just before her stomach growls loudly.

"A bit?" I question teasingly before I make my way to the kitchen and open the fully stocked fridge, pulling out ingredients to make a quick fish and veggie dinner for us.

Maliah joins in after a few minutes, walking around me to grab ingredients, brushing against me each time until I'm positive she's doing it on purpose. I fight with everything I have to keep my hard on from showing, but by the time the food is done, she's the only thing I want to eat.

I watch as she plates our dinner and brings it to the table, waiting for me to take a seat across from her, which I do.

"The fish looks good," she says, before cutting into hers.

"Does it?" I ask absentmindedly, as I watch her place her fork in her mouth, her perfect plump lips wrapping around it.

The corners of her lips lift, and I raise my eyes to hers only to find that she's watching me, amused. I clear my throat before I shove a piece of my own fish into my mouth. It tastes good but I know she'd taste better.

"So," Maliah says, picking up another piece of fish with her fork. "If we win, what do you plan to do with your half of the earnings?"

I hesitate before answering, weighing how much I'm willing to share with her. But it's a genuine question, and it deserves a genuine answer.

"You know that abandoned house up the street from The Shredder House?"

"The white and green one, just off the main beach?"

I nod. "I want to buy it, fix it up, and move in."

Her chewing slows as she looks at me, a mix of emotions running across her beautiful features.

"You're moving out of our house?"

"Out of the team residence." I nod, diverting my eyes back to my plate as I grab some of the vegetables. "I think it's time for me to start exploring life outside of the team."

A few beats of silence pass between us before she speaks again.

"Does that mean you're planning to leave the team, too?"

I watch as she places her fork down beside her plate and focuses on me entirely.

"I haven't decided yet," I admit, growing uncomfortable with the questions. "What about you, what's your big plan once you win the money?"

She ponders the question for a moment before picking up her fork and playing with her food.

"I've been teetering with the idea of starting my own small business," she says, pushing the vegetables around on her plate with her fork. "I just don't know how that would work with our strict surfing schedule."

"What kind of small business?" I ask, my brows jumping up in surprise.

I was positive her answer would be more along the lines of a closet refresh or an all-inclusive trip somewhere expensive. I never thought she'd want to stray away from surfing in any capacity, not with the amount of dedication she's poured into it over the years.

"I was thinking of a bakery," she says, her cheeks turning pink.

"That makes sense," I say, trying to sound casual. "You've always loved to bake."

Her head shoots up and her round eyes find mine. "You think it's a good idea?"

I nod, smiling at her encouragingly. "I think any idea you have is a good idea," I admit.

She scoffs. "Really? So what if I told you my plan was to buy that abandoned house and turn it into a bakery?"

I narrow my eyes at her, challengingly. "I guess we'll just have to see who outbids who."

"I guess so," she says, narrowing her eyes back at me before returning her attention to her plate.

I can't stop the small smile that tugs at my lips as I watch her, imagining how annoyed she'd get at actually being in a bidding war with me.

Something to look forward to.

When we both finish eating, I stand up and take our plates from the table before walking over to the sink and cleaning them, while Maliah wipes down the table. When we're both done, I start to walk towards the couch that I'll be calling my bed for the next two weeks.

"Wait," I hear her quiet voice say from the kitchen table.

I stop and look at her over my shoulder, raising a questioning brow at her.

"You can't sleep on the couch," she says, sounding both embarrassed and annoyed.

"And why not?" I ask, turning to face her.

She hesitates, bumping her palm against the side of her thigh nervously. I slowly walk up to her, stopping when we're just inches apart.

"Why not, Maliah?" I push.

"Well, because!"

I hold back my chuckle at her frown. "Because?"

"Because there isn't a mosquito net for the couch, and you could get bitten and die from...from...whatever disease the mosquito has."

I smirk as I watch her face turn crimson again.

"And we can't have me dying, can we?" I ask in a teasing tone.

"Oh, shut up," she says, smacking my chest gently as she rips her gaze away on a frown.

I reach up and gently take her chin, guiding her gaze back to me. Her eyes flicker between mine, then dart to my mouth, uncertainty written all over her face, as if she's unsure whether I'll make another move.

"So, is this your way of asking me to sleep with you?" I murmur, keeping my eyes on hers.

"No," she practically shouts, pulling her chin out of my grasp. "This is me offering my teammate the option to sleep next to me, not with me, to avoid a horrible death."

I chuckle before turning around and picking up my bag from the floor.

"Well, if my life depends on it," I smirk as I look back at her, "then I guess I don't have much of a choice, do I?"

Her face turns three shades darker before she turns on her heel in a huff. "Whatever," I hear her mutter as she speed-walks back to the room. I chuckle as I follow her, watching as she grabs a change of clothes from her bag and stomps over to the bathroom to shower.

Two weeks in a bed next to her. What's the worst that can happen?

TWELVE

MALIAH | TAVARUA, FIJI

I'VE OFFICIALLY LOST my mind. That's the only explanation for why I agreed to this death trap of an excursion. I should've faked feeling sick, or pretended to have injured my leg, but instead here I am. I can feel the cameras zooming in on every one of my shaky breaths, capturing the fear I'm doing a horrible job of hiding.

The ski lift jerks to life as it starts to ascend, the cables rattling in the most unsettling way. The air is warm on Tavarua, but the higher we go, the cooler the breeze becomes, and it begins to bite against my skin. My fingers are clenched so tight around the metal bar that they're turning numb. I can't look down. The lush canopy of trees below looks too far away—too distant, like something from a dream.

Or a nightmare. Yeah, definitely a nightmare.

"I'm gonna pass out," I mumble through gritted teeth, my voice small and trembling.

The thought of being suspended so high up in nothing but this flimsy seat causes my stomach to twist into knots.

Koa, of course, is completely unfazed. He sits beside me, legs relaxed, one arm casually draped over the back of our chair. He glances at me with that smug grin that always makes me want to punch him, and yet—God, why does he have to look so good?

"You could sit on me," he says, leaning closer with a mock-serious tone. "Might help with the passing out part."

I snap my head towards him, narrowing my eyes. "Say that again, and I'll throw you off this lift."

He laughs, a deep, rumbling sound that echoes in the air between us. The crew behind us probably got that on camera too, along with the audio from the mics attached to our tops—great. Now I'm not only terrified but also irritated. Koa knows just how to get under my skin, and right now that's the last thing I need.

The ski lift lurches again, and I nearly yelp, but I manage to keep my lips pressed shut. Koa's laughter fades as he watches me, his expression softening just a bit.

"You're going to be fine, Maliah," he says, his voice low, almost soothing. "I won't let anything happen to you. Besides, we're almost at the top."

As much as I hate to admit it, his voice calms me just a little. I keep my eyes forward, focused on the ridge that's finally coming into view. The second we hit solid ground, I jump out of the lift, my legs wobbling beneath me, and let out a deep breath I didn't realize I was holding. Koa hops out too, grinning like this is the best day of his life.

"I haven't seen your legs shake like that in a long time," he says, winking as he stretches his arms above his head with a smirk.

"I hate you," I mutter, though there's no heat in my words. All the heat has found its way to my face instead.

He has a horrible habit of saying things that remind me of what it was like when we were together. A time I'm trying to move on from, with horrible luck.

I turn around and see the zipline platform almost instantly, my stomach twisting all over again.

The towering trees seem even taller now that I'm standing at their level. The zipline cables stretch across the dense jungle, disappearing into the horizon. The other surfers along with their camera crews are already gearing up, helmets and harnesses in place, while the instructors prepare the lines. I can feel my heart pounding harder.

There's no way I'm doing this.

But before I can come up with an excuse to back out, a crew member approaches me with a harness in hand.

"Ready to zipline?" he asks, way too cheerfully for my liking.

I open my mouth to say no, to refuse outright, but Koa steps in next to me before I get the chance.

"Want to strap yourself to me? That way, if the cord breaks, I'll break your fall," he says, his tone light but his eyes holding that playful glint that drives me insane.

I glare at him. "You're the worst."

But somehow, the offer doesn't sound so bad. I mean, if I have to die, at least I'll take him down with me, right?

I sigh, nodding reluctantly. "Fine, but if you make one more joke about dying, I swear..."

He just laughs again and grabs the harness, stepping behind me to help strap me in. I hate how my skin tingles the moment his fingers brush against me, how my body reacts even though I try so hard to fight it. He pulls the straps tighter, securing them across my chest and waist before buckling my harness to his own, and then his arms are suddenly around me. I can feel the heat of him, the solid weight of his chest against my back.

"You okay?" he asks quietly, his lips dangerously close to my ear.

No, I want to scream. But my voice betrays me. "Yeah," I manage to croak.

He guides my hands to the straps in front of me, ensuring I'm holding on before he grabs on, his other hand slipping around my waist to pull me closer. I swear my lungs stop working as he presses me firmly against him, his breath tickling my ear.

"I'm so proud of you," he whispers.

I nearly melt at his words, my heart hammering wildly in my chest. Of course, he can't see the way my face flushes, but I know he feels the way I tense in his arms. My mind is a mess, spinning from the close contact, from his soft, low voice that sends heat straight to my core.

The next thing I know, we're off. The zipline jerks and suddenly we're flying, the wind roaring in my ears as the jungle blurs beneath us. I scream, clutching the straps for dear life as the trees blow past us in a blur, but there's something exhilarating about it too. The rush, the speed—maybe it's because Koa is holding me, grounding me, that I feel like I can breathe.

When we land on the next platform, I can barely stand. My legs feel like jelly, but Koa keeps me steady as the crew disconnects us and prepares for the next zipline. I should be terrified for the next part, but all I can think about is the warmth of Koa's body against mine.

As we get strapped in again, his lips brush against my ear, his breath hot against my skin. "Hearing you scream like that turned me on way too much," he murmurs, his voice sending a shiver down my spine.

I gasp, my heart jumping into my throat as he presses himself against me, the unmistakable hardness of him making my breath catch.

"Koa," I whisper, barely able to find my voice.

"Just being honest," he teases, his arm tightening around my waist again.

I bite my lip, refusing to scream this time as we take off again. But despite the flurry of nerves and heat coursing through me, there's a strange sense of comfort in the way he holds me—like nothing in the world could hurt me as long as I'm in his arms.

And that scares me more than anything.

By the time we finish with the ziplines, my entire body feels like it's buzzing. Part of it is the adrenaline that's still coursing through me, but the other part is most definitely because of Koa. Every touch, every whisper—it's like he's rewired my senses, and I'm not sure if I'll ever recover from it.

The crew is already guiding us toward the next activity, the cave tour. I'd hoped that by some miracle, I'd be able to catch my breath, but of course, we have to keep moving, and my heart hasn't stopped racing since Koa pressed himself against me on that last zipline.

"Come on, Princess. Try to keep up." Koa's teasing voice snaps me out of my thoughts. I glance up to see him grinning over his shoulder, as we follow the rest of the group into the mouth of the cave.

"Shut up," I mutter, "and I told you to stop calling me that." There's no bite to my words. I'm too distracted by the massive limestone entrance looming ahead. The opening is wide, and from the outside, it looks like nothing more than a dark hole in the earth. But as we step inside, the cool air hits me, and the temperature drops instantly. It's a welcome relief after the heat of the jungle, but there's something eerie about it too.

The guide ahead starts talking about the history of the cave —how it was formed, and the ancient tribes that used it for rituals—but my mind is elsewhere. The sound of dripping water echoes through the chambers, and every step we take seems to reverberate through the stone walls. Stalactites hang from the ceiling like jagged teeth, and pools of water glisten faintly in the dim light provided by our flashlights.

"Kind of spooky, isn't it?" Koa's voice is closer now, his shoulder brushing against mine as we walk side by side.

I nod, swallowing hard. "Yeah, a little." My voice sounds small in the cavernous space.

He chuckles, and for a moment, I wish I could be as calm as he is. The tightness in my chest hasn't gone away, but it's not the cave making me anxious. It's the fact that Koa is so close— again—and I don't know how to handle it. Every time I try to focus on the tour, a whiff of his scent or the warmth radiating off him pulls me back, drawing me into the storm of emotions he's awakened.

We stop at a large chamber, the ceiling towering above us. The guides pause to let us take in the view, explaining how the stalagmites were formed over thousands of years. The other surfers are taking photos, laughing, and chatting, but I'm distracted by the faint sound of water trickling somewhere deeper in the cave.

Without thinking, I step away from the group, my curiosity getting the better of me. I follow the sound, the dim light of the cave flickering on the damp walls as I move toward a narrow passage. The air smells earthy and cool, and the ground beneath my feet is uneven, covered in small rocks and puddles.

"Maliah, wait up." Koa's voice comes from behind me, and I turn just as he catches up, his flashlight illuminating the passageway ahead.

"What are you doing?" he asks, though his tone isn't accusatory—more curious than anything.

"I just...wanted to see where the water was coming from," I admit, my voice a little shaky. There's something about this place that feels otherworldly, almost magical, and I can't help but be drawn to it.

Koa steps closer, his arm brushing against mine again, sending another wave of heat through my body. "You really shouldn't wander off. What if you get lost?"

I scoff, trying to hide the way my pulse quickens whenever he's near. "I'm not a kid, Koa. I can handle myself."

But even as I say the words, I realize how much I've come to rely on his presence—especially in moments like this, when everything feels a little too big, a little too overwhelming. And of course, he picks up on that.

He smirks, leaning in slightly. "Are you sure about that? Because from where I'm standing, it looks like you're pretty rattled."

Before I can snap back at him, the narrow passage opens up into another chamber. This one smaller, more intimate, with a crystal-clear pool of water at its centre. The trickling sound I heard earlier comes from the water gently dripping off the rocks above, creating small ripples in the otherwise still surface.

"Wow," I breathe, momentarily forgetting Koa's teasing. The pool glows faintly, reflecting the pale light from the rocks. It's beautiful, serene, like something out of a dream.

"Not bad, huh?" Koa says, his voice softer now, less playful. He steps up beside me, and for a moment, we just stand there in silence, taking it all in.

The atmosphere in the cave feels different here—calmer, quieter. The tension between us, though still there, seems to ease a little, replaced by something else. Something softer.

"Sometimes," Koa says after a moment, his voice barely above a whisper, "you just have to let go and trust that everything will work out."

I glance at him, my heart skipping a beat. There's something in his tone, in the way he's looking at me, that makes my chest tighten. He's not talking about the cave anymore.

And maybe...maybe he's right. Maybe it's time to stop holding back, to stop being so afraid of what might happen again. I've been running from my feelings for him for so long, but here, in this quiet, magical place, it feels impossible to keep pretending.

I take a deep breath, the cool air filling my lungs, and before I can second-guess myself, I speak, "Koa, I—"

But before I can finish, the rest of the group calls out to us, their voices echoing through the cave. The spell is broken, and the moment slips away.

Koa smiles, that teasing glint back in his eyes. "Come on. We should catch up before they think we got lost."

I nod, my heart still racing as we turn around to rejoin the group. But even as we walk away from the pool, the feeling lingers—that unmistakable shift between us. No matter how much I try to fight it, I know there's no going back now.

THIRTEEN

KOA |TAVARUA, FIJI

AFTER THE LONG day of activities, my muscles are sore, and I can tell by the way Maliah keeps flexing her shoulders that she's feeling the same. I almost whimper in pleasure when I realize the cave tour ends with a spa. The production crew directs us towards the mud spa area, where a nearby hot spring has steam rising from the mud pools, a calming scent of lavender and eucalyptus drifting through the air. I notice Maliah eyeing the mud bath with equal parts curiosity and hesitation and I can't hold back my grin.

"Come on," I say, nudging her shoulder. "You've already faced your fear of heights today. A little mud isn't going to hurt you."

She rolls her eyes, but I catch the smile she tries to hide. We both grab robes and towels from the attendants before heading to the changing rooms. By the time we come out, the sun is starting to dip lower in the sky, casting a warm golden light over everything.

Maliah sits on the edge of the mud pool, her toes dipping into the warmth, testing it out. I take a seat beside her, watching as she gets used to the temperature. She leans forward slightly and slides in, so I follow right behind her, feeling the soft, warm mud squish under my feet as I lower myself in.

She sighs, closing her eyes as she sinks into the mud, clearly enjoying herself. "Okay, I'll admit," she says, "this is pretty nice."

"Told you." I smirk, leaning back and letting the warmth seep into my muscles.

We sit like this for a few minutes, just enjoying the quiet sounds of nature and the heat, but I can't resist reaching over, grabbing a handful of mud, and slowly smearing it along her upper arm. Her skin is soft under my fingers, and I feel the subtle tremor as my touch lingers just a moment too long. She opens one eye to look at me, raising an eyebrow.

"You really want to start that?" she asks, her voice dripping with playful challenge.

I grin. "Why not? It's part of the experience, right?"

She rolls her eyes but grabs her own handful of mud, smearing it along my arm in return. We go back and forth like this for a minute, the mood light and easy, until I smear some along her shoulder and down her back, my fingers lingering on her skin for just a little longer than necessary.

"You know," I say softly as I rub the mud across her shoulders, "I've been thinking about what you said before. About starting your own bakery."

She tenses a little under my touch but doesn't pull away. "Yeah?"

"Yeah." I pause for a moment, gathering my thoughts. "I really do think it's a good idea. I mean it. You've always had that passion for baking, and it makes sense for you to want to explore that."

She turns slightly, looking at me with wide eyes. "You really think it could work? Even with surfing and everything?"

"I do," I say, my voice steady. "You're good at juggling things. And who says you can't do both? Surf and bake? You can hire people to help with the day-to-day stuff while you're away, but it could be something that's yours, you know?"

I know how important it is to Maliah to have something that's *hers*. That was never surfing, she only joined The Saltwater Shredders because her parents had pushed her into it. Having her on this tour has been her father's dream for as long as I can remember.

Her lips tug into a soft smile, and she looks down, rubbing a bit of mud between her fingers. "It's scary, though. Stepping away from something I've known my whole life."

I nod. "But you can't let fear stop you from doing what you want. And besides, you're not really stepping away. You'd still be surfing. You're just...expanding. Trying something new."

She stays quiet for a minute, thinking about it. "I guess I'm just worried I'll fail. What if no one comes to my bakery? What if it flops?"

I chuckle, shaking my head. "Maliah, have you met you? You'd never let that happen. And honestly, I think people will be lining up for your pastries."

Her cheeks flush, and she dips her head slightly, clearly embarrassed by the compliment. "You really think I can do this, huh?"

"I know you can," I say, and there's no hesitation in my voice. "Besides, I'm already planning to move into that abandoned house we talked about. If you turn it into a bakery, I guess I'll just have to live above it or something."

She laughs softly, and it's a sound I could listen to for hours. "You'd love that, wouldn't you?"

I lean closer, my voice teasing. "Maybe. But only if you save me the best desserts."

She smirks, looking at me through her lashes. "We'll see."

I can sense the conversation dying off, but I'm not ready to stop talking to her yet, so I grapple at anything. "How do you picture it? How would you design it?"

"I've thought about it a lot," she admits, her fingers playing with the mud idly. "I want it to have an open, inviting feel. Rustic but modern. You know, lots of warm woods and big windows. I'd probably keep the exterior as is though, but give it a little facelift."

I raise an eyebrow, intrigued. "What about the inside? You gonna go all out on those cozy vibes?"

"Definitely." She scoffs. "I want it to feel like a place people can just hang out, you know? Maybe a bookshelf, plants everywhere...and a big display case right at the front with fresh pastries and desserts."

"What kind of pastries are you thinking of making?"

"I'd offer something new every week, just to keep it interesting."

"Like what?" I ask, my hand moving down her back now, carefully applying more mud as I go. "Signature bakes? Weekly specials?"

She looks at me over her shoulder, her eyes lighting up with excitement. "Exactly! Seasonal items too—fresh fruit pies in the summer, warm cinnamon rolls in the winter, maybe even themed cakes for holidays."

I smirk, leaning a bit closer to her as I slide my hands to her hips, pulling her muddy back against my chest. "Sounds like you've got it all planned out. And what would you call this bakery of yours?"

Her cheeks flush a deeper shade before she shrugs, trying to play it off. "I haven't landed on a name yet...maybe something to do with the beach, or—"

I press in closer, my lips near her ear now. "How about something like *Maliah's Temptations*?" I murmur, my tone playful.

She rolls her eyes but can't hide her smile. "You're impossible, Koa."

"Don't act like you don't love it," I tease, running my fingers lightly down her spine. The way her breath catches doesn't go unnoticed, and I feel a surge of pride knowing I'm affecting her.

She leans back slightly, her body pressed close against mine, and I can feel the tension rising between us. Her fingers dip into the mud, and before I realize it, she's turned herself around and smears it right across my chest.

"Looks like you need some help too." She grins mischievously.

I chuckle, enjoying the shift in her mood. "Oh, so we're playing that game?"

"Maybe," she says, her voice soft but teasing. Her hand lingers as she spreads the mud over my skin, her fingers trailing slow paths. The way her touch lingers feels far more intimate than it should.

I catch her wrist, stopping her before I lose control. "You know," I whisper, locking my gaze with hers, "you're going to have to share that bed with me again tonight. And after this..." I trail off, letting the implication hang between us.

Her eyes widen, and for a second, I think she's going to pull away. But instead, she smirks, a boldness coming through. "You wish," she shoots back, though her voice wavers slightly.

The conversation fades as we continue spreading the mud over each other's skin, the intimacy of the moment hanging between us. Every touch, every gentle caress, feels heavy with unspoken words, a quiet tension simmering just below the surface.

Eventually, she speaks again, her voice quieter now, "Last night...sleeping next to you...it was—"

"Comfortable," I finish for her, not wanting to make her uncomfortable.

"Yeah," she agrees, her eyes focused on the mud as she

continues to spread it over my chest. "It wasn't awkward or anything. It just felt…natural."

I nod. "It felt like that for me when we shared my bed back at the hotel in Australia too. If anything, sleeping next to you earns me the best nights of sleep I've had in a while."

She lets out a soft laugh. "Same."

There's a brief silence before she asks, "Do you think it'll be like that every night for the next two weeks?"

I smirk, my hands pausing as I meet her gaze. "I hope so."

"Me too," she whispers.

And just like that, the tension between us thickens, but it's not the kind that makes you want to run. It's the kind that makes you want to lean in, to see what happens next. The heat between us spikes, the tension crackling in the air. Just as I'm about to close the distance between us, an attendant clears their throat.

"Time to wash off so the next group can come in," she says politely, but the interruption is enough to break the moment. Maliah's face burns crimson as she glances away quickly. I can't help but smirk as I watch her climb out of the pool, the thoughts swirling in my head far from innocent. I can't wait to get back to the villa now.

THE MOON IS OUT, CASTING A BRIGHT GLOW ACROSS THE WATER when we get back to the villa. Maliah walks inside first, her hair still damp from the hot springs, skin practically glowing. I follow behind her, my eyes on her—always on her. She moves through the room with this quiet grace, even when she's pretending like she doesn't know I'm watching her.

"I'm so sore, I don't think I can move," she groans,

stretching her arms over head, her top riding up slightly to reveal a sliver of her waist. "That was way too much adventure for one day."

I smirk, leaning against the wall, crossing my arms. "What, you didn't enjoy me holding you for dear life on the zip line?"

She shoots me a playful glare, walking past me towards the bedroom. "Don't flatter yourself. I could've done it without you."

"Sure you could've," I call after her, chuckling as I head to the kitchen. "You want something to drink? Water? Wine?"

There's a pause before she answers, "Wine sounds good."

I grab two glasses and pour the wine, hearing her rummaging around in the bedroom. By the time she comes back, she's changed into tiny shorts and a cropped tank top, her hair tied up in a messy bun. She looks too comfortable, too damn tempting, and it's hard to keep my thoughts straight.

She sits beside me on the couch, keeping a little space between us, but I can still feel the tension hanging thick in the air, like we've been dancing around something all day. I hand her the wine glass, taking a sip of mine as I settle back, trying to act casual even though my mind is anything but.

After a few quiet minutes, I can't help myself. I glance at her, then ask, "Do you ever think about it?"

Her brows furrow, confused. "Think about what?"

"Us," I say, watching her closely. "Sharing a bed...last night...everything that's happened between us."

Her body stills for a second, and I can see the way her fingers tighten around her glass, like she's bracing herself. I don't rush her to answer though, I know she has a million thoughts running through her head right now, and I want to hear them—every single one.

"How could I not?" she finally admits, keeping her eyes on her wine.

I put my glass down on the coffee table, turning full towards her. "And what do you think when you do?"

She takes a slow breath, her eyes darting to mine for a split second before she looks away again. I can tell she's trying to find the right words, but I don't need much more than that—her hesitation says it all.

"I think…" she starts, but then stops, biting her bottom lip.

My eyes zero in on the motion, and it takes everything in me not to reach out and close the gap between us. Her breathing grows fast, and I can tell she's battling herself, trying to figure out what to say.

Finally, she speaks, "I think it scares me."

That wasn't what I was expecting, but I stay calm, leaning in a little closer. "Why?"

She shifts in her seat, looking more nervous now. "Because we were supposed to be over. But now…it feels like we never really were."

I move closer, my knee brushing against hers, just enough to let her know I'm right there, not backing down. "We weren't," I tell her softly. "You know that."

She looks down, and for a second, I think she might shut me out again, but then I see her shoulders relax, just a little. I'm not letting her hide this time.

"We can't just pick up where we left off," she whispers.

"Who says we're picking up?" I ask, my voice low. My hand finds her knee, my fingers brushing the soft skin there. "Maybe we're starting something new."

She looks at me then, really looks at me, and for the first time today, I can see the walls she's been putting up starting to crack. I know I'm pushing her, but I have to. I can't keep pretending like this tension between us isn't driving me insane.

Her breath hitches as my fingers trail up her thigh, slow, deliberate. The air between us is thick now, like we're standing on the edge of something we can't back away from. My hand moves up to her face, cupping her cheek gently, and she leans into my touch.

"Tell me you don't feel it, too," I whisper, my thumb grazing her bottom lip. Her eyes flicker to mine and I see her pulse quicken in the hollow of her throat. She's fighting it, just like she always does, but I know the truth.

She feels it.

She leans forward but stops just short of kissing me, her breath mingling with mine.

"I—" she starts, but the words get caught somewhere between her heart and her throat.

I lean in just a fraction closer, my lips barely brushing hers. "I can wait," I murmur, my voice rough with restraint, "but don't lie to me, Maliah. You feel it. Just like I do."

Her resolve crumbles, and before I can think, she's kissing me. It's soft at first, hesitant, but when my hand slips around her waist and pulls her against me, she kisses me harder, deeper. I can feel the urgency in the way her fingers tangle in my hair, the way she presses herself into me like she's been holding back for too long.

It's like the world stops. Every thought, every doubt I've been carrying, fades away, replaced by the feel of her lips on mine. Months of pent-up tension finally finds release in this single moment. I've kissed her before, a thousand times, even back in Australia, but this feels different. This feels like the first time all over again, like she's handing me a piece of herself that I thought I'd lost forever.

It's not just physical; it's emotional, raw, and real in a way that hits me right in the chest.

I'm about to deepen the kiss, but just as fast as it started, she pulls back, her eyes wide, breathless.

"We can't," she whispers, shaking her head. "I need to figure out my feelings first."

The warmth that had flooded through me begins to fade and my heart drops a little, knowing that whatever this moment was, it's not enough to fix everything—not yet.

"Alright," I say softly, pulling back a little but keeping my hand on her waist, not ready to let her go just yet. "But this isn't over. Not by a long shot."

She nods, her breathing still a little shaky. "I know."

THE ENERGY OF COMPETITION DAY CRACKLES AROUND ME LIKE static in the air, fuelling the adrenaline that's already pumping through my veins. The moment my feet hit the sand, everything sharpens—my focus, my breathing, my senses. The cameras, the crowd, the pressure—it all fades into the background. The only thing that matters now is the surf. Cloudbreak is roaring, the waves as massive and menacing as I expected, but that's exactly what we wanted.

I glance at Maliah beside me. Going forward on the tour, we'll all be going into the waters with our partners instead of splitting up the men and women's heats. She's adjusting her leash, her face a little tense, her brows furrowed in that way they do when she's trying to psych herself up. I can tell she's nervous, and hell, so am I, but I also know that once we're out there, the fear will burn away, leaving only instinct and adrenaline.

The camera crews are already in place, capturing every second of us as we prepare. I shove them out of my mind, focusing only on the surf ahead. Cloudbreak looks insane today—walls of water just waiting to crush anyone who dares take them on. Perfect.

I run a hand through my damp hair, glancing at the horizon. The wave of the day is forming out there, rising slowly, a beast waiting to strike. My heart pounds in anticipation. This is what I live for.

I look over at Maliah. "Ready?"

She nods, her eyes fierce, the nerves replaced by something else now. Determination. She's locking in, and I know she's going to kill it.

We paddle out together, side by side, slicing through the water with long, powerful strokes. The current's strong, but we've faced worse. The Point is where we're going to make our mark today, I feel it in my bones.

A massive set starts to build in the distance. I spot the perfect wave, a monster, and glance at Maliah. We lock eyes and I give her a quick nod. This one's hers.

"You take the first one," she calls out, but I shake my head.

"You go. Show 'em what you've got."

She hesitates for a second before turning her board toward the wave. Her paddling is strong, determined. I watch as she drops in, her timing perfect, the wave lifting her as she flies down the face. It's a beauty of a wave, and she's riding it like it's hers.

I sit back for a second, just watching her. Her cutbacks are sharp, her form perfect. She's hitting every section exactly like we talked about. When she hits the middle section, she crouches low disappearing into the barrel, completely tucked inside the tube. I hold my breath. She's in deep, but I know she's got it. The seconds tick by, and just when I think the wave might take her, she comes flying out, riding clean and sure.

Damn. She looks incredible out there. The announcer's voice crackles over the speaker as the crowd cheers, but I barely hear it. My heart's still hammering from watching her crush that ride.

My turn.

Positioning myself at The Point as the next set rolls in, I feel the wave begin to swell beneath me. I paddle hard, feeling the rush of the drop as I'm lifted, gravity pulling me down the steep face. The power of the wave hits me like a freight train, but I'm in control, moving with it, not against it.

I carve through the top section, pushing my board to the limit. Every cutback, every turn is sharp, deliberate. I'm showing them exactly what I've got, what Gabriel's drilled into us over the years. The water sprays in my face as I carve back into the wave, the wind rushing through my hair.

The middle section comes up fast, the barrel forming. I crouch low, lining up the tube perfectly. The world goes silent as I slip inside, the roar of the wave enveloping me. Inside the barrel, time seems to slow—just me and the ocean. The pulse of the wave thrums through my board, through my bones, and I can feel the ocean's raw power beneath me. It's risky, but that's what makes it so damn exhilarating.

I shoot out of the tube just as the wave starts to close, my timing perfect. Shish Kebabs is next, the section that's claimed plenty of surfers. The water speeds up as I hit the inside section, and I know I've only got seconds before this thing turns deadly. With one sharp curve, I pull out of the wave, just before it swallows itself.

I ride it all the way to the shore, heart pounding, chest heaving. The crowd erupts as I kick out, and I can hear the announcers calling out my score. I look over at Maliah, who's waiting for me at the shore, her face lit up with a huge grin.

"Not bad, huh?" she teases, clearly buzzing from her ride.

I laugh, running a hand through my hair. "Not bad? You killed it out there."

She scoffs playfully, but there's something softer in her eyes when she looks at me today. "You didn't do too bad yourself."

I flash her a grin as the world around us blurs. The cheers of the crowd, the cameras—none of it matters. It's just me and her, riding the high of the competition and that unspoken connection between us.

The scoreboard flashes our combined scores, and I feel a surge of pride as we lock in first place.

"We did it," I say, unable to hold back my grin.

Maliah nods, her eyes sparkling as she smiles up at me. "Yeah. We really did."

FOURTEEN

MALIAH | TAVARUA, FIJI

THE DAYS since our big win at Cloudbreak have been filled with a quiet kind of tension—more so on Koa's part. I, on the other hand, have been enjoying bugging him every chance I get. Subtle, small touches here and there, just enough to get under his skin. And I *love* watching him try to control himself each time.

We walk side by side from the beach back to our villa, the warm Fijian air thick with the scent of frangipani. I purposely let my hand drift just slightly, grazing Koa's as we walk. I watch from the corner of my eye as he stiffens beside me, his fingers twitching, but he doesn't pull away. A smirk tugs at my lips as I glance up at him, his face unreadable—at least to anyone who doesn't know him as well as I do.

"You okay?" I ask innocently.

His grey eyes flicker down to mine, a mixture of amusement and something darker hidden behind them. "Just fine, Mal," he says, voice strained but steady.

I chuckle softly and look away, knowing I'm driving him crazy, but not quite ready to let up yet.

When we reach the villa, I collapse onto the couch,

stretching out with a groan. My damp hair clings to my neck, and I push it aside lazily, trying to cool off. My shirt rides up a little, exposing my stomach, but I don't care. I'm too drained from our practice to worry about modesty right now. Plus, it isn't anything Koa hasn't already seen.

"Finally," I breathe, sinking deeper into the cushions. This couch feels like a cloud after being out in the sun all day.

Koa stands a few feet away, dropping his board by the door and kicking off his sandals. I can feel his gaze on me before he speaks.

"You look comfortable," he says casually, though there's a teasing edge in his voice. It's the same playful tone he always uses when he's trying to stir something in me.

I give him a sly smile. "You should try it sometime."

His lips quirk into a small smirk, and I see the challenge flicker in his eyes. "I'm perfectly relaxed."

"Really?" I arch an eyebrow at him, trying to sound casual, but there's a twinge of daring in my voice. "Because you seem pretty tense for someone who claims to be relaxed."

He doesn't answer me right away, instead stepping closer and taking a seat beside me—closer than necessary, if I'm being honest. I catch a whiff of saltwater and the faint smell of his skin, making it harder to ignore the heat simmering between us. He's not touching me, but the air between us feels electric, and I can't stop my pulse from racing.

"Maybe you're the one who's tense," Koa says in a low voice, leaning in just enough for me to feel the heat of his breath against my cheek.

I stiffen for a split second, but quickly narrow my eyes at him, trying to hold my ground. "I'm perfectly relaxed, thank you," I shoot back, hoping my voice sounds steady, though my heart is now in overdrive.

His smirk grows, and I know he's enjoying every second of this, but I won't let him turn the tables on me.

"Really? Because you look a little...flustered," he says, his eyes flickering down to my lips briefly before meeting my gaze again. He leans in a bit more, his arm casually draping along the back of the couch, so close that the edge of his fingers brush against my shoulder. It's almost imperceptible, but I feel it like a spark.

I roll my eyes, refusing to let him get the upper hand. "Don't flatter yourself, Koa," I say, though my voice is a little breathier than I intended.

He chuckles under his breath, his eyes glinting with mischief. "I don't have to. You're doing a pretty good job of that yourself."

I open my mouth to throw a snarky comeback at him, but it gets caught in my throat when his hand moves. He reaches out, his fingers brushing lightly against my arm, trailing down slowly until they reach the edge of my shirt. My skin burns under his touch, and I suck in a quiet breath, determined not to show how much he's getting to me.

"You sure you're relaxed?" he murmurs, his fingers playing with the hem of my shirt, barely lifting it. His voice is low, teasing, but there's something else in it too—something that makes my stomach flip.

I shove at his chest lightly, forcing a laugh. "You're such a tease," I mutter, trying to sound exasperated, but it's hard to ignore how fast my heart is racing.

Koa grins, his eyes locking on mine with that infuriatingly confident look. "Maybe. But I'm pretty sure you like it."

I snort, crossing my arms over my chest in defiance. "In your dreams."

"In my dreams?" he echoes, pretending to be offended. His fingers brush my side again, and I feel a jolt of electricity shoot up my spine. He leans in, close enough that I can feel his breath against my neck. "I'm positive you like it, princess, and I'm wide awake."

My breath catches in my throat, and I find myself leaning ever so slightly towards him before I realize what I'm doing. I force myself to pull back, shaking my head. "Keep telling yourself that," I say, standing up abruptly, needing space before this playful teasing becomes something I can't handle.

He laughs behind me as I start walking towards the bedroom to shower and change into clothes for the evening excursion.

"Running away already?" he calls after me, and I can hear the smirk in his voice.

I pause in the doorway, glancing over my shoulder. "Just preparing for the next round of this little game we're playing, Koa. Don't get too comfortable."

His eyes linger on me, that slow smile tugging at the corner of his lips. "I'm ready whenever you are, Maliah."

TONIGHT'S GROUP EXCURSION IS MORE LAID BACK THAN THE recent ones we've been on, and I couldn't be more grateful. After piling into a van, we're taken to the Garden of the Sleeping Giant. It's stunning, lush greenery surrounding us, orchids of every colour peeking out from the trees, and the sun setting just behind the mountains, casting a soft glow over everything.

"So we're just supposed to wander through this place? That sounds boring," one of the girls complains as we wander through the garden.

"Let's make it fun then," Reese chips in, turning to face everyone. "Have you ever played Murder in the Dark?"

For the next five minutes he explains the rules of the game, but I notice he's put a twist on how it's traditionally played. If the murderer can kill everyone before the time's up, they win. But if anyone is left standing, the murderer has to come forward as the loser.

"So, it's basically like Hide and Seek?" Koa asks, coming to stand next to me, his arm brushing against mine subtly. I feel the hairs on my arms stand.

"Yeah, something like that," Reese agrees.

The group loves the idea, so we all agree to play, and soon enough, we're all scattering into the dark forest, each of us searching for a hiding spot to start the game. I run deeper into the trees, the sounds of laughter and footsteps fading behind me. The sun has almost fully set now, leaving just enough light to make out shapes in the distance, but shadows creep between the trees, making it difficult to see much else. Perfect for a game like this.

The night deepens as I weave through the trees, branches scraping against my arms, the ground soft beneath my feet. I pause, leaning against a thick tree trunk to catch my breath. Charles—the one I'm certain is the murderer—is fast, but I'm faster. I can spare a few moments here.

That is until I hear it—footsteps, faint but steady, coming from behind me. I glance over my shoulder, thinking it's Charles, but my heart skips a beat when I catch sight of a figure moving through the trees. *Koa.*

He's walking slowly, purposefully, like a predator stalking his prey, his tall frame moving effortlessly through the underbrush. His eyes lock on mine, a devilish smile stretching across his lips. My stomach flips, and I instinctively take a step back, even though I know it's useless. He's caught me.

"Are you going to try and outrun me?" Koa's voice is low, teasing, and it sends a shiver down my spine. His footsteps quicken, and in a rush of panic, I turn and sprint, trying to get away, even though a part of me knows I don't really want to.

I dart between the trees, my breath coming faster as I hear

him closing in behind me. My heart pounds as I push myself harder, my legs burning with the effort. But it's no use. Koa is faster and I feel his hand wrap around my arm, pulling me back towards him.

"Gotcha," he growls playfully, spinning me around to face him.

I gasp, but not from fear. There's something dark and heated in his gaze as he towers over me, his chest rising and falling with controlled breaths. He presses me back against a tree, his body close—too close. The rough bark digs into my skin, but all I can focus on is the way Koa's eyes are practically smouldering as they roam over me.

"You've been teasing me all week," he murmurs, his voice husky as his hands slide to either side of me, pinning me in place. "What are you going to do about it?"

My breath hitches. The space between us feels electric, every inch of my body hyper-aware of his closeness, of the heat radiating off him. I try to speak, but the words catch in my throat.

"Koa—" I manage, my voice barely a whisper.

He leans in, his mouth hovering near my ear, his breath warm against my skin. "What do you want, Maliah?" His voice is low, intimate, making my stomach tighten.

For a second, I can't think straight. My heart is racing, my skin tingling everywhere he's touched me. I should push him away, but instead I find myself wanting to close the gap, wanting to feel him pressed even closer.

"I..."

Before I can say anything else, he pulls back slightly, just enough to look me in the eyes, and the intensity of his gaze nearly melts me on the spot. "Tell me," he demands softly, his thumb brushing over my jaw. "What do you want?"

I swallow hard, my pulse thudding in my ears. My resolve

crumbles under the weight of his gaze. The truth is, I don't even know what I want anymore—except him.

I bite my lip, my voice trembling as I finally whisper, "You."

A satisfied grin spreads across his face as he leans in again, his lips brushing just below my ear. "That's all you had to say," he murmurs before his mouth captures mine in a kiss that's deep and consuming. His hands slide down to my waist, gripping me firmly as his body presses me back against the tree.

Every thought, every ounce of tension from the day melts away as I give in to the moment. It's just us, lost in the darkness, wrapped up in each other. Koa's kiss isn't gentle. It's hungry, demanding, like he's been waiting for this as long as I have.

Although my mind is spinning, my body knows exactly what it wants. I melt into him, my hands sliding up his chest, feeling the hard muscles beneath his shirt, my fingers curling into the fabric as I pull him closer. His grip tightens on my waist, strong and possessive, and the way he holds me makes my heart ricochet around my chest. His body is so warm, so solid against mine, and *every* inch of him is pressing into me, making it impossible to think about anything other than how much I want him.

His tongue teases mine, and the low, rumbling sound he makes in the back of his throat sends shivers down my spine. The rough bark of the tree digs into my back, but the slight discomfort only makes the heat between us more intense. Koa's hands move lower, slipping under the hem of my shirt, his fingers grazing the bare skin of my waist, and a gasp escapes me. It's like every nerve in my body is suddenly on fire, my skin tingling everywhere he touches me.

I can feel his heart pounding just as fast as mine, his breathing uneven, and it turns me on even more knowing I'm affecting him just as much. I arch into him, feeling the heat pooling low in my stomach, the ache between my thighs becoming impossible to ignore.

He pulls back slightly, just enough for me to catch my breath, but he doesn't give me any space. His forehead rests against mine, our noses brushing as his breath fans across my lips. His eyes, dark and full of desire, lock onto mine, and my heart stutters in my chest.

"You feel that?" His voice low, rough with need as he presses his hardness against me. "That's what you do to me, Princess."

I can't respond, not with the way my body is trembling from the intensity of it all. My chest is heaving, and all I can do is nod because the truth is, I'm feeling it too. It's like every inch of me is attuned to him, to the way his body fits against mine, the way his touch sends sparks through my veins.

He doesn't wait for an answer. His lips crash into mine again, harder this time, more desperate, and I lose myself in him. His hand slips up my side, fingers brushing the curve of my breast, and my breath hitches. I can't help the soft moan that escapes me as my body reacts instinctively, pressing closer to him, needing more.

His other hand tangles in my hair, pulling just enough to tip my head back, giving him full access to my neck. His mouth moves from my lips, trailing hot, open-mouthed kisses down the column of my throat, and I swear my knees almost give out. Every touch, every kiss, is like gasoline being poured on a fire that's already raging inside me.

"Koa..." I whisper, my voice trembling, but I'm not sure if it's a plea for him to stop or a plea for him to *never* stop. His teeth graze my skin, and another shiver runs down my spine.

I can feel him against me, hard and unyielding, his body pressed so tightly to mine that it's impossible not to notice how much this is affecting him too. It makes the heat between us even more unbearable, the want twisting into something raw and desperate.

He pulls back again, just enough to look at me, his breath coming in ragged bursts. His eyes are dark, intense, and the way he looks at me sends another rush of heat straight through me. His hand starts to move with an intentional slowness, trailing down my waist. Anticipation rushes through me as his fingers deftly navigate the soft fabric of my pants, sliding beneath the waistband, teasingly brushing against my skin.

He lowers his hand further, sending a rush of adrenaline coursing through my veins, until he's cupping me. His fingers glide along my slick entrance and he gently pushes two inside of me, claiming me, and I can't help but arch into him, as he works them in and out of me.

"You drive me crazy, you know that?" he murmurs, his thumb circling over my clit as he continues to work his fingers in and out, bringing me closer and closer to release.

I can barely speak, my body buzzing from his touch, but I manage a breathless, "I know."

He smirks before bringing his lips back to my neck, finding my sensitive spot and slowly licking in a circular motion as he edges me along with his fingers. I can feel my pussy starting to flutter, as my eyes close on their own and breathy moans escape from my lips.

"Are you about to come, Maliah?" he asks, his lips brushing along my neck.

I whimper in response as his words tip me over the edge and I feel myself getting lost in the insatiable feeling. He pulls back so that he can watch me orgasm, a devilish smirk playing on his lips.

"I can feel your pussy trying to cut off circulation in my fingers," he says with a satisfied smirk. "That's it, baby, keep coming for me."

My body begins to shake, my legs starting to feel like jelly, as he continues to work his fingers in me. Black dots start to fill my vision so he slows his movements until he can gently pull his fingers free.

He slides his wet fingers into my mouth, surprising me.

"Taste how much you want me," he says in a low voice, his eyes dark as he watches me close my mouth around his fingers and clean up my mess.

"Fuck," he whispers, his gaze intense.

We both hear the final whistle echo in the distance, signalling the end of the game. Koa smirks before leaning down and pressing a soft kiss to my forehead.

"Right on time," he says, retreating backwards towards the others, until he disappears in the darkness.

I'm rooted in place, trying to wrap my head around the whirlwind of emotions swirling inside me. What just happened? I replay the moment in my mind, his lips brushing against my skin, his fingers working me to an orgasm, leaving me both exhilarated and confused. Warmth floods my cheeks as I start to walk towards the meetup spot, the moment on replay in my mind the whole time. How am I supposed to sleep next to him after what just happened?

FIFTEEN

KOA | RIO DE JANEIRO, BRAZIL

SURFING SAQUAREMA IS AN ADRENALINE RUSH. The beach break here is wild—powerful, unpredictable, and constantly shifting under my feet. Every second on my board feels like a battle between chaos and control.

The waves are peaking high, coming in strong and fast. I feel the energy in the air, the raw power of the ocean, and it has my blood pumping. Maliah is quiet, but I see the same determination on her face that she always has when we're about to compete. It gets me going, seeing her like that—focused, eyes sharp, and completely in her element. There's something about knowing we're about to take on the same beast together that makes the whole experience electric.

We have enough time this competition to catch a few waves each. The first one I catch throws me into the barrel faster than I expect. The walls are thick, but I stay low, carving through the lip as it begins to close in. Not my best start, but enough to give us a solid base to work with. My next wave will be better.

I watch as Maliah takes on the next set with confidence. The wave is steep, but she handles it effortlessly, sliding into a perfect roundhouse cutback. I can't take my eyes off her. Every time she takes a wave, it's like she's dancing with it—reading every shift, every swell like it's second nature. And she makes it look easy. She always does.

We spend the rest of the heat picking off waves, feeding off each other's energy. The final waves are nothing short of perfect. I go for the most technical part of the wave, where it's bigger, faster, and more unpredictable. I catch one of the biggest waves of the day, riding the lip before tucking into a clean barrel. The spray hits me in the face as I come out and I hear the crowd on the beach losing it.

When Maliah catches her final wave, she angles her board just right to carve through the section, hitting a sharp bottom turn that leaves a clean spray behind her. The way her body shifts and her eyes lock onto the next section of the wave is flawless. She even pulls off a cheeky cutback before heading to the shore, a signature move I've seen her do a hundred times, but it never fails to impress me.

The whistle blows and we paddle back to shore. I'm not surprised to learn we've managed to keep our spots in first place.

"That was insane," Maliah says, breathless but smiling wide. "I can't believe we nailed it."

I smirk, pushing my hair back as I shake the water from my face. "You crushed it out there."

She glances away, a modest shrug lifting her shoulder, but I can see the pride in her eyes. "You weren't so bad yourself."

We start walking to our rental van with the rest of the production crew, but I let myself fall back so that my gaze can wander over her as she walks ahead of me. My mind drifts back to Fiji—to the feel of her body against mine, the heat of that kiss, the way she had looked at me right before I—

"Are you even listening?" the cameraman beside me asks, his voice breaking through my thoughts and snapping me back to reality.

"Huh?" I blink, realizing I've been zoned out, staring at Maliah's ass. "Sorry, I missed what you were saying."

Maliah looks over her shoulder at me, raising an eyebrow curiously. I shove my hand into the pocket of my wetsuit, trying to look casual.

"I was saying the production team is wrapping up early here so we can prepare for later tonight, we'll catch a different car to our accommodations," he repeats.

"Right," I say, pulling my gaze away from Maliah and back to him. "Okay then, have a good night," I say before rushing away from him toward the van.

We load our boards into the van and climb into the back of the car, our driver not bothering to wait for us to fasten our seatbelts before he starts to drive. I glance at Maliah out of the corner of my eye, wondering if she's been thinking about what happened in Fiji too, or if she's doing everything she can to forget it.

We never spoke about it again for the rest of our time there. Each night, she would slip under the sheets quickly, lying silently until her breathing slowed, signalling she'd finally fallen asleep.

My heart stutters when Maliah turns her head and catches me staring.

"What's going on with you?"

I ponder whether I should tell her the truth or make something up, but curiosity gets the better of me. "I've been thinking about what happened in Fiji."

Her eyes flick up to mine, guarded but curious. "Is there something you want to say?"

I open my mouth to respond but close it again, the words getting stuck. "Not yet," I say, keeping it simple.

She doesn't push me on it, instead giving me a small nod before returning her attention out the window. I follow suit, wondering how long we can keep dancing around what's been happening between us.

Once we get back to the tour house we've been assigned, Maliah barely spares me a glance before heading straight to her room, shutting me out like she's always done. I watch her disappear down the narrow hallway, her door clicking shut behind her, and it hits me harder than I want to admit.

I stand there for a moment, still holding my board, staring at the closed door. Did I push her too far? Did I cross a line back in the forest that we can't uncross?

The tension's been building between us for weeks—hell, maybe longer than that. It's like every time we're together, the air gets heavier, thicker, charged with something neither of us can fully control. And then the kiss. The way her body felt pressed up against that tree, her breath warm and uneven against my lips, the sound of her moaning while she came for me...it's all I can think about.

But now, she's avoiding me, and I'm left here, wondering if I've completely messed this up.

I drag our boards to the back deck, the warm Rio air wrapping around me as I hang them on the board hooks out here. I pull my phone out of my pocket and call Griffin and Colton in a group video call, hoping for a distraction.

Griffin picks up first, his voice crackling through the speaker. "So you finally decided to call," he says in mock annoyance. "How's Brazil treating you?"

I lean against the railing, looking out at the pool as I talk. "Not bad. We placed first again today at Saquarema."

Colton's voice cuts in next. "Hell yeah! I knew you two would kill it."

They start filling me in on what's been going on back home, updates on the surf scene, parties, some new faces at our usual spots. I'm listening, kind of, but I keep my responses vague, not really wanting to dive into what's been happening between me and Maliah. I'm not even sure what I'd say. Griffin and Colton are like my brothers—they can tell something's up.

"You good, Koa?" Griffin asks after a beat, his tone softening. "You seem off."

I open my mouth to respond, but then the sliding doors open, and out walks Maliah in a black bikini, her skin glowing in the soft light of the pool. My throat goes dry instantly. She's all legs, hips swaying as she walks with a sort of quiet confidence, and I can't take my eyes off her.

I hear Colton and Griffin whispering to each other, their voices distant now, but I'm not listening. My attention locked on her. She steps into the pool, the water lapping around her waist as she turns to look at me. The way her eyes find mine—like she's daring me to follow her.

She leans back against the edge of the pool, water glistening on her skin, and gives me this look, her eyes filled with something that sends a jolt straight to my cock.

"Bro, is he drooling?" Colton's voice cuts through the fog in my brain.

"Yup, definitely drooling," Griffin agrees, his voice filled with humour.

I blink, realizing they've caught me staring at Maliah like an idiot, mouth half-open.

"I've got to go." I hang up the call, not even bothering with a goodbye.

Maliah watches me, her lips curving into a small, knowing smile. "Are you coming in?" she asks, her voice low, almost teasing.

Hell. Yes.

I don't waste a second, running inside to change out of my wetsuit and into my swimming trunks before running back out to the pool and diving in, the water cooling the heat that's building inside me. When I surface, I swim right up to her, water dripping from my hair, and place my hands on either side of her head against the pool edge. I lower myself to her level, close enough to feel the warmth coming off her skin despite the cool water.

She stares at me for a moment, her eyes flickering with something I can't quite put my finger on—lust, maybe curiosity or desire. Her breath hitches slightly, and I notice the way her chest rises and falls, like she's trying to control it.

I'm so close, I can see the tiny flecks in her eyes, gorgeous shades of blue. She shifts slightly under my gaze before asking, "Why are you looking at me like that?"

I tilt my head, smirking. "Like what?"

"Like that," she repeats, her voice a little breathless now.

I let my gaze travel over her face slowly before I meet her eyes again, my tone playful. "Your eyes are really pretty up close."

She narrows her eyes, lips pursing slightly. "Shut up."

I grin, my voice dropping lower. "Make me."

She scoffs, but there's no real anger behind it, just that teasing edge we've always had. "I hate you."

I lean in just a little closer, brushing a thumb along the edge of the pool beside her. "No, you don't."

She opens her mouth, probably to argue, but then stops. Her breath catches again, and for a second, I think she's going to close the distance between us. The tension is thick, the space practically buzzing.

"What do you want?" she asks finally, her voice soft but steady, and it catches me off guard.

The question reminds me too much of that moment we

shared in Fiji. My first thought is simple—*you*. It's all I want. But if I say it out loud, if we kiss here, it won't just be like last time. This time, there's no way we'd stop and I'm not sure if she's ready for that yet.

"I think I've made it clear what I want, Princess," I say instead.

She breaks eye contact, submerging herself in the water. She swims a lazy circle around me, and I stay still, letting her move freely. My gaze follows her, heart pounding. She's drawing me in without even trying.

After a few seconds, I pull myself up to sit on the edge of the pool, water cascading down my body, and watch as she moves to the deep end. When she finally surfaces, our eyes meet again. Her expression is unreadable, but something in the way she's looking at me keeps me rooted to the spot.

She swims over to the stairs, slowly climbing out of the pool, water dripping down her beautiful body as she wraps herself in a towel. Without another word or glance, she heads back into the house, leaving me alone by the pool.

I wait a few minutes, trying to sort out the whirlwind of thoughts racing through my mind, then push myself up and follow her inside. The coolness of the air conditioning hits my skin, and I hear the sound of water running from her ensuite bathroom. She's in the shower. I pause outside her door, listening for a second before turning away and heading to my own room.

Carnaval is tonight. We're going with the others, and I still need to get ready. I peel off my wet swim trunks and head for my bathroom, turning the shower on to full blast, hoping to clear my head. I'm about to step in when there's a knock at the front door.

I grab my towel, wrapping it around my waist, and make my way down the hall to the door, opening it to find someone delivering our costumes for the night. Great timing. I grab the package, thanking the courier before I shut the door, and head back down the hall, stopping outside Maliah's room.

The sound of her shower is still going when I knock softly, and without waiting for a response, I open the door. Steam fills the room, curling out from the open bathroom door, and I catch a glimpse of her silhouette through the frosted glass. My throat tightens before I drop her costume on the bed and turn to leave, but then I hear it—her moan.

It's soft, barely there, but it echoes through my head like a gunshot. My body reacts instantly, heat pooling low in my stomach as I grit my teeth and force myself to leave her room. I close the door behind me, my heart hammering, and make my way back to my own bathroom.

The water is still running as I step into the shower, letting it pound against my skin, but it doesn't cool me down. My mind keeps flashing back to her, to the sound of that moan, and before I know it, I'm jerking myself off to the thought of her.

Again.

MALIAH | RIO DE JANEIRO, BRAZIL

I STARE at myself in the mirror, fingers nervously fidgeting with the hem of my Carnival costume. The vibrant colours were meant to stand out, but I feel almost naked in this outfit, more exposed than I've ever been outside of the ocean. My mind flashes back to finding it laying on my bed after my shower, and I wonder when Koa had dropped it off and whether or not he heard me in the shower. My face flushes at the thought, and I quickly push it away, trying to focus on something else.

My eyes drift down to the pink, puffy scar on my hip, just visible above the waistband of my costume. A wave of nostalgia washes over me, pulling me back to the day it happened when I slipped from a tree, the branch ripping into my side as I crashed to the ground.

I wince at the memory of how scared Koa had been, jumping out of the tree with that familiar mix of panic and concern in his voice, trying to joke and calm me down. He'd been my rock back then, always there to help me back up after I fell. Now everything feels different—complicated. I brush my fingers over the scar, a reminder of a simpler time when being around Koa didn't make my head spin.

With a deep breath, I force myself to shake off the nostalgia. *It's Carnival,* I remind myself. *You can do this.*

I gather enough courage to open my bedroom door and walk into the living room, only to stop dead in my tracks. Koa is leaning against the edge of the couch, shirtless. My heart races as I take in the sight of him—his bronzed skin glowing under the soft lighting. He's wearing a beaded necklace that hangs loosely around his neck, and the relaxed carnival themed pants he's wearing sit low on his hips, emphasizing every chiseled muscle in his torso.

My breath catches in my throat. He looks incredible—too incredible. The pull I feel towards him is immediate and overwhelming, a rush of heat spreading through me like wildfire. I can hardly breathe as I watch him, my body responding to him in ways I can't control.

"Did they forget the rest of your costume?" I ask, swallowing past the dryness in my throat. My voice comes out weaker than I intended, betraying my attempt at teasing him.

He scoffs, his lips curling into that familiar, cocky grin. "I could ask you the same question." His eyes roam hungrily over my body, pausing momentarily on my scar before continuing their slow journey downward, sending shivers over my skin.

I shift on my feet, feeling self-conscious under his gaze, even though I shouldn't be. The way he's looking at me...it's as if he's memorizing every inch, every curve, every flaw. "We should go," I murmur, fighting the urge to cover myself. "The others are probably waiting for us."

His gaze lingers on me for a moment before he nods and rises from the couch. As we step out of the penthouse, the tension between us hums in the air, unspoken but undeniable —thick and electric.

The moment we step outside, we're instantly swarmed by

production. Glitter rains down on us from all directions as people rush to make sure we're covered in it before the cameras start rolling. The energy around us is buzzing with excitement, and I feel it seep into my veins, making my nerves tingle. A producer approaches us, clipboard in hand.

"You two will have your own float to wave to the fans and cameras as you pass," she says with a smile. "If you're up for it, you can try to samba on the float, but please make sure you do so safely. Stick together, and don't accept drinks from anyone, okay?"

I nod, my heart thudding in my chest. The idea of being on a float with Koa in front of thousands of people should feel exhilarating. I should feel proud that we'll be up there representing Saltwater Springs, but I'm suddenly aware of the weight of his presence beside me, the magnetic pull between us.

Moments later, we're boarding the bus that'll take us to the carnival with the others. As I slide into a seat, Koa settles in next to me, his leg brushing against mine. The touch is subtle, but it sends a jolt through me. I start to nervously tap my leg, trying to shake off the nervous energy bubbling inside me.

Without a word, Koa's hand finds my knee, resting there gently but firmly. His touch instantly grounds me, offering me a comfort I wasn't expecting. I glance up at him, and he gives me that quiet, knowing look, as if telling me everything's going to be fine. Somehow that simple act calms me.

The problem with trying to force myself to move on from Koa is I truly don't think anyone else in this world will understand me the way he does. He just feels right.

When we finally arrive at the carnival, it's complete chaos. People are everywhere—laughing, dancing, singing in the streets. The music is loud, the lights are blinding, and I'm immediately swept up in the wild energy. The crowd presses in, pushing and pulling in every direction, and panic starts to build in my chest. I lose sight of Koa in the sea of people.

I barely have a second to react before I feel a strong hand wrap around my wrist, tugging me back into safety. I turn and see him, his face intense as he pulls me close to him, his arms wrapping around my waist protectively. The warmth of his body against mine is overwhelming, but I don't care. I don't feel scared anymore. His presence shields me from the chaos, making me feel safe and secure and that's all I want right now.

Koa keeps his arm around me, guiding me through the crowd as if I'm the only thing he's focused on. Even with the frenzy around us, it feels like we're in our own bubble, his grip tight and sure. When we finally reach our float with the production team, I glance up at him, breathless and grateful, his eyes meeting mine with a look I can't quite decipher.

"Alright, let's get you both onto your float," the same producer from earlier says as she walks us towards the float. "Remember to be careful up there—it's going to move slow, but it can be slippery."

My nerves are buzzing as we're led towards the float. It's bigger than I imagined, adorned with vibrant flowers that remind me of Saltwater Springs and glittering decorations, the whole thing swirling with coastal colours. The platform is high up, and a set of steps leads to the top. Koa helps me up first, his hand resting firmly on my back as I steady myself at the top.

The cameras follow our every move, and I can feel the weight of the lenses on us as we take our places. When the float starts to move, it jolts slightly and I instinctively reach for the railing, but Koa's hand finds mine first, steadying me.

The music starts pumping louder as the float lurches forward, and we're suddenly moving through the heart of Carnaval. The crowd below cheers and waves, the energy infectious as we wave back, plastering smiles on our faces for the cameras.

The more the float moves, the more the atmosphere starts to loosen me up. The other surfers on their floats are attempting to dance samba—some with more enthusiasm than talent. Laughter ripples through me as I watch their clumsy moves. A few waves of encouragement from the crowd later, Koa gives me a nudge, his eyes bright with mischief.

"We can't let them have all the fun," he says with a wink, pulling me closer as the beat of the samba music pounds through the speakers.

"You know I can't dance." I laugh, a hint of embarrassment crawling its way up my throat.

"Neither can they," he says, tilting his head over his shoulder at the others.

We start dancing together, his body moving in sync with mine as the rhythm pounds around us. At first, it's playful, filled with laughing and teasing, but as the music gets more intense so does our proximity. His hands find my hips, pulling me closer until we're dancing so tightly together that I can feel every breath he takes, every shift in his muscles. My skin feels like it's on fire wherever he touches me, and my heart races.

Minutes later, the float eventually reaches the end of the parade route, and we're ushered off into a private area to watch the rest of the floats pass by. It's incredible, the lights, the costumes, the sheer creativity of it all. I'm in awe, watching the artistry unfold in front of me. Turning to see if Koa's just as amazed, I find him already staring at me, his expression intense. His gaze ignites something inside me, a warmth that spreads from my chest down to my toes.

"Do you want to go back to the penthouse instead of heading out with the others after this?" he asks, his voice low, carrying a weight that hints at more than just the question.

I nod, not trusting myself to speak, because I know that if I do, my voice will betray just how badly I want him.

We find the producer from earlier and explain we'd like to head back early. Surprisingly, she agrees. The ride home is quiet—too quiet. The air between us is charged with so much tension that it's almost suffocating. Every slight movement feels amplified in the small space of the car; every breath I take seems to sync with his. The silence is heavy with everything we're not saying, everything that's been building between us.

As soon as we step into the house, Koa doesn't waste a second. Before the door even fully closes behind us, he pushes me up against the wall, his hands grabbing my waist with a sense of urgency that makes my breath catch. His lips crash into mine, hot and demanding, and I instantly respond, melting into him. My back presses against the wall as he deepens the kiss, one of his hands sliding up my side, the other gripping the back of my neck, keeping me locked against him.

His hardness presses against me, and before I know it, he's lifting me up effortlessly, my legs wrapping around his waist as I cling to his shoulders for support. I can feel his heart pounding as hard as mine. We're making out like we can't get enough of each other, and I don't want it to stop. He carries me, his lips never leaving mine, as he walks us toward the back door.

"This glitter's going to be impossible to get off," he says, pulling back from the kiss. "Want to just jump in the pool to rinse off?"

I see the playful spark in his eyes, and I know it's more than just a way to get rid of glitter. I bite my lip and nod.

"Yeah," I say, my voice barely audible as he lowers me to the ground.

I tug at the strings of my costume, letting it fall to the floor. Koa's gaze immediately darkens, and I can feel his eyes on me —on every inch of my body as I stand there completely naked. My pulse quickens, pounding loudly in my head as heat creeps up my neck, but I don't break eye contact.

His clothes come off next and I allow myself to admire his body—lean, muscular, toned in a way that makes my breath hitch every time. The pool lights reflecting off the water cast shadows over his skin, and I feel that familiar deep craving for him, stronger than ever.

"Come," he says, his voice thick, holding out his hand.

I take it, the warmth of his fingers wrapping around mine. We walk toward the edge of the pool, the cool night air doing absolutely nothing to chill the heat radiating inside of me. Our hands stay intertwined as we leap in, water crashing over us, the world disappearing for a moment beneath the surface.

When we emerge, Koa's already pulling me toward him, his hands slipping around my bare waist, tugging me closer until my body is pressed against his. The water ripples around us, but all I can focus on is him. His lips hovering just above mine, his breath hot against my skin.

He presses his lips into mine, gently at first, and I lose myself in the kiss, in the feel of his body against mine, the water swirling around us. My hands are on his chest, tracing the hard lines of his muscles as his mouth begins to move hungrily against mine, his hands exploring every inch of me too.

If Koa Foster wants me, he's going to get all of me.

"I want you," I whisper against his lips, my voice barely a breath, but heavy with desire as I slide a hand down his torso into the water, until I wrap my fingers around his hard length.

He pulls back, his expression tight, conflicted, his jaw clenched as he tries to resist. "Mal, maybe we should talk fir—"

"I want you, Koa," I say, shaking my head before pressing my lips to his neck, my words a soft plea against his skin. "I have an IUD...you don't have to worry."

I pump his cock once, feeling him shudder beneath my touch. His breathing grows heavier, his eyes searching mine as if he's trying to find the strength to hold back. But then, something shifts. His resolve snaps, and his hands tighten on my hips, spinning me around and forcing me to grip onto the cool tile of the pool's edge, as he presses his body against mine until there's no space left between us. I feel his cock slide between my thighs and my pussy clenches at its nearness.

"Are you sure?" His voice is a low growl, his lips brushing against my ear.

I nod, my grip on the edge of the pool wall tightening in anticipation. "Yes."

Without hesitation he grips his cock and brings it to my entrance. I spread my legs wider, giving him better access, before he slides in, stretching me to my limit. I let out a breathy moan, feeling him completely fill me before he pauses inside.

"Fuck," he groans, one hand gripping my breast and the other gently wrapped around my throat as he begins to pull out before slamming back into me.

I gasp on the impact, my eyes shutting from pure bliss. "I forgot how big you are," I say, breathlessly.

"I missed your tight pussy," he replies, thrusting into me faster now. The water splashes around us, each movement sending waves rippling outwards, and I feel my entire body respond, melting into him.

Koa groans, the sound vibrating against my skin, and I bite my lip, trying to contain the rush of emotion and pleasure coursing through me. I've missed this, feeling him worship me until I'm crying out, his hands roaming over my entire body as if memorizing it in case I disappear. The water splashes against our bodies, but all I can focus on is the sensation of him, the feelings I have for him, the way we move together like we're the only two people to exist in this world.

Carnival fireworks burst above us, and it feels like a celebration just for us—a sign that everything is right and I'm exactly where I'm meant to be.

He pulls out of me, and I feel the loss instantly, my heart sinking, but he spins me around so I'm facing him and lifts me up by my thighs so that I'm straddling him. I wrap my arms around his neck before crashing my lips to his.

He re-enters me, more forcefully this time, and I moan into his mouth as he pounds my pussy relentlessly. My head falls back as my mouth falls open and the sound of the fireworks mask the loud moans that escape from me.

"Is this what you wanted, princess?" he asks, watching me with that lust-filled look in his eyes.

I nod, but that's not good enough.

"Say it," he commands.

I feel my face heat, feeling shy for some reason.

"Say it," he repeats, stopping the thrusts all together.

"Don't stop," I say in a panic, my eyes widening as I find his.

"Why not?" he asks, a smug smirk playing on his lips as his thrusts begin again, agonizingly slow.

"Because," I say, my face heating even more.

He watches me, fascinated and amused. "Use your words, Princess. Why don't you want me to stop?"

"Because I want you to make me come until I can't even remember my own name," I say in a rush, pursing my lips as I look away from him, certain I'm crimson.

He lets out a boyish chuckle before slamming into me once, forcing a moan out of me, before he returns to the slow thrusts. "Anyone could make you come until you can't remember your own name," he says, moving his head in my line of vision, forcing me to look at him again. "Why do you want me to be the one to do it?"

"I highly doubt every man out there is capable of that," I say, avoiding the question.

He pauses, the humour slowly fading from his face. "Why me, Mal?"

I stare into his eyes, feeling him twitching inside of me distractingly, a lump forming in my throat as I catch the vulnerability in his gaze. "Because...because I still love you, Koa," I say, my voice shaking, "and I don't know how to stop being afraid of all the what-ifs that come with you, but maybe this is a start."

He looks at me like I'm the most incredible thing he's ever seen, and it makes my heart skip a beat. His lips curl into that half-smile, and I feel my knees weaken, grateful that he's holding me up right now.

"I lov—"

"Don't," I say quickly, interrupting him. "Don't say it. Please. With how things ended, I'm going to need more than just words to believe that, Koa."

He nods, understanding, before his gaze intensifies, like he's taking in every part of me, devouring me with his eyes. There's something about it. Dark and hungry. Like I'm the only thing that matters at this moment. It's more than just desire. It's like he's in awe, as if he can't believe I'm here in front of him, completely exposed.

"Don't worry, princess," he finally says as he starts to move again, pulling out almost completely before slamming into me as deep as he can. "I promise, when I say those words again, you won't doubt me."

His eyes meet mine and I see that quiet look of determination in them that makes it hard to breathe. He pounds into me, tipping us over the edge at the same time as the water splashes around us, and I know I've never wanted anyone like this before.

KOA | RIO DE JANEIRO, BRAZIL

I WAKE up to something warm and soft pressed against me, the steady rise and fall of her breathing against my chest. For a second, I almost don't believe it's real. I blink my eyes open, adjusting to the dim light, and there she is—Maliah, naked and tangled in the sheets beside me. Her body draped across mine like she belongs here.

Because she does belong here.

Last night plays back in my head like a dream I don't want to wake up from. The way she looked—her skin glowing in the moonlight, the fireworks lighting up the sky, the water splashing around us in the pool while we fucked. The way she felt. I can still feel her soft gasps, the way her body trembled and tightened around me when she came. It was...breathtaking. More than that, it was everything.

She's everything.

I gently brush a strand of hair from her face, careful not to wake her. Watching her now, so peaceful, it hits me like a punch to the chest—she's the one. I've always known it deep down, but after last night, it's like everything snapped into focus. I've been an idiot, letting her slip away, letting her think I didn't want her. But now...now I'm so close to getting her back. It feels within reach, like one more step and we could be together again, for real.

I shift slightly, trying to grab my phone from the nightstand without waking her. It's early, barely dawn, but I can't stop thinking about her. About us. I open my phone and start searching for things we can do in Rio today. We were given a free day from the tour to explore, and I want to make it perfect for her. I want to show her that I'm not just playing games—that when I say I want her, I mean all of her.

I scroll through a few places—Christ the Redeemer, Sugar-loaf Mountain, some beaches—and start planning it all out. A full day for just the two of us. No distractions, no cameras, just...us.

Maliah stirs beside me, and I look down just as her eyes flutter open. For a moment, she looks at me, sleepy and a little confused, and then jumps back, pulling the sheet up to cover her naked body. I can't help but smirk at the sight.

"Really?" I say, raising an eyebrow. "There's no point in covering yourself up. I saw it all last night."

Her cheeks flush bright pink, and she glares at me like she's trying to be mad, but I can see the smile she's trying to hide. That's the thing about her—no matter how much she tries to act tough, I can always tell when she's flustered.

"Shut up," she mutters, clutching the sheet tighter.

I chuckle, leaning back against the pillows, my eyes tracing the curve of her shoulder, her back. "I'm serious, Mal. You don't need to hide from me."

She glances at me, then looks away quickly, still holding the sheet to her chest like a shield. I reach out and take her hand, gently tugging the fabric down just a bit, enough to see her skin. She doesn't stop me.

"Last night," I start, my voice low, "was perfect."

She bites her lip, looking like she's not sure what to say, but I don't push her. Not yet. I'll wait. I'll give her time. But in my head, one thing is clear—there's no going back now. I'm not letting her slip through my fingers again.

I reach out again and gently push her back onto the bed. Her eyes widen slightly, and I can see the conflict there—she wants to push me away, but I can tell she's torn.

"Koa..." she starts, her voice soft but edged with protest, "I need to shower."

I shake my head and spread her thighs apart, my hands gliding down her legs as I settle between them. Her breath hitches as I look her dead in the eyes, my voice low and steady. "The shower can wait. I'm feeling hungry."

She opens her mouth to argue, but I don't give her a chance. I lower my head, and the second my mouth touches her soft pussy, her body arches off the bed. I feel her hands press against my shoulders, half-heartedly trying to push me away, but it doesn't last. Her fingers tangle in my hair instead, and the only sounds left are her breathy moans filling the quiet room.

I lose myself in the sweet taste of her, every shiver, every gasp pushing me further. I can feel the tension in her body build as she tugs on my hair and her thighs squeeze around my head, as if she's trying to pull me deeper. It doesn't take long for her to come, and it's like the world pauses for a second, her body trembling against me.

I pull back, a satisfied smile stretching across my face. Her chest is rising and falling rapidly, her face flushed, and I know I've done my job when she grabs the nearest pillow and chucks it at my head. I laugh, dodging it easily.

Before she can get too in her head, I reach for her hand and give it a playful squeeze. "Go shower and get dressed. We've got plans."

She looks at me with a raised brow, not fully trusting me. "Plans? What kind of plans?"

I shrug. "Gabriel's idea. Team building sessions. You know how he gets." I keep my face as straight as possible, selling the lie, though I can see she's still skeptical.

"Uh-huh," she mutters, clearly not convinced but going along with it anyway. "Fine, but if this is some stupid prank, you're dead."

I watch her get out of bed and trot out of my room; my eyes glued to the way her ass jiggles as she walks.

That girl is going to be the death of me.

THE CITY VAN PULLS UP TO THE CHRIST THE REDEEMER STATUE, and I can feel Maliah's excitement radiating through the car. Her eyes light up as she looks around, taking in the massive monument towering above us. I keep my hand on her thigh the whole time, a quiet connection that I don't want to break. She doesn't move it away either.

I follow her as she steps out of the van, her eyes wide while she soaks in the view. I lean back against the side of the van, watching her in awe. There's something about the way she lights up in moments like this that gets to me every time. Without thinking, I take out my phone and snap a picture of her. She looks over her shoulder at me, catching me mid-snap, and rolls her eyes playfully.

"Really?" she says.

"Gotta capture the moment," I say, pocketing the phone. "It's not every day you're standing in front of something like this."

I glance up at the iconic statue, feeling small—like, really small. The statue towers over us, arms outstretched like it's embracing the entirety of Rio. It's way bigger than I expected. I follow her as she gets closer to examine the statue and I'm amazed at the details, from the folds in the robe to the serene expression on the face—it's all so still, yet powerful. I glance at Maliah next to me and a feeling of pride fills my chest at pulling this off. She had always said she wanted to check off the seven wonders of the world and she definitely hadn't checked this off yet.

It's peaceful up here, despite all the tourists snapping pictures and whispering. You can see the whole city, stretching out under a blanket of blue sky, but it's the statue that holds all the attention. There's something about the way it stands, over-looking everything—like it's watching over us, reminding us of how small our problems really are in the grand scheme of things. It's humbling.

We spend some time exploring the area, learning about the statue's history, but my focus keeps drifting back to her—how she moves, the way her lips curve when she smiles, the sound of her laughter mixing with the murmurs of the crowd. I can't help but wonder what it would be like to bring her here again in the future, to share moments like this without the weight of everything hanging over us.

After a while, the city van returns to take us back down to our car. We climb in, the only two leaving at this time, and begin the drive down Corcovado Mountain.

"Thank you," she says, her voice low but clear, breaking the comfortable silence.

I turn toward her, eyebrows raised. "For what?"

Her lips curve into a small smile, and she shrugs. "Gabriel would never plan something like today as a team building event," she says, turning knowing eyes towards me. "So, thank you...for today. For planning it. It was...nice."

Nice? That's an understatement. But I get it. I nod, feeling a strange mix of relief and embarrassment at being caught. I wanted to give her a perfect day, to take her mind off everything —to show her something more than the usual chaos we're stuck in on this tour, to remind her how easy it is between us. I wanted to give her something real, something she could remember that wasn't tied to all the messy stuff between us.

She leans her head back against the seat, her eyes still on the view, but I catch the way her body relaxes, just slightly. She's finally letting herself breathe a little easier around me. I want to hold onto this moment. Hell, I want to hold on to her, to everything we have.

The van hits a curve, and I rest my hand on her thigh. Just a light touch, like an anchor, reminding her that I'm here. She glances down at my hand, then back up at me, and for a split second, there's that spark again. But just as quickly, her body tenses beneath my hand and the spark dims. I see it in the way she shifts her gaze, closing herself off again, putting those damn walls back up.

She clears her throat softly, eyes still on the window. "Koa..."

I know that tone. It's the kind of tone that comes right before something I don't want to hear.

She sighs, finally turning to face me. "About last night...and this morning." Her fingers fidget in her lap, like she's trying to gather the right words. "I think we might be moving too fast."

My stomach drops. The high I've been riding all day crashes down hard. I try to keep my face neutral, but inside, it's like a punch to the gut.

"What do you mean?" I ask, though I already know where this is headed.

She lets out a shaky breath. "I mean, maybe we should take a step back. Try rebuilding the trust between us...as friends first."

Friends.

The word feels like ice, chilling me from the inside out. It's not what I expected. Not after last night, not after how she looked at me this morning. It's like I was so damn close to getting her back, and now she's pulling away again.

I swallow hard, trying to keep my voice steady. "I don't think I can go back to being just friends, Maliah. Not after everything."

Her eyes meet mine, and I can see the uncertainty, the way my words freak her out. But it's the truth. "You've always been the one for me," I say, my voice lower, almost pleading. "I don't think I could ever see you as just a friend."

Her eyes flash with something sharp, and before I can say anything more, she snaps.

"I've always been the one for you?" Her voice rises, frustration spilling out. "You're the one who broke up with me, Koa. You're the one who stood there and told me you didn't love me anymore—remember? So how can you sit here and say I've always been the one for you?"

Her words hit me like a slap to the face, and I feel my chest tighten. She's right, and I know she has every reason to be angry. But I can't tell her the real reason why I did it. I can't let her know it wasn't about not loving her anymore. It was about protecting her—even if she'll never understand it that way.

"Maliah..." I start, but my voice catches. I run my hand through my hair, struggling to find the right words. "I...I never wanted to hurt you."

Her eyes are blazing now, and it's like every bit of hurt I caused is coming to the surface. "But you did," she says, her voice trembling. "You broke me, Koa. And now you're sitting here saying I've always been the one? How am I supposed to believe that?"

I want to tell her everything, but I can't. Not here, not now. It would only make things worse. So instead, I bite my tongue, keeping the truth locked up where it's been since the day I ended things. "I know what I said, but...it's complicated."

She shakes her head, letting out a bitter laugh. "Complicated. Right."

By the time we pull into the parking lot, the tension between us is suffocating. We climb out of the van and into the car, but the silence between us speaks louder than any words. I grip the steering wheel, overthinking every damn thing I said, wondering if I've already ruined whatever chance we had.

She doesn't say a word on the drive back to the penthouse, and I feel like I'm losing her all over again.

WE PULL UP TO THE BUILDING, AND AS SOON AS I PARK THE CAR, I see a group of surfers, including Charles and Reese, gathered outside the entrance. They're all laughing and talking loudly, clearly in the middle of planning or debating something. As Maliah and I step out of the car, they spot us and wave us over.

"Yo, Koa! Mal!" Reese calls out with a grin. "We're heading to a samba show and pub crawl for our last night in Rio. You two coming with us?"

I'm just about to decline, not even remotely in the mood for partying after everything that just went down between me and Maliah, but before I can say a word, Maliah speaks up.

"Yea, sounds fun!" she says, her voice a little too enthusiastic, like she's trying to drown out the tension that's still hanging between us.

I blink, caught off guard by her sudden shift. My instinct is to still turn them down, maybe just head back upstairs and keep stewing in my thoughts. But one look at the smirk that spreads along Charles' face is enough to convince me otherwise.

"Sure. I'm in," I say, forcing a small smile.

The group cheers, hyped up for the night, while I follow Maliah inside with the feeling that this night is going to be a lot longer than I expected.

EIGHTEEN

MALIAH | RIO DE JANEIRO, BRAZIL

THE SAMBA SHOW IS VIBRANT, alive with colours and energy, and I'm trying my best to focus on it. The music is infectious, the dancers moving with grace and rhythm that almost feels like magic. A few times, I catch bits of conversations about the history of samba—how it was born out of African and Brazilian roots, how it's not just a dance but a way of life, a symbol of resistance, culture, and celebration. It's fascinating, and for a moment, it pulls me out of my own head.

But as incredible as the show is, my mind keeps wandering back to what Koa said earlier.

You'll always be the one for me.

Those words are on repeat in my head, gnawing at me, making me feel things I don't want to. I should be flattered, right? I should be relieved. But instead, I feel this overwhelming sense of fear, like I'm teetering on the edge of something that could either save me or destroy me. And the fact that he broke up with me, *he* ended it, makes it all the more confusing. He said he didn't love me. So why now? Why say I'm "the one" now?

I feel like I can't breathe.

When we leave the samba show and move onto the pub crawl, I'm desperate for some kind of distraction, anything to get my mind off Koa and the mess I'm in. I order drink after drink, each one going down easier than the last, and the tipsiness starts to creep in like a welcome relief.

That's when I spot Charles.

He's laughing with the others, his arm slung casually over the back of one of the bar stools, and I don't know why, but I make my way over to him. It's not that I'm actually interested in Charles—God, no. He's sweet, and we've been friendly, but this isn't about him. This is about me needing to feel *something else*, to shift the focus off of Koa.

"Hey," I say, sliding into the seat next to him, my voice lighter than usual, more playful. "How are you enjoying Rio?"

Charles grins, his eyes lighting up. "How could I not? This place is incredible."

I nod, leaning a little closer, just enough to blur the lines. "Yeah, it is. You know, I think I've underestimated how fun you are, Charles."

He laughs, a little flustered, clearly not expecting me to be so forward. "You? Underestimating me? Never."

I flirt back, more openly now, my hand brushing his arm as I smile at him. It's not real. None of it is. But it's easier to do this than to sit with the feelings Koa stirred up. I keep telling myself it's harmless, that I'm just having fun, but deep down, I know what I'm really doing.

I'm running. Running from Koa, from his words, from the possibility of getting hurt again.

And it's not working.

The group of girls surround me before I even realize what's happening. They're giggling, nudging each other as they drag me away from Charles. Their eyes are filled with curiosity, and I already know what's coming.

"So," one of them says with a smirk, "what's going on with you and Koa?"

I blink, trying to play dumb. "What do you mean?"

"Oh, come on," another chimes in, leaning closer. "We all saw you two at Carnival. You were all over each other."

The memory of last night—of Koa's hands on me, his lips, the way my body responded to him—floods my mind. It's almost too much, and I feel a pang of something I don't want to acknowledge. I glance towards the bar where Koa is standing, and sure enough, he's watching me, his dark eyes tracking my every move. The way he looks at me, it's as if he's still claiming me, like I belong to him.

It pisses me off.

I turn back to the girls, forcing a smile. "Koa? Nah, he's all yours. Go ahead and take him."

They exchange a few shocked glances before breaking into laughter. One of them claps her hands together, almost in disbelief. "Really? You're saying he's free?"

"Completely free." The words taste bitter as they leave my mouth, but I push through it. "I'm not holding him back."

The moment the words are out, I feel a sharp stab of regret. But I don't let it show. I just watch as the girls giggle excitedly and make their way over to him. And to my surprise—no, to my *horror*—Koa doesn't seem to mind. He actually *interacts* with them. He's smiling, laughing, his eyes lighting up in a way that feels like a slap to my face.

What the hell?

Jealousy surges inside me, hot and fierce. I hate the way he looks so damn unbothered. He's enjoying the attention, and I'm left standing here, feeling like an idiot for caring. For a second, I can't even think straight, the rage boiling up inside me.

I need to do something. *Anything* to get back at him.

My eyes dart to Charles. I flash him a flirtatious smile, step closer, and before I know it, we're dancing. My body moves to the rhythm of the music, my hips swaying, and I make sure Koa sees.

I'm dancing, probably horribly, with Charles for one reason only—*to piss Koa off.*

Every now and then, I glance over at Koa. He's still at the bar, but now his expression has changed. He's no longer laughing with the girls. His jaw is tight, his eyes narrowing as they lock onto me and Charles.

Good. I want him to feel the way I felt.

I can feel his anger simmering from across the room, his eyes tracking my every move. It should make me feel good, maybe even satisfied that I got the reaction I wanted out of him. But instead, something tight and uneasy coils inside me. This isn't who I am. I don't play these games—yet here I am, dancing with Charles, trying to make Koa feel something.

Charles leans in closer, whispering something I barely register over the pounding music and his thick accent, and before I know it, he's tugging me toward the back of the pub. I hesitate, glancing back, but Koa is still by the bar, glaring at us like he wants to rip Charles apart. For a second, I think about pulling away, but Charles' hand is firm on my wrist, and I stumble into a dark corner of the back room before I can even process what's happening.

"Wait—" I start, my voice shaky as I try to pull back, but he doesn't listen. His hands are suddenly everywhere, rough and fast, tugging at my clothes, his mouth coming down on mine without warning.

"No!" I shove at his chest, panic rising in my throat, but he's stronger than I expected. My heart races, my breaths shallow as I try to push him off. "Stop!"

He doesn't stop. Instead, he presses harder, his hands roaming where they have no business being, and fear grips me. My mind goes blank, trapped in the growing terror of the moment.

Suddenly, I hear a familiar voice—a roar of fury.

"Koa?" I manage to gasp just as Charles is ripped off me, his body flying back against the wall with a hard *thud.*

Koa is on him in an instant, his fist smashing into Charles' face. One punch, then another, each hit fuelled by a rage I've never seen in him before. Charles slumps to the ground, groaning in pain, but Koa doesn't stop. He's going to destroy him, and all I can think is that he's going to kill him if I don't do something.

"Koa, stop!" I rush forward, grabbing his arm, my voice breaking. "Please, stop!"

He pauses, breathing heavily, his chest heaving as he stands over Charles. His eyes are wild with fury, the muscles in his jaw clenched so tight I think they might snap. Then he turns to me, and the intensity in his gaze makes me shrink back.

"He fucking touched you, Mal!" His voice is raw, full of venom. "Do you even get that?"

I flinch at his words, my heart racing for a different reason now. I'm at a loss for how to respond, my thoughts still tangled from what just happened. But before I can speak, Koa pushes himself off Charles, his body trembling with barely contained anger.

Without another word, he grabs my wrist as he storms past me, yanking me behind him. I stumble after him, barely able to keep up with his long angry strides as we push through the crowd, out of the pub and into the cool night air. My wrist stings where he's gripping it, but I don't say anything. I don't even think I could if I wanted to.

He drags me to the car, still furious, his jaw clenched tight as he pulls open the door. I slide into the passenger seat silently, my heart pounding in my chest. The silence between us is thick, suffocating. He slams the door shut and rounds the front of the car, slamming his door behind him too and gripping the steering wheel so hard I think it might break under the pressure.

The entire drive back to the penthouse is filled with nothing but the sound of his heavy breathing and the roar of the engine, rage simmering between us, threatening to explode at any moment. My heart pounds, not just from the fear of what almost happened in the back of that pub, but from the energy radiating off Koa.

We pull into the parking garage thirty minutes later, and the car comes to a screeching stop. Koa is out before I can even unbuckle my seatbelt, opening my door for me and then slamming it shut as soon as I'm out. My legs feel shaky as I follow him into the building and up the elevator.

The moment we step into the penthouse, the tension boils over.

"What the hell were you thinking, Maliah?" he snaps, pacing in front of me like a caged animal. "Dancing with Charles? Letting him take you off like that?"

My chest tightens. "I wasn't—I didn't let him—"

"Does it even matter?" he cuts me off, his eyes blazing. "You could have been hurt. He could've—"

"I know!" I yell, my voice breaking. "I know, okay? I was just —I was trying to—" I don't even know what I was trying to do anymore. Distract myself? Punish Koa for what he said earlier? Make sense of the chaos between us?

But it all sounds so stupid now, standing here in front of him, seeing the hurt and fury in his eyes.

"You don't get it, do you?" Koa's voice drops, lower, more dangerous. He steps closer to me, his presence overwhelming. "No one can mess with you. With us. I can't...I can't lose you, Maliah."

My heart skips a beat at his words, but I try to push it down. "We're moving too fast, Koa," I say, my voice trembling. "We need to slow it down. We should—"

"What?" he scoffs, closing the distance between us in one stride. "Go back to being friends?"

His words sting, and I try to hold my ground. "I don't know what we're doing anymore. It's all so confusing."

"I don't care about labels, Mal," he says, his voice rough. "We don't have to call it anything. We don't need a title. We can just be us. Koa and Maliah. That's it."

His voice is raw, and it hits something deep inside me. I'm still angry, still scared, but hearing him say that...it does something to me. I stare at him, my chest heaving, and the next thing I know, he's closing the gap between us, pulling me towards him in one swift motion. His lips crash against mine, rough and demanding, and all the pent-up anger, frustration, and fear explodes between us.

I kiss him back, hard, my hands fisting in his shirt as I push him towards my bedroom. His hands are everywhere—tugging at my clothes, pulling me closer, like he can't get enough of me. And maybe I can't get enough of him either.

We stumble inside, and the second my back hits the mattress, he's on me, his weight pressing me down, his mouth hot against my neck, my collarbone, anywhere he can reach. His hands grip my thighs, spreading them apart, and I arch against him, needing him in a way that scares me.

"I need you, Mal," he breathes against my skin, his voice thick with desperation. "I don't care what we call it. I just need you."

"Then take me," I whisper, my voice shaking with want.

He doesn't need any more encouragement. His lips claim mine again, and before I know it, he's fingering me. His touch is demanding, almost possessive, as he thrusts his fingers into me with an intensity that leaves me gasping, moaning his name like it's the only thing that matters. He keeps going until I'm shaking, blubbering nonsense, and the sheets are soaked.

He gently removes his fingers, and I watch in fascination as he slides them into his mouth, a low growl escaping him.

"You always taste so good," he says as he unbuttons his pants, pushing them lower to allow his cock to spring free.

I stare at it in bewilderment, always shocked at the sheer size of it. He gently strokes it as I watch, a bead of pre-cum forming on the head. He uses his thumb to spread it around before he positions himself at my entrance and thrusts into me. I gasp at the feeling of him, my pussy fighting to allow him fully inside.

This isn't 'making love' sex, this is wild and messy and raw, and I can feel how much he needs this—how much *we* need this. It doesn't take long for me to come again, the sound of his name on my lips. Everything else in the world fades away as his thrusts become more frantic and his breath heavy and ragged in my ear.

Every thrust is hard, purposeful, as if he's trying to pour everything he feels into me—his anger, his need, his despera-tion. I can feel the tension in his body, the way his muscles tighten and coil, like he's holding onto control by the thinnest thread.

His hands grip my hips, pulling me even closer to him, and I can barely keep up with the intensity of it. I hear his breath hitch, his pace faltering for just a moment, and I know he's close. The weight of him on top of me, the sound of his rough groans filling the air, it's all too much.

He leans down, burying his face in my neck as his move-ments become more erratic, his body trembling with the effort of holding on. "Mal..." he groans, his voice tight, like he's trying to hold back but can't. "Fuck..."

And then with one final thrust, I feel him break. His entire body shudders as he comes, releasing into me with a deep, guttural sound that vibrates through my skin. His grip on me tightens, almost painfully, as if he's afraid to let go, as if he needs this moment to last.

For a second, time stands still. The world narrows to just the two of us, tangled together, our breathing heavy and uneven.

As his breathing slows, he stays pressing against me, neither of us moving, the weight of what just happened hanging between us. His forehead rests against mine, our bodies still intertwined, but the fire from moments ago has cooled, leaving only the quiet aftermath.

I close my eyes, trying to steady my heart, unsure of what this means—what any of it means. There are no words left, just the sound of our breathing, and the steady rhythm of his heart against my chest.

For now, we're just Koa and Maliah. Nothing more, nothing less.

But for how long?

NINETEEN

KOA | LA LIBERTAD, EL SALVADOR

THE WAVES at Punta Roca are something else—sharp, clean, and relentless. They peel perfectly, letting you catch multiple airs, carve tight turns, and then shoot into a barrel like the ocean's pulling you in just to spit you out in triumph. It's every surfer's dream, the kind of conditions that make you feel alive, like you're one with the water.

As soon as my feet hit the wax, I know this is going to be good. The board cuts through the wave, and I drop into the pocket, the lip curling over me. The feeling of being inside a barrel is indescribable, like time stops and all that exists is the roar of the water around you, the tunnel of blue pulling you deeper in. My heart thunders in my chest, but my mind is completely clear—no thoughts, no worries, just the thrill of riding it out.

I emerge from the barrel, catching air before landing the final turn, and the rush is pure adrenaline. The nearby crowd roars, but all I hear is the ocean in my ears. This is where I belong.

We come in first place, Maliah buzzing with excitement as we get out of the water. Other surfers high-five us and pat us on the back, adrenaline-fuelled smiles all around. Except for Charles. He stands farther down the beach, watching me with a glare through his two black eyes and busted lip. I smirk at him before looking down at Maliah next to me, her skin glistening with the ocean's salt, and I can't help but feel like I'm on top of the world. Not just because of the win, but because of her.

As we get pulled over for the post-heat interview, the interviewer grins and congratulates us. Then, out of nowhere, she asks, "Fans around the world are shipping you two pretty hard. The first six episodes of SurfFlix have aired, and people are dying to know—what's the deal? What's the status of Koa and Maliah?"

I open my mouth to say something, but before I can, Maliah jumps in, "We're just Koa and Maliah."

Her voice is steady, confident, and when she says it, my grin stretches wide. Because yeah—she gets it. We don't need a label, and maybe that's enough. For now, at least.

The interviewer raises an eyebrow, clearly intrigued, but I just laugh as I throw my arm over Maliah's shoulder, pulling her into my side as I give her a sideways glance. "Just Koa and Maliah," I repeat, feeling the truth of it settle in.

And damn, I don't think I've ever felt so good hearing my own name.

We head back to our tent and hop on a video call with Gabriel. The connection flickers for a second, but when his face finally appears on the screen, I'm hit with two things. One, he actually looks better. A lot better than the last time we saw him, when he was grumpy as hell. And two, Zalea is walking around in the background, but something's off. She's pale, her steps unsteady, and she looks like she might be coming down with something.

Before I can ever say anything, Maliah's already leaning closer to the screen, her brow furrowed. But Gabriel notices us staring and snaps, "Mind your business."

We both back off immediately, and he shifts his attention back to the competition. "Congrats on the win. Let's go over the race before I send over my notes." His voice softens a bit as he glances at Maliah. "And, uh, I've been meaning to say sorry about springing the shared bed situation on you guys in Fiji. Poor planning on my part. I've arranged a team building event for you guys to make up for it."

Maliah gives him a teasing smile. "No worries, Coach. But seriously, another team building event? We just had one in Rio." She nudges me playfully.

Gabriel's face scrunches in confusion. "Another one? What are you talking about?"

Panic grips me as I realize Maliah's hinting at the day out that I planned for us. "Oh, uh, Gabriel, the production crew is calling us over for more interviews." I laugh awkwardly, feeling my face heat up. "Text me the details for the next event and any notes you had from today, yeah?"

Before he can ask more questions, I hang up. Too quick. Way too quick.

When I turn to Maliah, she's doubled over, laughter spilling out of her. I rub the back of my neck feeling like an idiot. "What?"

"You should've seen your face!" she says between giggles. "You were so flustered. I've never seen you like that."

"Yeah, well, you almost blew it," I say, though I can't help but laugh too. Even through the embarrassment, seeing her smile like this makes it all worth it.

The sun is starting to dip below the horizon when we pull up to *Parque el Espino*, also known as Sunset Park, in La Libertad. The sky is painted in warm oranges and pinks, casting a soft glow over the ocean in the distance. The breeze carries the scent of saltwater mixed with grilled street food, and the air buzzes with laughter, chatter, and the sound of carnival games. It's like something out of a movie—the kind of place where everything feels alive.

Maliah and I step out of the van, two camera guys trailing behind us, capturing every moment like we're some kind of reality TV couple. I take in the scene around the park: brightly coloured stalls, neon lights flickering to life, and the buzz of excited voices filling the air. The scent of pupusas and fried plantains wafts over from the food stands, making my stomach growl.

Maliah's eyes widen as she takes it all in, her expression caught between wonder and amusement. "I've never been on a date somewhere like this," she says, mostly to herself, but I catch it.

A slow grin creeps onto my face. "You just called it a date."

Her cheeks flush instantly. "No, I didn't! I just—" She fumbles, her flustered reaction making her even more adorable.

"You did," I tease, leaning in a little closer, ignoring the way the cameramen behind us inch closer. "But don't worry, I'll make it the best date ever."

She glares at me playfully, but I can see she's trying to hide her smile. That blush? Yeah, that's fuel to my fire. I'm going to make sure tonight is one for the books.

We start wandering through the park, and I slip into full-on carnival boyfriend mode. First stop: the games. I spot a simple ring toss booth and nudge her. "Think you can beat me?"

Her competitive side kicks in, and before I know it, we're both chucking rings at bottles. I'm aiming with laser focus, but it's not long before she wins a small stuffed iguana. Maliah holds it up, triumphant, as if she's just claimed the championship trophy. I pretend to be bitter about it, but seeing her smile that big? Worth the fake defeat.

"Not bad," I say, giving her a playful nudge. "Now let me show you how it's done."

I manage to win her a small cotuza—a stuffed toy resembling the cute little agouti, a rodent native to El Salvador. It's tiny, but I figure it won't take up much room in her suitcase. She giggles when I hand it to her, but the look in her eyes tells me she appreciates it more than she's letting on.

And then she surprises me. "Your turn," she says, tossing a ring at another booth and, after a few tries, she wins me a stuffed torogoz—El Salvador's national bird. Its vibrant colours are bright against the fading sunlight.

I take the bird from her outstretched hand, feeling a strange warmth spread through my chest. It's just a stuffed toy, nothing big. But knowing she put the effort into winning it for me? That's a different kind of feeling.

"Guess we're even now," I say, giving her a grin, though I can't shake how good it feels to be on the receiving end of something from her. Not just anyone—it's Maliah.

As we continue through the carnival grounds, my eyes drift to Maliah again, and damn, she's stunning tonight. She's got this effortless beauty that just pulls me in without even trying. Her hair, those golden waves, flow down her back and catch the light from the neon signs around us. They move with the breeze, soft and wild all at once, and I have to resist the urge to reach out and run my fingers through them, especially because I know we're being filmed for the world to see.

She's wearing a simple but perfect outfit. A white sundress that clings in all the right places and flares out as she walks, giving her that easy, carefree look. The fabric moves with every step she takes, like it was made to be worn in the warmth of this carnival night. Her skin has this golden glow under the sunset, and the contrast of the dress against her tan makes her stand out even more.

But it's her eyes that get me every time. Those big, blue eyes, brighter than the lights of the park, wide with excitement as she looks around, taking everything in. She's got this infectious energy tonight, like she's a kid in a candy story, and it makes her even more beautiful. When she catches me staring, she raises a brow, the corner of her mouth lifting into a smirk.

"What?"

"Nothing," I lie, because how the hell do I explain that she's the most beautiful thing I've seen all night? Even in this whole vibrant, colourful carnival, it's her that keeps pulling my attention.

She shakes her head, probably thinking I'm just being weird, but I don't miss the light pink that dusts her cheeks. That little blush, the way she tries to hide it, makes her even harder to look away from.

As we wander through the park, choosing games to play and passing by food stalls, a feeling of pride settles over me. Everyone around can see her—how amazing she looks—and she's here with me.

TWENTY

MALIAH | LA LIBERTAD, EL SALVADOR

WE'RE SITTING ON A BENCH, finishing up the last of our food, and I have to admit it's been a while since I've felt this carefree. The air is thick with the scent of grilled meats, sugary churros, and popcorn. I take a bite of my arepa, savouring the crispy outside and the warm, cheesy filling. Koa's munching on some skewers, his eyes sparkling as we laugh over how competitive we were at the ring toss earlier.

The sun's starting to dip lower now, casting this warm orange glow over everything. It feels like time's slowing down, just a little. We talk about the games we've played, the ones he won me stuffed animals at, and how he claims to have a secret technique for every single one. I roll my eyes, but it's hard to hide my smile. There's something about tonight that feels... different. Almost like we're tiptoeing closer to something more, but neither of us is ready to call it that and that's perfectly fine for me.

"Hey," Koa says, breaking into my thoughts. "Do you want to go on the Ferris wheel? Escape these cameras for a bit?" He nods over to where the wheel is lighting up, colourful lights flashing as it spins slowly in the distance.

I freeze for a second, trying not to let the spike of anxiety show on my face. I hate heights. And that thing looks massive.

"Uh..." I glance at it, then back at him, trying to think of a way to say no without sounding like a loser.

"You scared?" He smirks, raising an eyebrow, like he's daring me.

"Of course not," I lie through my teeth. I think I manage to sound casual, but inside, I'm freaking the hell out.

He studies me for a second, his face softening. "It's okay if you don't want to go, Princess. But if you're up for it, I promise we'll be fine. I'll be right there with you." His voice is gentle, reassuring, and somehow that makes it worse.

I know I should say no. The last time I was up high, I could barely keep it together. But something in the way he's looking at me, the way he said he'd be there with me, makes me want to take that step. Just for tonight.

"Fine," I say, trying to sound more confident than I feel. "But if I throw up, I'm aiming for you." I point at him, narrowing my eyes.

Koa laughs, shaking his head. "Deal."

The entire walk to the Ferris wheel, my stomach twists in knots, and I pray to God I don't actually puke when we reach the top. I swear, I'll die from embarrassment if I do. We stand in line, and I can feel the nerves creeping up my spine. Heights have never been my thing, but Koa is next to me, calm and collected as ever. When it's finally our turn, my feet hesitate, rooted to the ground. Koa notices right away, of course. He always does.

He takes my hand in his, kisses the back of it gently, and looks straight into my eyes. "Trust me," he says, his voice low and reassuring.

And I do. I trust him, despite everything we've been through. So I take a deep breath and step into the carriage with him.

As soon as the Ferris wheel lurches forward, I screech involuntarily, clutching the safety bar with all my strength. My stomach flips, and I'm ready to beg them to let me off, but before I can even say a word, Koa wraps his arms around me, pulling me into his chest. His body is warm and solid, and I find comfort in the way he holds me so close.

"It's okay," he murmurs into my ear, his lips brushing against my temple. "I've got you."

I exhale slowly and sink into him, trying to calm my racing heart. We rise higher and higher, the carnival lights twinkling below, and the ocean stretches out in front of us, meeting the horizon where the sun is beginning to set.

"It's beautiful," I say softly, my eyes glued to the view. The sky is painted in shades of pink and orange and the waves shimmer under the fading light.

"Yeah," Koa says, but when I glance up at him, he's not looking at the ocean. He's looking at me.

I feel a flutter in my chest, but I need a distraction before I get lost in the way he's staring at me. So I shift the conversation.

"Why are you considering leaving the team if you love surfing so much?"

Koa's face changes slightly, his jaw tensing. He doesn't answer right away, and I can feel him mulling over the question. His arms tighten around me, like he's holding onto something deeper than just the moment.

He finally sighs and leans his head back against the seat. "It's not that I don't love surfing. I do," he begins. "But it's been years. It's all I've known for so long, and I've been away from my family for most of it. I miss them. I want to make more time to be with them, to live, not just surf."

I nod, understanding what he means, but the thought of him not being there during practices, not being on the team, makes me uneasy. I've had him by my side for so many years now—it's hard to imagine what it would be like without him.

"I get that, but don't you think you'll miss competing? The thrill of it?" I ask.

He shrugs slightly. "Maybe. But I don't think competitive surfing is what I want to do forever. I love it, but there's more to life than just riding waves for scores, you know? I want to figure out what else I'm passionate about. Like you and your baking. Maybe that house I want to buy is a start. And who knows, we might end up in a bidding war over it."

I laugh softly at that, but there's a weight in his words that lingers in the air. I hadn't realized how much he'd been thinking about life beyond surfing.

The conversation slows as we near the top of the wheel. The city below us is alive with lights, the ocean reflecting the last glimmers of the sun. The view is breathtaking, but I can feel something else building in the air—something between us that's been simmering all night.

The carriage rocks slightly, and I clutch Koa's arm without thinking, earning a quiet laugh from him. "We're almost at the top," he says, his voice soft. "You okay?"

I nod, but my heart races for a different reason now. There's something about being up here, with the world spread out beneath us, that makes everything feel more intense. Like the air is charged.

As the wheel comes to a gentle stop at the very top, we sit there, hovering about the carnival. It's just us, the vast sky, and the hum of the world below. I glance at Koa, and he's already looking at me, that familiar intensity in his gaze.

"You know," he says, his lips curving into a small smile, "this would be the perfect moment in a movie for fireworks."

I'm about to laugh when, as if on cue, fireworks explode in the distance. Bright streaks of colour shoot into the sky, lighting up the night. The sound of the first boom startles me, but then I relax, laughing as the sky fills with bursts of red, blue, and gold.

"Did you plan that?" I tease, my heart racing.

Koa grins, his eyes reflecting the fireworks above us. "Not this time."

He turns toward me, his face close enough that I can feel the warmth of his breath against my cheek. The fireworks crackle in the sky, but all I can hear is the sound of my own heartbeat, thudding louder with each passing second. I feel the weight of the moment, the electricity between us building to something undeniable.

My breath catches as his hand moves to cup my cheek, his thumb brushing lightly over my skin. He leans in slowly, his gaze flicking to my lips before locking back onto my eyes. There's no hesitation, no doubt. I know what's coming, and I want it.

I want him.

And then he kisses me.

It's soft at first, gentle, like he's testing the waters. But the second I respond, the kiss deepens, and everything around us seems to fade away. His lips move against mine with a tenderness that makes my heart swell, and I melt into him, my hand sliding up to the back of his neck. The world falls away until it's just him, me, and this kiss.

The fireworks continue to explode above us, a kaleidoscope of colour lighting up the night, but all I can focus on is Koa. How his lips taste like the sweetness of the cotton candy we shared earlier, how his hand feels against my cheek, and how this kiss feels like a promise. A promise of everything that could be.

When we finally pull apart, I'm breathless, my chest rising and falling rapidly as I meet his eyes again. He smiles, that goofy, boyish smile that makes my heart skip a beat every time.

"See?" he murmurs, brushing his thumb across my lips. "Fireworks."

I can't help but laugh, a mixture of disbelief and pure happiness bubbling inside me. "Yeah...fireworks."

As the Ferris wheel starts moving again, slowly lowering us back to reality and back to the cameras, I realize that whatever happens next, this moment—this kiss—will stay with me forever.

TWENTY-ONE

KOA | TAHITI, FRENCH POLYNESIA

THE SUN barely rises over the horizon, casting a golden morning glow across the beach as we gather for morning yoga. The sky is painted in colours that would make you stop and take a breath, appreciating where you are. But all I can focus on is Maliah—directly in front of me, stretching her arms above her head in perfect form, her body moving like it's made for this.

And damn, it's distracting.

Her curves are on full display in those tight lavender leggings and that little matching sports bra, the one that hugs her in all the right places. Her blonde waves cascade down her back, catching the light of the sunrise like a halo, and I swear, every time she bends forward, my mind goes places it really shouldn't.

Stop. Breathe, Koa.

This is supposed to be relaxing. Centring. A time to clear the mind and find peace. But how the hell am I supposed to find peace when she's right there in front of me, moving like that? It doesn't help that I haven't had nearly enough sleep between the other night, still buzzing from the Ferris wheel kiss, and the eighteen-hour flight to Tahiti. And now here I am, fighting the urge to grab her, toss her over my shoulder, and march us straight back to our shared villa.

I glance up and catch one of the camera guys pointing his lens in our direction, reminding me that SurfFlix is still a thing. Great. I'm not only dealing with my own personal torment but doing it on camera. I can already imagine how they'll cut this together—me trying to focus on yoga while clearly eye-fucking Maliah.

She shifts into another pose, this time a deep lunge, her body arching just enough to drive me out of my damn mind. My fingers twitch at my sides as I force my eyes to stay on the instructor, trying to focus on her gentle voice. It's either that or give in to the primal urge to drag her out of here.

The instructor calls out another stretch, but it's no use. I can barely keep up with the movements because all I can see, all I can think about, is her.

After yoga is finally over, I'm on a mission to get Maliah back to our villa as quickly as possible. My body's still buzzing, and I've had enough of holding back for one morning. As we walk back, I reach for her hand, my mind already racing with the thought of taking her in the shower. The warmth of the water, her skin slick against mine—it's almost enough to make me forget we're not even alone yet.

But then, just as I'm about to suggest we make a detour to get back faster, one of the female surfers jogs up to us, eyeing me like I'm her next meal.

"Hey, you two! A bunch of us are hitting the jet skis this morning. You in?"

Maliah's eyes light up like she's a kid on Christmas. "Jet skis? I've never done that before! Sounds fun, right?" She's practically bouncing on her toes as she looks up at me, excitement radiating from her, and just like that, I'm screwed.

I was about to suggest something a lot more...private, but how can I say no to her when she looks like that?

Still, there's a feeling of hesitation in my chest, and it's not just because I wanted some alone time. Off to the side, I see Charles standing near a group of surfers, glaring at me again like he's ready to explode. His face is still bruised from the bar incident, the evidence of my punches clearly visible. He hasn't said a word to me or Maliah since then, but he doesn't have to. The way he's been watching me says enough.

There's a dangerous tension in the air whenever he's around. I felt it from the moment I met him, and I can't help but think it's only a matter of time before he does something stupid to get revenge. For now, he hasn't acted on it. He knows that if he escalates things, we both could be kicked off the tour, and neither of us wants that. Still, Charles gives me the impression that he isn't the type to let things go.

"Jet skis sound awesome!" Maliah says, dragging me into this decision.

I grit my teeth and force a smile. "Yeah, sure, why not?" The words feel heavy in my mouth. I don't want her anywhere near Charles, especially not in open water where things could get messy.

I glance back at Charles, who's smirking now, like he's already won something. I want to deck him again, but I can't risk it. Not just because of the tour, but because if I lose my cool, Maliah's the one who'll end up hurt the most. So I agree, knowing damn well I'll have to keep a close eye on her the entire time.

We board our jet skis after changing into our swimwear, and I try to hide that I'm not exactly in the best mood. I'm wound up so tight I'm pretty sure I could snap, and now, instead of relieving some of that tension back at the villa, we're out here on jet skis.

Great.

"No life jackets?" I ask.

"Come on, we practically live in the ocean. We don't need those," Charles calls out, as if I was speaking to him.

Everyone starts revving their engines, ready to take off, but when Maliah tries hers, nothing happens. She frowns, giving the thing a few more tries, but it's dead.

I pull up beside her, shaking my head with a grin I can't help. "Looks like you're riding with me. Hop on."

She doesn't hesitate, hopping on the back of my jet ski, wrapping her arms around me. I can't lie, having her pressed against me like this helps my mood a little. Maybe this won't be so bad after all.

"Why don't you steer?" I suggest.

Her eyes light up and she quickly shuffles herself so that she's sitting in front of me instead. We take off, speeding over the water, her laughter filling the air as we zoom around, weaving between the others. It's exhilarating, the way she leans into the ride, throwing herself into every turn. It takes the edge off.

But after a few minutes, I spot something. A cove, hidden just behind a rocky outcrop, barely noticeable unless you're really paying attention. My mind clicks into gear.

"Let me take over for a second," I say as I steer us towards the cove, aiming for that narrow gap between the rocks.

As we slip inside, the whole world changes. We're surrounded by this secret cave beach, with an open top where the sun filters through, reflecting off the water. It's like we've stumbled into a hidden paradise.

Maliah looks around, wide-eyed, taking it all in. "Wow...this place is unreal," she whispers.

And all I think is, *yeah*, and *we're here alone.*

I pull the jet ski to a slow stop, letting it bob gently in the water as we sit in this hidden spot. The cave is quiet, except for the faint echoes of waves lapping against the rocks. The sunlight streams in from above, casting a warm glow across everything; especially her.

Maliah's still staring around in awe, but I can't take my eyes off her. My body is still buzzing from the morning, from having her ass in my face the entire yoga session, and being this close to her now? It's a test of every bit of restraint I have.

I shift, and her gaze snaps back to me. Our eyes lock, and something flickers between us, that familiar electricity crackling to life. I see it in her eyes too, she's feeling it.

"You're driving me crazy; you know that?" I murmur, leaning in closer, my hands finding their way to her hips, fingers curling into her skin.

She doesn't pull away. Instead, she turns herself on the jet ski so that she's facing me and lets out a soft laugh, but it's breathless, and I know she feels it, too. "Am I?"

Before she can say anything else, I crash my lips onto hers, gripping her tighter as the heat ignites. She gasps into my mouth, her hands coming up to my chest, but she doesn't push me away—she pulls me closer.

Without breaking the kiss, I slide my hands down her body, tugging at her bikini bottoms, and she shifts on the jet ski, letting me strip them off. My head spins from the feel of her, how soft she is, how much I want her right now. Her breath is ragged against my lips, her nails digging into my back as I push her onto my lap, her legs straddling me.

"Right here?" she whispers, but there's no hesitation in her voice.

I smirk, grabbing her hips as I settle her right where I want her. "Right here."

With a quick movement, I slide her down, a low groan escaping both of us as she sinks fully onto me. The sensation is overwhelming—her warmth, her tightness, the intimacy of being so deep inside her in this hidden cave. It's almost too much, but I don't stop. I guide her movements, letting her ride me slowly as the jet ski rocks beneath us.

Her moans fill the cave, echoing off the walls, and it drives me insane. I grip her tighter, pushing deeper, faster, until she's gasping and clutching onto me like I'm her lifeline. Every thrust, every movement brings us closer, and I can feel her body tensing, shaking as she nears the edge.

"Come for me," I growl, my voice rough with need.

Her head falls back, eyes squeezing shut as she cries out, her body trembling with her release. The sight of her falling apart on top of me, the sound of her calling my name, sends me over the edge. With a few more hard thrusts, I come too, gripping her tightly as the intensity of it crashes through me.

For a moment, the world is still, just the two of us breathing hard, tangled together on the jet ski, the water gently lapping at our legs.

I press a kiss to her shoulder, still catching my breath. "We should probably head back before someone comes looking for us." I give her a lazy grin. "Though I don't mind staying here a little longer."

She laughs softly, leaning into me. The noise from behind catches both our attention, and my body tenses as I look up, spotting Charles riding his jet ski into the cave. His cocky smirk and the dangerous energy in his movements send a surge of fury through me.

Maliah yelps, startled, scrambling to pull her bikini bottoms back on, while I do my best to shield her. My jaw clenches as I quickly tuck myself back into my shorts, not breaking eye contact with him for a second. Charles grins, clearly enjoying himself, his eyes narrowing in on Maliah.

"Real classy, Maliah," he says, his thick accent dripping with sarcasm and venom. "Throwing yourself at half the guys on this tour. Such a slut."

Her body stiffens, and I feel the hurt radiating. It ignites something fierce inside of me, and I turn towards Charles, my jaw clenched, rage boiling just beneath the surface.

"Shut your mouth," I growl, keeping my voice low but firm. "If you even *think* about ruining her reputation, I'll make sure you're behind bars for sexual assault." I meet his gaze, my expression hard. "Don't forget what you did. It'll only take one call."

Charles blinks, and for a second, I see the doubt flash in his eyes. The smirk falters just enough for me to know I've got him. He straightens up, revving his engine a little, like he's trying to regain control of the situation.

"Yeah, right," he mutters, trying to act tough, but there's no real confidence behind it. His eyes flick to Maliah again, but he quickly looks away when I lean forward slightly, my hands gripping the jet ski handles tighter.

"You think I'm lying?" I say, voice calm but threatening. "Go ahead. Blink in her direction one more time, and I'll make the call. You know what you did, you really think I won't follow through?"

His smirk fades completely now. He knows he's cornered, that what I'm saying isn't bullshit. He gives a half-hearted scoff, more out of trying to save face than anything else.

"Whatever," he grumbles, revving his jet ski harder now, clearly uncomfortable. He starts backing out of the cave, shooting me a final glare over his shoulder. "You two have fun while it lasts."

The moment he's gone, the tension in the air seems to lift, but I'm still seething, watching the last ripples of his wake as he disappears out of sight. I take a deep breath and turn back to Maliah, who's hastily adjusting her bikini, her expression shaken but composed.

I reach out, brushing my thumb gently along her arm. "You okay?" I ask softly.

She nods, her lips pressing together in a tight line. "I'm fine."

She's quiet, too quiet, and I hate it. "Princess," I say gently, wrapping my arms around her waist, pulling her closer to try and give her some sense of comfort. "What's going on in that head of yours?"

She doesn't answer me right away, but I feel her shift a little, her body tense under my touch. After a long pause, she finally speaks, "What if he's right?"

Her voice is quiet, almost lost under the echo of the water lapping against the cave walls.

"Right about what?" I ask, pressing a kiss to the back of her neck.

"About us," she admits, her voice shaky. "About...this. He said 'have fun while it lasts.' What if it doesn't last, again, Koa? What if we're pretending this is more than it is?"

I feel a flicker of frustration, not at her, but at myself. This doubt she has is my fault, for destroying the trust she had for me years ago. I tighten my grip around her, pulling her even closer to me.

"Don't let him get in your head like that."

She leans back into me, but I can tell the doubt is still there, gnawing at her. Torturing her. "But we've never said what this is between us, Koa. And maybe it's not anything. Maybe he's right and this...whatever we're doing...won't last."

I can't help the low growl of frustration that escapes me. She's questioning us because of him, because of me, and it's pissing me off. But I take a deep breath, trying to calm myself before I answer.

"It's not just anything," I say firmly, my lips brushing her ear. "This is real. I don't care about what Charles thinks or anyone else for that matter. All I know is I want you, you have me, and I'm not going anywhere."

She's silent for a moment, and I feel her tense again, her hands gripping the handlebars tighter. "But how do you know? We've been through so much already, and...what if it's not enough?"

Her voice cracks a little, and it makes my chest tighten. I press my forehead against her shoulder, taking a deep breath. "Because I know what I feel for you, Mal. I know this is more than just a fling. I don't care about labels or what people think. I'm not going anywhere. You've got to trust me."

She shifts slightly, turning her head just enough to glance back at me. "But what if—"

"No what-ifs," I cut her off, my voice more certain this time. "I'm here. I'm not leaving. Not again."

She's quiet for a few more seconds, her gaze dropping to her hands. I can see the internal battle playing out in her mind, the doubt that Charles planted. But slowly, I feel her body start to relax against mine. Her hands loosen their grip on the jet ski, and she lets out a shaky breath.

"I just don't want to lose you again," she whispers.

"You won't," I promise, my arms wrapped around her tighter. "I'm right here, Mal. We're not letting some French asshole like Charles decide what we have. We're good."

She's still for a beat longer before she gives a small nod, her back finally softening against me, her trust starting to seep back in. "Okay," she says quietly.

I breathe a little easier, relieved to feel her tension fading. I kiss the top of her head and nudge her gently. "Are you ready to get out of here?"

She hesitates for a moment but then nods, turning the engine back on. "Yeah...let's get out of here."

As we pull out of the cave and back into the open ocean, I feel her settle into me, her body relaxed against mine. It feels different now—like maybe, just maybe, she's starting to trust this, to trust us again.

IT'S LATER IN THE DAY AND WE'RE WANDERING THROUGH THE bustling marketplace, the sun beating down on the brightly coloured stalls. The scent of tropical fruits and salty sea air mix together as vendors call out to us trying to lure us to their stands. Maliah's been talking about getting her hands on soursop since we arrived, something about how rare it is back home, and now we're on a mission to find it.

I watch her move through the crowd, her excitement bubbling over every time she spots something new. She's always been like this—curious, open, taking in every little detail. It's one of the things I love most about her.

As we pass by a jewelry shop, I notice her slow down. She's staring at a necklace in the display case—a delicate set of pearls, the matching earrings gleaming in the sunlight. She doesn't say anything, just stands there for a moment, admiring the way the light dances off the smooth surfaces.

"Pretty, huh?" I ask, stepping up beside her.

She looks up at me, her cheeks flushing a little. "Yeah...I've never owned anything like that before."

I glance back at the pearl set before returning my attention to her. "C'mon, let's find that fruit you've been dreaming about."

We continue walking through the market, passing by stalls selling all kinds of things. Handmade jewelry, woven baskets, fresh seafood. It's not long before I spot the spiky, green soursop she's been searching for.

"Hey, Mal," I call out, waving her over. "Found it."

She hurries over, her eyes lighting up the second she sees the fruit in my hand. "Oh my god, you found it!" She practically snatches it out of my hand, grinning from ear to ear.

I can't hold back my smile too, satisfied by the way her happiness seems to radiate in waves. She looks up at me, holding the fruit close to her chest like she's found gold.

We start walking back through the market, her arm linked with mine while the other holds her bag of fruit. I'm happy to see her smiling, completely in her element. I glance at the pearl shop, memorizing where it is as we pass, before glancing back at her with a feeling of contentment. The simplicity of this moment makes everything else fade away until it's just us.

Just Koa and Maliah.

TWENTY-TWO

MALIAH | TAHITI, FRENCH POLYNESIA

THE SUN IS bright as it peeks through the curtains of our villa, bathing the room in a warm golden light. I stretch out, the cozy blankets slipping off my shoulders, and take a moment to soak in the quiet before the day starts. I glance to my left and notice Koa isn't next to me. We've shared a bed every night since Rio, and he's always been there fast asleep when I wake up.

I shrug, guessing he probably went out for an early practice before our excursion. Today's the snorkelling and lunch trip, and I feel all the excitement rush to my chest. I love snorkelling, ever since seeing the whales in Ningaloo Reef, Australia.

After a quick shower and small breakfast, I throw on my favourite swimsuit, a vibrant blue bikini that compliments my skin tone, and a breezy cover-up. I grab my bag and head out, the salty breeze tousling my hair as I make my way to the boat dock. The laughter and chatter of the other surfers fills the air as they gather, anticipation buzzing like electricity.

Koa stands among the group, looking effortlessly handsome as always. He's wearing a loose knit polo and board shorts, and my heart does that familiar flutter when his grey eyes catch mine. His tanned skin glows in the sunlight, and I can't help but admire how at ease he seems.

"Hey, beautiful," he calls out as I approach, and I feel a rush of warmth spread through me.

"Hey," I reply, trying to sound casual, but my heart races.

As we board the boat, the excitement intensifies. The crew goes over the safety rules, but I barely register their words as my eyes wander back to Koa. The boat rocks gently on the waves, and I lean against the railing, the ocean stretching out before me like a vast canvas.

The boat ride isn't long before we arrive at our destination—a secluded cove surrounded by lush greenery. The water sparkles under the sun, inviting us in like a cool oasis. Koa grabs my hand, pulling me towards the edge of the boat.

"Ready to dive in?" he asks, his voice laced with enthusiasm.

I nod, my nerves mingling with excitement. "Let's do it."

We throw on our gear and jump off the side of the boat together, the cool water enveloping me like a refreshing blanket. I resurface, spluttering and laughing as I push my hair back. Koa swims close, and I can see the mischief in his eyes.

"Race you to the coral," he challenges, and before I can respond, he's off, cutting through the water with powerful strokes.

"Hey, no fair!" I shout after him, my competitive spirit igniting. I kick my legs and dive after him, my laughter echoing through the water.

The underwater world is breathtaking—colourful fish darting around, vibrant corals swaying gently with the current. I lose myself in the beauty, following Koa as we explore the hidden treasures beneath the waves.

After some time, we resurface, our lungs burning from the exhilaration. I glance over at him, and he grins back, the sunlight glinting off the droplets of water clinging to his hair and skin. We swim around, diving back under to investigate the coral formations. Koa takes my hand, guiding me deeper into the water. The fish swim around us, unbothered by our presence, and I can't help but feel like we've entered a whole other world.

Finally, we make our way back to the surface, breaking through the water at the same time. We float on our backs, staring up at the blue sky above us.

"This feels incredible," I murmur, letting the gentle waves rock me.

Koa turns his head to me, his expression serious. "You'd love Hawaii."

I glance at him from the corner of my eye before returning my attention to the sky. "You really miss it, huh?"

I hear him release a breathy chuckle. "More than you know."

I swallow hard, feeling sad for him. He hasn't seen his family since he was seventeen, I can only imagine how hard that must be. I'm not the closest with my father but I at least see him every few years. I can't imagine what it must feel like for Koa, going so long without being back home.

"Hawaii is our last stop on this trip," I say, turning to look at him now. "Are you planning to visit your family when we're there?"

He smiles to himself. "Hell yeah," he says, his face bright. "I'd love it if you'd come with me too. I want you to meet my mom."

The weight of his words nearly drowns me as I quickly reposition so that I'm treading water instead. Meeting his mom...that means something, doesn't it?

"Your mom?" I ask, unable to hide the hesitation in my voice.

"Yeah," he says, letting his feet drop into the water so that he's treading too. "I think you'd like her."

I want to say no. I've never met anyone's mother before, not someone I'm interested in. What if she hates me and convinces him to end what we have? I'd lose him again, and I don't know if I could recover from this one.

He must sense my inner panic because he paddles over and cups my cheeks, forcing me to look into his eyes.

"I already know she's going to love you," he says, reassuringly. "So, will you come with me?"

I let out a shaky breath, knowing this would mean a lot to him. Instead of saying no like I want to, I find myself nodding slowly instead.

I watch as the widest grin spreads across his face in return, causing my heart to flutter. We paddle back towards the boat and climb back on board. Laughter echoes around the deck as everyone shares their favourite moments from their snorkelling experience.

Just before lunch, Koa pulls me aside, a playful glint in his eyes. "I have something for you," he says, his voice low and teasing.

"What is it?" I ask, curiosity piquing as he gestures for me to follow him away from the group.

He leads me to the edge of the boat, where the water glimmers below us. In one fluid motion, he reaches into his bag and pulls out a small, elegantly wrapped box. My breath catches in my throat as he hands it to me.

I can't help my brain from thinking back to the day he broke up with me, the day I thought I'd be getting proposed to. I quickly shake the reminder out of my mind and stare down at it.

"You didn't have to get me anything," I protest, suddenly feeling nervous as I unwrap it. I gasp as I open it and find the pearl necklace and earrings I had been admiring at the market yesterday, their iridescent beauty mesmerizing.

"I went back this morning while you were sleeping," he explains, his expression earnest. "I wanted you to have them."

So that's where he was when I woke up.

"This must have cost a fortune," I say, trying to push the box back towards him. "I can't accept this."

He shakes his head, his jaw set with determination. "You deserve it. You're worth every penny."

Koa's words warm me from the inside out, but the weight of the gift feels heavy in my hands. "I really appreciate it, but—"

"No buts," he interrupts, taking my hands in his. "You can just say thank you."

I look into his eyes, searching for any hint of insincerity, but all I see is affection. Taking a deep breath, I decide to surrender to the moment.

"Thank you," I whisper, my heart swelling.

Without thinking, I lean in and press a soft kiss to his lips, feeling the warmth of his smile as he kisses me back, a gentle spark igniting between us. It feels right, natural.

"Now, let's go eat," he says, grinning widely, and I can't help but smile back.

We return to where the others are gathering for lunch, the delicious aroma of freshly prepared food wafting through the air. The tables are set with an array of colourful dishes—fresh fish, tropical fruits, and a spread of local delicacies. Wine flows freely as everyone settles in, sharing stories and laughter.

Koa pours us each a glass, the crisp white wine sparkling in the sun. As we eat and drink, I lose myself in the moment, surrounded by friends and the beauty of Tahiti.

THE SUN HAS SET BY THE TIME WE RETURN TO THE VILLA AND I'M still riding high from our amazing day, but there's something else building inside me. A desire to do something special for Koa after his sweet gesture with the pearls.

I watch as he climbs into bed after his shower, his hair still wet as it glistens in the dim room light. I pad into the bathroom after him, stripping off my clothes and taking a quick shower, careful not to wet my hair as I feel a thrill run through me.

I dry myself off and walk over to the mirror, my bare body reflected back at me. The box holding the pearls sits on the edge of the sink and I slide it over, opening it and removing the necklace. I put it on, followed by the earrings. They glimmer against my skin, making me feel beautiful and powerful.

I walk over to the door, gently opening it and leaning against the frame in the most seductive pose I can manage, my heart racing. Koa is sprawled on the bed, his gaze locked on me, a mix of surprise and awe crossing his face.

"Wow," he breathes, his voice low and gravelly.

I soak in his reaction, revelling in the way his eyes widen, drinking me in. "What do you think?" I ask playfully, running the tips of my fingers along the necklace as I push off the door frame and walk towards him.

He doesn't answer right away, just stares, completely mesmerized. I strut over to him, swaying my hips, knowing how much he loves when I take control. The distance between us feels electric, the air thick with tension.

As I kneel before him, his breath hitches, and I can see the heat pooling in his gaze. I lean in, giving him a teasing smile before I slowly pull his boxers down and wrap my hand around him, feeling him harden beneath my touch.

Koa's hand finds my hair as I take him into my mouth, swirling my tongue around the tip, then taking him deeper, savouring the taste of him. I can hear the soft gasps escaping his lips, the way he bites back a groan, and it fuels my desire even more.

I work him slowly, feeling the way his body responds to every movement, every flick of my tongue. I pull back for a moment, looking up at him with a sultry smile, and then dive back down, letting myself get lost in the rhythm.

"Mal," he murmurs, his voice thick with need.

I pick up the pace, relishing the way his muscles tense and the pleasure radiating from him. I can feel him inching closer, teetering on the edge, and it's exhilarating to know that I'm the one bringing him there.

With each deliberate movement, I watch his face transform, and the tension builds. I can tell he's about to come so I take him as far as I can, his cock deep in my throat when he does, sending waves of heat coursing through me. His groan is guttural as I feel the warm liquid pouring into me. When he's finished, I pull away, swallowing any remaining come in my mouth, breathless and satisfied, looking up at him with a smirk.

Koa leans back on his elbows, running a hand through his hair, his chest rising and falling rapidly. "That was the best blowjob of my entire fucking life, princess," he says, his eyes dark and hungry as he looks at me, and I can't help but smile wider.

I sit back on my heels, feeling a sense of triumph wash over me, but also a warmth. Koa's gaze locks onto mine and everything fades away.

"You're incredible," he finally murmurs, his voice low and filled with awe, sending a thrill through me.

I lean forward, brushing my lips against his, savouring the taste of him, the connection that feels deeper than ever. "I just wanted to thank you for the pearls," I whisper playfully, a smile tugging at my lips.

"Consider me thoroughly thanked." He grins back, a playful glint in his eyes.

He pulls my bare body against his and I snuggle against him, feeling the warmth radiating from his body and the soft, rhythmic sound of his breathing. I close my eyes, allowing the peace of this moment to wash over me, feeling hopeful about tomorrow and every day after.

KOA | TAHITI, FRENCH POLYNESIA

THE MORNING SUN hangs high in the sky today, casting a shimmering glow over Teahupo'o, the legendary waves crashing against the reef. The air is electric with excitement and nerves, a familiar tension that thrums in my veins. Maliah and I huddle close to the edge of the beach, our phone set up for a video call with Gabriel.

"Alright, listen up, you two," Gabriel says, his voice crackling through the speaker. His face fails the screen, Zalea nowhere in sight, and I can see the anticipation in his eyes. "Today those waves are going to be intense, especially on that southwest peak."

Maliah nods, her big blue eyes focused on Gabriel. "We're ready for it."

"Good," Gabriel continues, glancing down at his notes. "Just remember—commit to your line and don't overthink it. Trust the wave, and you'll be fine."

We both reply with a confident, "Got it," but inside, I can feel the pressure mounting. Maliah's been struggling in practice in Tahiti, and the last thing I want is for her to panic out there.

She's an amazingly talented surfer, but the weight of expectation can crush anyone.

The call ends, and as we make our way to the water, I can sense her nerves. I lean over, whispering, "You've got this, Mal. Just remember to breathe."

She offers me a shaky smile, and I can't help but feel that surge of protectiveness for her. If I could protect her from the world, I would. We make our way into the water, paddling out to the lineup, the ocean's surface shimmering beneath us. I glance at the southwest peak, the towering wave beckoning with its raw power, but something shifts in the air—a hesitation in Maliah's movements.

When her turn comes, she paddles towards the wave, but as she stands, I can see the uncertainty in her stance. The wave crashes down, and she falls, taking us out of the point standings. I grit my teeth, frustration boiling inside me. I know we can't afford to lose points now, not when we've worked so hard to get back to first place.

"Fuck!" I mutter under my breath, knowing I have to step up and make this right.

Instead of following her lead, I turn and paddle toward the southern peak. It's riskier, this part of the reef is known for its dry, sharp edges, but I need to make a statement. I can't let Maliah's mistake cost us, she'll never forgive herself for it. I see the wave rising in the distance, a monstrous wall of water ready to break. My heart races as I push myself forwards, feeling the rush of adrenaline.

I catch the wave, and it's everything I expected. I carve through it, feeling the familiar thrill as I angle into the barrel. I feel the rush of water around me, the world narrowing to just me and the wave, a dance that only the ocean and I know. Time slows, and I find my rhythm, riding it to perfection.

But as I finally eject from the board, the realization hits me like a punch to the gut; the reef isn't forgiving. I land hard on the dry surface, the sharp coral ripping into my skin. Pain shoots up my leg, a million tiny cuts slicing through my adrenaline fuelled high. I grit my teeth, trying to swallow the agony that flares as I scramble back onto my board.

Blood mixes with seawater, but I can't let it show. Not now. I paddle back to the lineup, heart pounding with the thrill of victory and the sting of pain. As I near Maliah, I can see the look of concern in her eyes, but I put on a brave face.

The moment I stand and stumble onto the sand, the pain flares. I try to shake it off, but I feel the searing sting of my leg with every step.

"Koa!" Maliah's voice breaks through my haze, and I glance back up to see her rushing towards me, concern etched on her face. "Are you okay?"

"Yeah, I'm fine," I reply, but the lie tastes bitter on my tongue. I can see her gaze drop to my leg, and her eyes widen.

"Koa..." She steps closer, and I watch as her expression shifts from worry to horror. "What happened?"

I glance down and see the tear in my wetsuit, the crimson streaks seeping through the fabric. "It's nothing," I insist, but that only pisses her off.

"Nothing? That's not nothing!" She grabs my arm, her grip firm, and I can't help but feel a twinge of guilt for worrying her. "You need to see a medic. Now."

I want to argue, but as I catch the look of pure worry on her face, I realize I can't dismiss this.

The medic tent feels like a blur as we walk in, the reality of the situation crashing down on me as the adrenaline fades away. The medics pull my wetsuit down, and as it falls away, I see my leg—covered in deep angry cuts.

"Shit," I mutter, trying to mask my fear as I see Maliah's eyes begin to glisten.

"Stay still, Koa," the medic instructs, and I nod, swallowing hard.

They have me lay down on a gurney as they begin cleaning the cuts to assess which ones will need stitches. The pain intensifies, radiating up my leg. I grit my teeth, determined not to show how much it hurts, for Maliah's sake, but as the alcohol swabs touch my skin, a scream bursts from my lips, echoing in the small space.

Maliah grips my hand, her fingers intertwined with mine, and I can feel her trembling. I turn to her, and tears pour down her face. "I'm okay," I try to reassure her.

"No, you're not," she whispers, her voice thick with emotion.

The medics continue to work, and I can't help but squeeze her hand tighter, each burn and sting punctuating my cries. I hate this—hate that I'm making her worry and cry, hate that I can't be the strong one right now.

They stitch up a few of the deeper cuts before bandaging my leg with fresh gauze, wrapping it snuggly. "You're good to go," the medic says, but I feel anything but good right now.

Maliah leaves to our tent to grab my change of clothes before returning with both of our bags. She helps me stand, and the moment I do, the pain lances through me again. "Just breathe," she murmurs, supporting my weight as I change into my clothes.

She continues to support me as we step back into the sunlight, cameras swarming us, their flashes blinding. Questions rain down about my leg, the competition, and my performance, but I barely register them. The only thing I hear is that we managed to keep our first-place ranking, despite my injury, and a sense of relief washes over me. After that, all I can focus on is climbing into the waiting vehicle, Maliah following behind me before shutting the door and cutting off the media from any more questions and pictures.

The ride back to the villa is tense. I lean back against my seat, trying to find a comfortable position that doesn't exacerbate the pain radiating from my leg. Maliah is silent, her fingers gripping the phone tightly as she calls Gabriel.

I pretend to sleep, hoping to shield her from my frustration, but the tightness in my chest tells me I'm failing miserably.

"Hey, it's me," she says, her voice shaky, and I can hear the worry lacing her tone. "Koa got hurt at the competition. He...he hurt his leg on the reef at the southwest peak."

A curse escapes Gabriel's lips, loud and clear even from the other end of the line. "Is he okay?"

"He's bandaged up with a few stitches on some of the deeper cuts. It looks really bad, Gabriel," she replies, her words tumbling out in a rush. "I've never heard him in that much pain before."

"Damn it, Maliah. I'm sorry. I should have prepared you guys better for the conditions out there...I've been distracted lately. Don't worry, I'm going to use a wildcard to bring in someone from the Saltwater Shredders for the next competition. Koa needs time to heal."

I feel a surge of anger mix with self-recrimination. Will this cost us the overall win of the tour? Because of my carelessness?

"Okay, thank you," Maliah says, her voice softer now, yet still tinged with anxiety. "I'll take care of him, I promise. I'll make sure he rests for the rest of today."

"Good. Get him settled and keep an eye on him," Gabriel instructs. "I don't want him pushing himself. He needs to heal."

I can't help but tune back into the conversation, my heart sinking at the thought of letting everyone down. I hear the click as Maliah ends the call, and she glances at me, concern etched on her face.

"Coach said you need to take it easy," she says softly. "We're heading back to the villa now, and I'm going to make sure you rest. So don't make it hard on me, please."

I nod, a mix of frustration and gratitude swirling inside me.

"I should've been more careful out there," I mutter, my voice laced with self-doubt.

"It was an accident, Koa. You did great before the fall. You can't blame yourself for that," she reassures me, but the words don't fully penetrate the fog of disappointment in my mind.

As we drive on, I rest my head against the window, watching the blur of palm trees and ocean views pass by, the weight of today's reality settling in. I can't afford to let anyone down.

I need to heal.

TWENTY-FOUR

MALIAH | PENICHE, PORTUGAL

WE FLEW to Peniche just a day after the competition in Tahiti, and the change in scenery hasn't done much to ease the knot of guilt twisting in my chest. Koa's been putting on a brave face, but I know him well enough to see through it. The way his jaw tightens every time he moves, the forced smile when he says he's fine—it's all just a cover for the pain he's in.

I glance over at him now, asleep on the couch in the upgraded house Gabriel managed to score for us. It's bigger than what we've been used to on tour, with a few extra rooms, no doubt to accommodate the wildcard who's arriving soon. Koa's leg is bandaged up from thigh to ankle, and even though his breathing is steady, there's no peace on his face. I can only imagine how uncomfortable he is, especially after the long flight we just had.

It's my fault. If I hadn't screwed up that wave, if I hadn't lost focus, Koa wouldn't have had to make up for it by taking the risk that got him hurt. My mistake, my distraction...and now here he is, sidelined because of me. The thought keeps circling in my mind like a vulture, picking at my self-doubt.

Are we just doomed to keep hurting each other? First the breakup, and now this—maybe we're never going to get it right.

I sink down into the armchair across from him, my phone in my lap. It's been unusually quiet between us since Tahiti. Koa hasn't said anything about what happened, hasn't blamed me once, but that just makes it worse. I can feel the weight of it all, hanging in the air between us, unspoken.

Just as I'm about to lose myself in that spiral of guilt again, my phone buzzes. Gabriel. I hesitate before picking it up, making sure to keep my voice low as I answer.

"Hey."

"Wildcard's landing in thirty minutes. Are you ready to head out?" His voice is brisk, as usual, but there's a hint of concern underneath it. I can't tell if it's for Koa or me, or both of us.

I glance over at Koa again. His brows furrowed in his sleep, and the sight of it makes my chest tighten all over again. "Yeah," I murmur. "I'll head out now."

"Good. And Maliah," Gabriel pauses for a beat, "don't stress yourself out too much about Koa. He's tougher than you think."

"Right." I force the word out, but the guilt still gnaws at me.

I grab the keys and slip out of the house quietly, shutting the door behind me as I head for the car we've rented. The private landing strip isn't far, but the drive feels longer than it should. My mind is still stuck in the past few days. I can't shake the feeling that maybe Koa would be better off if I wasn't such a distraction for him. If I hadn't let my feelings interfere at Teahupo'o, would Koa be healthy and uninjured, instead of wrapped in bandages and unable to compete?

The sun is setting by the time I pull up to the landing strip. I take a deep breath, trying to shove down the wave of anxiety building up inside me. Gabriel didn't mention who the wildcard was, and I'm too nervous to even guess. It could be anyone from our old team, or someone completely new.

The plane is already on the runway when I get out of the car. I watch it taxi closer, the engine roaring before it finally comes to a stop. The door eventually opens, the golden light of the afternoon spills out onto the tarmac, casting a soft glow on the figures stepping down the stairs.

I stand frozen for a moment, squinting against the sunlight as they come into focus. My heart skips a beat.

It's Griffin and Eliana.

Before I can even react, she spots me, her face lighting up with a huge smile. "Mal!" she shouts, sprinting towards me with her arms wide open. I barely have time to register it before she crashes into me, pulling me into a bone crushing hug. I laugh, squeezing her back just as tightly.

"I can't believe you're here!" I exclaim, my voice muffled by her long brown hair.

Eliana pulls back, her eyes sparkling with excitement. "Believe it! When Gabriel called us, we didn't even hesitate. I missed you, and this tour is about to get way more fun."

I grin, warmth filling my chest. Having her here, especially after everything that's happened with Koa, feels like a breath of fresh air.

Griffin steps forward next, towering over us but wearing that same calm, confident expression I remember. "Good to see you, Malipop," he says with a nod and smirk, his voice steady and reassuring. "Heard you and Koa had a rough time in Tahiti."

My smile falters for just a second, the guilt about Koa's injury creeping back in, but I force it away and nod. "Yeah, but we're glad you're here. We need the boost if we want to stay in first place."

I glance at Griffin, the legend, the guy who came back from an injury that could've ended his career. Having him on the team feels like a second chance.

As we head to the car, Elian's arm loops through mine, and I feel lighter, like maybe things will start looking up again with them here.

As we drive back to the house, the hum of the engine fills the silence between our conversations. Eliana is leaning against the window in the passenger's seat next to me, soaking in the views of Peniche's coastline, while Griffin sits quietly in the back, his presence calm but commanding. I glance in the rearview mirror, catching his eye before turning my attention back to the road.

"So...about Koa's injury," I start, my voice softer than I intend. "He's putting on a brave face, but he's in a lot of pain. It's really hard to watch."

Griffin leans forward a little, his brows knitting together with concern. "What happened?"

I sigh, gripping the steering wheel a little tighter. "He went to the Southern peak at Teahupo'o to make up for the points I lost. He wiped out and landed right on the dry reef." I pause, the image of Koa's leg covered in cuts, his leg pouring out blood, flashes in my mind. "His leg's a mess. They stitched him up, but he's really been pushing through the pain."

I can feel Griffin watching me closely, his gaze heavy. "And how are you holding up with all this?" he asks, his tone gentle but direct.

I hesitate, trying to keep my voice steady. "I feel like it's my fault. If I hadn't screwed up that wave...he wouldn't have felt the need to take the risk."

Griffin shakes his head, a faint smile tugging at the corner of his lips. "Mal, you can't think like that. Koa's always been the daredevil type when it comes to surfing. Even if you hadn't made a mistake, he'd still push the limits because that's who he is."

I glance at him through the rearview mirror, my heat squeezing at his words. Griffin's calm reassurance feels like a lifeline, but the guilt still clings to me like a shadow.

"We're in first place," I continue, trying to shift the focus. "But there's only a one-point difference between us and second. We need a solid performance in this upcoming competition to hold our lead."

Griffin leans back, crossing his arms. "Then that's what we'll focus on. Don't carry the weight of something that's out of your control, Maliah. Koa's made a career out of taking risks—this won't be the thing that brings him down."

His words linger in the air, and I try to absorb them, but it's hard. Seeing Koa hurt because of me, because of a mistake I made, makes it impossible not to carry the blame. But maybe Griffin's right. Maybe Koa would've taken the risk regardless. That's who he is after all.

Eliana looks over at me and nudges my arm with a smile. "You've got this. Both of you do."

I offer a small smile in return, grateful for the support. As we pull up to the house, the weight in my chest feels a little lighter, and I take a deep breath, hoping that with Griffin and Eliana here, things will start to feel a little less overwhelming.

TWENTY-FIVE

KOA | PENICHE, PORTUGAL

IT'S the day after Griffin and Eliana arrived, to my surprise, and we're out on a dolphin boat safari, cruising along the turquoise waters off the coast of Peniche. The sun's beating down, but the breeze off the ocean cools things just enough to make it bearable.

I sit on the edge of the deck, my bandaged leg stretched out in front of me. The salt air burns a little as it brushes over my skin, reminding me of the countless cuts beneath the gauze. I glance down at my leg. It's still a mess, no doubt red, raw, and swollen. The tour medics came to check on me at the house today and said it's healing, but every step I take feels like some-one's dragging a serrated knife across my skin.

I grit my teeth, trying to ignore the pulsing pain. This isn't how I wanted the tour to go. And if I'm honest, I feel like I let Mal down. First place means nothing if I can't even get back in the water to keep us there.

I let out a slow breath, shifting my gaze away from my leg to the water, where she and Eliana are swimming with dolphins. They're both laughing, splashing around as the dolphin's dart around them. The single cameraman that joined us on this tour captures everything, of course—always. Maliah's hair floats around her like a dark halo, her smile wide and carefree, and for a moment, all I can think about is her.

She moves effortlessly through the water, as if she's meant to be there. I can see this is her element, and as I watch her, a twinge of regret stirs within me. I should be out there with her, not stuck on this boat feeling like a useless idiot.

Griffin's next to me, lounging with a casual ease that only someone like him could pull off. His leg bounced back from injury like it was nothing, but I know he worked his ass off to get back to this point. Part of me wonders if I've got that same strength in me or if this is the beginning of the end.

"You alright, man?" Griffin asks, his voice low enough that only I can hear over the sound of the waves and the girls.

I nod, though it's a lie. "Yeah, just watching Mal." He follows my gaze, a small grin tugging at the corner of his mouth.

He lifts his sunglasses to the top of his head, making sure our eyes meet. "I've been wondering," he says, his tone casual but with a hint of curiosity. "What exactly happened that night you called me and Colton and then abruptly hung up?"

I feel my face heat up, and I look away for a second, trying to play it cool. There's no way in hell I'm about to tell him what happened between Maliah and me that night...or the next. My eyes drift to her again. She's swimming with a dolphin that plants a kiss on her cheek, and she explodes in giggles, her laughter carrying over the water.

"I don't know what you're talking about," I mutter, my voice flat.

Griffin chuckles, clearly not buying it. "Right," he says, dragging out the word like he's onto something. "So how are things between you two? I noticed the burning rage and hatred she had for you seems to have disappeared."

I shrug, not really sure how much to share. "We're working through stuff."

"Oh, come on," Griffin teases, leaning back against the boat's railing. "We're going to see it on SurfFlix anyway, you might as well tell your friends before the media does."

I sigh, knowing he's right. "We're trying to repair things," I admit. "Taking it slow, but I don't know if I messed all of that up with this injury."

Griffin looks at me for a moment, serious now. "You didn't mess anything up, Koa. If she's still here, swimming with dolphins while you sit here moping about your leg, that's gotta mean something. She's in this with you."

I nod, but the doubt still lingers in the back of my mind. I glance at Maliah again, watching her smile, completely at ease. Maybe he's right, but the fear that I'll screw this up again is always there.

"We'll see," I say, not fully convinced, but trying to believe it.

Griffin nudges me with his elbow, a grin tugging at the corner of his lips. "You know, for a guy who flew across the world to be here for you, you're not really paying me much attention."

I glance over at him, chuckling. "Yeah, yeah, sorry, man. Just...got a lot on my mind."

He leans back, folding his arms. "That much is obvious," he jokes, but then his tone shifts. "Speaking of which, I had to pack up your stuff at The Shredder House temporarily. Gabriel brought in a few new team members to fill the gap while you and Mal are on tour."

I raise an eyebrow. "You packed my stuff?"

He nods, reaching into his pocket before pulling out something small—something familiar. It's a ring box. My chest tightens at the sight of it. The box that holds the ring I was going to propose to Maliah with...the same day I broke up with her instead.

Griffin holds it up between us. "Found this in your drawer," he says quietly, eyeing me as if waiting for an explanation.

Every emotion I buried that day crashes back into me, heavy and overwhelming. The sense of worthlessness, of not being good enough for her, floods my chest, suffocating me. I swallow hard, shaking my head as I stare at the box. "It doesn't matter," I say, my voice low. "I'm not good enough for her, Griffin. She deserves better."

Griffin's eyes widen in disbelief, and he shakes his head firmly. "You seriously think that?"

"I know that," I correct him, bitterness slipping into my voice. "I screwed up. I hurt her. She deserves someone who won't do that."

Griffin leans forward, his voice softer but insistent. "You're the best thing that could have happened to her, Koa. Everyone makes mistakes, but it's what you do after that matters. And I know you—you're not the kind of guy who gives up when things get hard."

"But I did. I did give up, and I broke her heart in the process."

He eyes me, as if seeing right through me. "I have a feeling there's more to that story than you're willing to share."

I don't respond. I just stare at the ring box in his hand, the weight of my past mistakes settling in.

Griffin places the box in my palm, his eyes locking onto mine. "Just in case you want to join the fiancé squad," he says with a grin.

I blink, confused for a moment. "Fiancé squad?"

Maliah lets out a screech, and my head snaps in her direction. She's gripping onto Eliana's hand staring at an emerald ring on her ring finger. I look back to Griffin with wide eyes and his grin broadens.

"Eliana and I...we're engaged."

"What?"

He nods, laughing softly. "Yeah, man. I popped the question literally minutes before Gabriel called us and asked us to come here."

I shake my head, a smile tugging at my lips despite everything. "That's crazy. Congratulations, Fin."

"Thanks, brother," he says, clapping me on the back. "Now, maybe it's your turn. That is, if you stop telling yourself you're not good enough for her."

I look back at the box in my hand, the weight of it suddenly feeling heavier.

Eliana bursts back onto the boat, her wet hair flinging water everywhere as she runs straight into Griffin's arms. She's laughing, carefree, and without hesitation, she wraps her arms around his neck and plants a kiss on him, soaking him in the process.

Griffin laughs, not caring in the least about the water dripping from her. "You're drenched, sunshine," he teases, but pulls her closer anyway.

I look away, giving them their moment, but the second I do, my eyes lock with Maliah's. She's standing at the edge of the boat, water glistening on her skin, but her gaze is fixed on the ring box in my hand. Her expression unreadable.

Before she can say anything—or before I can explain—I stuff the box into my pocket and lean back in my seat, closing my eyes as if that would hide everything. My chest tightens, and the weight of everything presses down on me, but I can still feel her eyes watching me.

I keep my eyes shut, pretending it doesn't matter. But deep down, I know it matters more than anything.

IT'S BEEN A FEW DAYS SINCE THE DOLPHIN SAFARI, AND TODAY IS competition day at Supertubos. Maliah and Griffin spent the last few days practicing the waves together and giving each other pointers on how to handle them the best. I'm confident they'll be able to pull it off today. The sky is clear and the conditions couldn't be more perfect—solid sets rolling in, forming those signature Supertubos barrels that swallow surfers whole before spitting them back out.

Eliana is on the beach next to me, holding her phone steady as she captures content for the team's social pages. She's already snapped about a million pictures of Griffin, but now her focus is on Maliah. Every so often, she glances down at the screen, switching between video and camera mode, determined to get the best shots.

"Look at them go," Eliana says, grinning and zooming in as Maliah carves through the face of a wave.

I lean forward, my eyes glued to the water. Maliah's form is clean, confident. She paddles with power, and the second she catches another wave, she's up and slicing across the surface. Her movements are fluid, each turn precise. She crouches low, tucking herself into a barrel, disappearing into the tunnel of water for a few seconds before the wave spits her out clean, leaving a spray of whitewater in her wake.

Griffin's right behind her on the next wave, making it look effortless. His timing is perfect, just like I've seen him do a hundred times. He leans into the wave with a kind of fearlessness that only someone who's conquered pain like his could pull off. He's a damn powerhouse, accelerating as the wave curls over him, his body low and in control as he threads through the pocket.

"They're killing it," Eliana says, clearly proud.

It should be me out there with her. I shake my head, pushing the thought away. Maliah deserves this moment, and I'm not going to ruin it with my own frustrations. My eyes follow Maliah as they both begin their return to the shore, and I almost don't notice the medic that approaches me just as she paddles in, her hair dripping wet and her face glowing from the adrenaline rush.

"Koa," the medic says, "let's take a look at your leg."

I glance over at Maliah, who's watching me with concern. She drops her board in the sand next to Eliana before walking over to join me as we head toward the medic tent. She's quieter than usual, her smile from the competition quickly fading into something else.

Once we're in the tent, the medic gets to work, carefully unwrapping the bandage around my leg. The relief of air hitting the skin is immediate, but the sight beneath the wrappings isn't pretty. Most of the smaller cuts have closed, leaving behind pink, puffy lines where they once bled. The deeper ones, the ones that had been stitched still cling to scabs. The stitches have dissolved, but the skin's fragile, healing over slowly.

"Looks like you're healing well," the medic says, inspecting my leg. "No more wrapping it. Just make sure to wash it carefully. Watch those scabs, though. If any of them open up, you're risking infection."

I nod, but my mind is elsewhere. Maliah stands off to the side, her arms crossed as she watches, still not saying much. There's tension between us I can't shake. Ever since the injury, things have felt off. She's been distant, quieter than normal. I can't help but wonder if she's mad at me—if she blames me for almost screwing everything up. I wouldn't be surprised if that was the case. It *is* my fault.

The medic finishes up, gives me a pat on the shoulder, and lets us go. Outside the tent, Griffin and Eliana are waiting, both of them grinning.

"Dinner tonight," Griffin says, clapping me on the back. "It's our last night before we fly out tomorrow, so let's do something nice. I know a spot."

I glance at Maliah, who forces a small smile, but she doesn't say much. I agree to dinner, hoping it'll give us a chance to talk, to work through whatever this tension is between us.

THE RESTAURANT GRIFFIN PICKED IS A SMALL, COZY PLACE tucked away in the heart of Peniche. The kind of spot that feels like a hidden gem, with candlelight on every table and the faint sound of Portuguese music playing in the background. We're seated at a booth near the back, away from most of the other diners.

Eliana and Griffin are chatting away, trading stories about the new Shredder Youth Team that Griffin's been coaching. Maliah, on the other hand, is barely speaking. Every time I try to bring her into the conversation, she diverts it right back to Griffin or Eliana, as if she's actively avoiding talking to me.

As I sit there, watching her laugh at something Griffin says, I force myself to push the thoughts aside, but I can't help but feel like I'm losing her, little by little. And I have no idea how to stop it.

The food arrives and despite my anxiousness toward Maliah's behaviour today, my mouth begins to water. Baked salted cod, and roasted mini potatoes sits on my plate but it smells so good that my stomach growls loudly.

"Hungry?" Eliana teases, cutting into the grilled chicken on her plate.

"Starving," I reply, digging in without a second thought.

When we finally get back to the house, Griffin and Eliana head straight to their room, calling it a night after the long day. It's just me and Maliah now, alone in the quiet living room. I've been waiting for this moment all night. For the chance to talk to her and figure out what's going on.

Maliah walks over to the couch and sits down, staring out the window at the dark ocean. I take a deep breath and sit next to her. "We need to talk," I say quietly, trying to ease into it.

She doesn't look at me. "About what?"

"About Teahupo'o. About us. You've been different ever since the accident."

Her body stiffens at the mention of Teahupo'o, and she finally turns to face me, her blue eyes blazing with frustration. "It's my fault, Koa! I messed up the wave! If I hadn't, you wouldn't have gone out there and got yourself hurt. I cost us points, and you tried to fix my mistake. It's my fault you're hurt."

I shake my head, already feeling the argument spiralling. "No, Mal, it wasn't like that. You didn't make me do anything. I made the decision to surf that peak because I wanted to. Even if your surf was perfect, I think I still would've gone over there and tried to surf that spot. I've been pushing myself my whole life, you know that. What happened was a stupid accident— nothing to do with you."

Tears well up in her eyes, but she fights to keep them from falling. "You could've been seriously hurt, Koa. Or worse. How am I supposed to not feel responsible for that?"

Her words hit me hard. I can see the guilt eating her alive, the way she's been carrying this weight since it happened. I move closer, taking her hand in mine.

"Listen to me," I say firmly, "you didn't force me to do anything. I made my own call out there. Surfing is dangerous, you know that. We take a risk every single time we hit the water. I'm fine. I'm here. I'll heal. But I need you to stop blaming yourself."

She stares at me, searching my face for something, her hand trembling slightly in mine. "What if I keep messing things up for us?"

I squeeze her hand tighter. "You're not messing anything up. We're a team, Mal. We've always been a team. And yeah, things get rough sometimes, but we figure it out. We always have."

A tear finally slips down her cheek, and she wipes it away quickly, trying to pull herself together. I can see the guilt starting to crack, like maybe she's starting to believe me. But there's still a bit of hesitation.

"It wasn't your fault," I say again, softer this time, leaning in until our foreheads almost touch. "It's not your fault, Princess. You need to let it go."

She closes her eyes and takes a deep breath, her whole body relaxing for the first time in days. "Okay," she whispers, her voice shaky. "Okay, I'll try."

I pull her into a hug, relief washing over me as I feel her finally lean into me, the weight between us finally lifted. And, for the first time in days, we're back on the same page.

After a while, I pull back and smile at her. "Let's do something fun tomorrow," I say, trying to lighten the mood. "Griffin and Eliana are leaving in the morning, and we could use a break. What do you want to do?"

Maliah's face brightens slightly, and she looks up at me with a small, hopeful smile. "Actually, I was thinking...maybe we could visit my father. He doesn't live too far from here, and it's been a while since I've seen him. The waves by his house are also insane."

I freeze, my stomach dropping. Her father? Of all people... he's the last person I want to see. Ever. My body tenses at the thought of facing him. The history between us isn't exactly good. He's never approved of me, and I've done nothing to change his mind. But when I look into Maliah's eyes, that hopeful glint I haven't seen in days...I can't say no.

I nod slowly, forcing a smile. "Yeah, okay. If that's what you want."

Her eyes light up as she quickly grabs her phone and starts texting him to arrange everything. I lean back into the couch, watching her, trying to ignore the sinking feeling in my gut.

TWENTY-SIX

MALIAH | PENICHE, PORTUGAL

KOA and I stand just outside my dad's massive beachside mansion, the sound of waves crashing against the rocks below filling the silence between us. The air smells like salt and distant rain, and I can't help but feel this strange mix of nostalgia and dread. The big wooden door looms in front of us, like it's judging me for even being here. I glance at Koa, who's been quiet ever since we dropped Griffin and Eliana off and made our way here. He's tense, his jaw tight, and I know this is the last place he wants to be. But I asked, and he's here anyway.

I take a deep breath and knock.

The door swings open almost immediately, and there's my dad, tanned and glowing like he just walked off the beach. His brown hair and beard are streaked with white now, a little older than the last time I saw him, but still holding that same rich arrogant vibe with his slightly unbuttoned shirt. His arms stretch out wide, reminding me of the Christ the Redeemer statue Koa and I visited in Rio.

"My little girl is home," he says, pulling me into a hug that smells like expensive cologne and the ocean.

This is his home, not mine. After my mother passed away

from cancer, he packed his bags and dropped me off at The Shredder House before flying out here and planting new roots, starting a new family.

"Hey, Dad," I reply, a bit awkwardly, the warmth in his embrace not quite reaching the tightness in my chest.

As I pull back, I catch the way his eyes flicker toward Koa, a weird look passing over his face, but it's gone in an instant. He quickly refocuses on me, all smiles again as he steps aside and gestures for us to come in.

I'm struck by how quiet it is—no loud voices, no slamming doors, none of the usual chaos. I glance around, noticing the stillness in the air.

"Where is everyone?" I ask, my voice low.

Dad waves a hand like it's nothing. "Oh, your stepmother, or I guess ex-stepmother took the boys and left months ago. Apparently, she was tired of the life I provided her," he says, like it's no big deal. "But don't worry, I've got a new girl now. Younger, hotter...still upstairs getting ready."

I stare blankly at him. "Why didn't you think to tell me that they left?"

He shrugs, his smile never faltering. "Figured you wouldn't care. You were never close to them anyway."

I bite the inside of my cheek, resisting the urge to snap back. It's typical of him, brushing things off like they don't matter. And maybe they don't, to him. But still...they were my family, in some twisted way.

I hear the soft click of heels descending the staircase, and when I turn, I feel a wave of nausea roll through me. A woman who looks no more than five years older than me, maybe even younger, walks over with a smile that's just a little too perfect, placing a gentle kiss on my dad's lips before turning to me. She's tall, with long dark hair cascading in waves down her back, wearing a tight dress that leaves very little to the imagination.

"You must be Maliah. I'm Victoria," she says in a soft, breathy voice, holding out her arms for an awkward air-hug. I force a smile, though my stomach twists as I oblige.

"Nice to meet you," I manage to say, trying to be polite.

But then I notice as Victoria's gaze shifts to Koa, her eyes lingering a little too long, like she's sizing him up. When she hugs him, it's not the same weird air-hug she gave me. No, she makes sure their bodies brush against each other, her hand gliding down his arm. Koa stiffens instantly, his discomfort visible as he glances at me, his face trying to mask the awkwardness. I feel my hands ball into fists.

God, why did I want to come here?

"The chefs are still preparing our food," my dad announces with a grin, completely oblivious to what's happening. "How about a house tour, eh? I don't think your boy toy has ever been to a house this big."

My stomach plummets. Mortified, I see Koa tense next to me, his jaw ticking with the effort of holding back.

"His name is Koa, Dad. You've met him before," I snap, my voice sharper than intended. "And your house isn't even that big."

I don't miss the way my dad's smile tightens, the flash of annoyance in his eyes at my remark. He leans in slightly, his voice calm but icy. "It's the biggest house on the whole coast, so I'd beg to differ. And I'm pretty sure the last time I saw *Koa*, you two were broken up."

Tensions brews in the room, thick and heavy, and I can feel the heat rising in my chest. Just as I'm about to say something I'd probably regret, Victoria jumps in, smiling brightly as if to smooth things over. "Let's start the tour, shall we?" she says, leading the way, her voice all sweetness.

We follow behind them, my dad's arm draped possessively over Victoria's shoulder as she chatters about the house like it's a damn palace. I let out a long, shaky breath, trying to calm myself. The whole situation feels surreal, like a nightmare.

I reach for Koa's hand, needing some sort of anchor. As soon as my fingers brush his, I feel a shock run through me. His hand is ice cold, and when I press my thumb into his palm, I can feel his pulse racing.

He's furious.

I squeeze his hand, trying to pour reassurance, and maybe even an apology, into the gesture. But I'm met with silence, Koa's gaze fixed ahead, jaw clenched so tightly I can see the muscle in his neck twitching.

After the stupidly long tour, mostly long because Victoria took every chance she got to show us each room in detail as if we were stupid; from how the lamps turn on when you clap, to how the bed raises for you so you don't have to in the morning. By the time we make it to the dinner table, I'm starving.

Dinner feels like a bizarre spectacle with us all seated around my dad's stupidly long table, like we're in some medieval castle. Dad, of course, sits at the head, his little throne of power, while the rest of us line the sides. Even Victoria. No one ever gets to sit at the end, except him. His weird way of maintaining control, I guess.

Victoria can't seem to stop talking, her voice sugary and high-pitched as she rambles on about the house tour. She's got that same fake cheer plastered on her face, like she's hosting a reality show.

"How's the tour going, anyway?" she asks with a bright smile, glancing at Koa like he's the next item on tonight's menu. "Your dad's been following all the headlines and live streams, you know. And I've been watching too. Saw the first six episodes of SurfFlix...but wow, Koa, you look way better in person than on TV."

My hands form tight fists under the table, nails digging into my palms. I force out a laugh—fake, brittle. The kind that's meant to avoid conflict. Beside me, Koa clears his throat. "Thanks for the compliment," he says smoothly, trying to be polite but obviously eager for her to stop gawking at him. He picks up his fork, and we both start eating in tense silence.

A few moments later, my dad speaks up, steering the conversation into territory I'd rather avoid. "I saw your accident, Koa," he says, casually cutting into his steak. "Watched the whole thing on a live stream. Stupid mistake to make, wasn't it?"

My pulse quickens, anxiety blooming in my chest. My gaze shifts to Koa, praying he won't snap at my dad. Koa pauses, clearly thinking it through before he answers. "You're right," he says, his tone measured. "It was a stupid mistake. But I guess that's why it was called a mistake. I've learned from it."

Dad scoffs, not quite making eye contact as he offers a half-grin. "Well, at least you learned from *that*."

There's something dark in his words, a hidden jab. Koa and my dad lock eyes, the tension between them tightening like a rubber band about to snap. They stare at each other for a long beat, and I can't quite figure out what my dad's trying to insinuate, but it leaves a sour taste in my mouth. My brow furrows as I glance between them, sensing something beneath the surface that I'm missing.

When dinner finally ends, I'm more than ready to bolt before the dessert can be served. Victoria, already halfway through her second glass of wine, slams the rest back and stands up, stretching.

"I need some air," she announces dramatically, tossing her hair over her shoulder. "Maliah, let's take a walk on the beach, hmm? Too much male testosterone in the air for me."

I hesitate, glancing at Koa. I don't like the idea of leaving him alone with my dad, especially after that weird exchange. But Koa catches my eye and nods, his expression calm, though I can still see the storm brewing behind his eyes.

"Go ahead," he says quietly. "I'll be fine."

Reluctantly, I stand up and follow Victoria towards the patio doors.

The air is still warm, even though the sun's starting to dip behind the horizon. I walk next to Victoria, the sand shifting under our feet. The waves crash gently in the distance.

"Phew, those two really don't like each other, huh?" Victoria says, bending over to take off her heels, her bare feet sinking into the cool sand. "I thought someone was going to throw a steak knife for sure."

I let out a small laugh, but it's forced. "Yeah, that was weird," I mumble, more to myself than to her. My mind is still replaying the awkward standoff between my dad and Koa, trying to make sense of it.

Victoria straightens up and glances over at me, as if she's been waiting for me to ask something.

"So, uh, how'd you meet my dad?"

She smiles like she's got the best story in the world. "Oh my gosh, I thought you'd never ask. It's kind of funny. I was on a horrible date at this fancy restaurant with some guy in finance, he was cute and all, but boring as hell, and then I spotted your dad sitting at the bar, looking all broody and mysterious. I thought 'there's a problem I can fix,' so I ditched my date and went over to him. We hit it off right away, like literally, he moved me in with him that very night. Haven't been apart since."

I blink at her, waiting for the funny part of the story, but it never comes so I nod. The first thought that pops into my head is *gold digger*. The words just sit there, hanging heavy in my mind, but I don't say anything. Instead, I try to smile, but it doesn't quite reach my eyes.

"Right."

Victoria doesn't seem to notice. She's too busy looking out at the ocean like we're in some cheesy romance movie. "He's got this...powerful presence, doesn't he? Hard not to fall for that."

My stomach twists at her words, and suddenly, I can't stand being out here anymore. "You know what?" I cut her off, my voice sharp. "I'm not really feeling the beach right now. I think I'm going to head back inside."

Victoria looks at me surprised, but then waves it off like it's nothing. "Okay, no problem. I'll be in soon. Just want to walk off that meal," she says, stretching her arms above her head again, her underwear basically on full display.

The meal you barely ate, I think but don't say.

Instead, I just nod and turn back towards the house, quickening my pace. Being here, with her, with *them*—it doesn't feel like home. It feels like I'm a stranger in my own dad's life.

TWENTY-SEVEN

KOA | PENICHE, PORTUGAL

I WATCH as Malia's dad stands from the table, walking over to his bar with deliberate, heavy steps. He pours himself a glass of whiskey, the amber liquid swirling in the crystal tumbler, but he doesn't bother offering me any—not that I'd take it if he did. His grip on the glass tightens as he brings it to his lips, the tension clear in his posture.

"I was surprised to find out you'd be joining my daughter on tour for a year. I was certain you'd left the team after you broke up with her." His words are sharp, but the anger in his eyes is what cuts deepest. It's like he's holding back an explosion, just barely.

I keep my face blank, refusing to let him see that his words are getting to me. "I'm not sure what gave you that impression," I say, standing from my seat and moving casually around the room. I pretend to admire the décor, my hands sliding into my pockets, trying to project confidence. I won't let him intimidate me, even if this situation makes my blood boil.

"Well," he starts, his voice thick with disdain, "I just figured you wouldn't be stupid enough to stay on the team after breaking my little girl's heart." He sneers, swirling the whiskey in his glass before taking another sip. "Not that you were ever good enough to be on that team anyway. You're just Gabriel's charity case, his little scholarship project."

I bite the inside of my cheek, holding back the urge to react. It's the same thing he said the last time we met in person, and just hearing it again makes my muscles tense. But I won't give him that power over me.

"You know," I say, finally turning to face him, my eyes locking on his, "you said the same thing before. 'Gabriel's charity case.' Surely, you can't still think that's true, not after all I've done to prove I deserve my spot on this tour and on the team."

He scoffs, shaking his head as if I've said something ridiculous. He walks back to the bar, pouring himself a second glass without a word, and for a moment, there's a flicker of doubt in my mind.

Did Gabriel pull strings for me? Did he do more than I realize?

No. I earned this. I earned my place.

"I earned my spot on this tour," I say firmly, my voice steady. "And I prove that every time I go out there and compete. So I don't understand—what exactly is your issue with me?"

He swings around, his eyes blazing, finger pointed directly at me as he stomps closer. "My issue *is* you!" he shouts, the words echoing through the room. "You're a nobody, from some poor island with a poor family, and you think you can just come in here on your scholarship and *brainwash* my only daughter into being with you?"

I stand my ground, keeping my voice level. "I didn't brainwash her."

He laughs, but it's a hollow, bitter sound. "Oh, you absolutely have. I told you the last time we met, when you came to me with that *ugly* and *cheap* engagement ring, asking for my blessing—*my* blessing—to marry her, that you weren't good enough. And guess what? You listened. You broke up with her, just like I knew you would. And I swear, I believed in God that day. My prayers were answered."

I grit my teeth, my chest tightening as his words hit a nerve. He's right, in a way—I did break up with her. I let myself believe he was right. That I wasn't good enough for her. But now? Now I see through him, and I see the fear behind his anger. He's scared of losing control.

"And yet," he continues, his voice dripping with disgust, "here you are, slithering your way back into her life, showing up at *my* door with the audacity to think you still have a chance with her?" He steps closer, his finger nearly jabbing into my chest. "You'll never be good enough for her. You'll never be anything but the island boy who doesn't know his place."

The urge to hit him is almost overwhelming, but I won't. I won't stoop to his level. Instead, I take a deep breath, looking him dead in the eyes, refusing to flinch, when something behind him catches my eye. I look over his shoulder, and my heart sinks. Maliah is standing there, her face frozen in heartbreak as she stares at me, her eyes filled with a mix of confusion and betrayal.

"Is that true?" she whispers, her voice barely audible, but her gaze never leaves mine. "Were you planning to propose to me?"

Her father spins around at the sound of her voice, his eyes wide with shock, and in his haste, he drops the glass in his hand. It shatters against the floor, pieces scattering everywhere. "Maliah, my darling, I didn't realize you came back so soon. Where's Victoria?" His voice is suddenly soft, placating, but she doesn't even look at him. Her eyes are locked on mine, burning through me.

"Is it true?" she repeats, her voice firmer this time, more demanding.

I can't move, can't breathe. This isn't how I wanted her to find out. I wanted to protect her from the truth, but now that it's out, there's nowhere to hide. I swallow hard, trying to push down the lump in my throat. "Yes," I finally say, my voice tight.

Her expression falters for a split second, like I've hit her with something too heavy to bear. But then, she squares her shoulders, her anger rising. "But instead of proposing to me, you broke up with me because of what my father said?"

I see her dad shifting uncomfortably, his eyes flickering between the two of us, his mouth twitching as if he's unsure whether he should step in or stay silent.

"I broke up with you because I believed you deserve someone better," I say, the words sounding hollow even to my own ears.

Maliah's lips tremble, and for a moment, I think she might cry, but then her expression hardens. "So I had no say in it?" Her voice cracks, shaking with the weight of her rage. "You both made that decision for me? Decided who I should and shouldn't end up with?" She looks between me and her father, her eyes burning with betrayal.

I open my mouth to respond, but no words come. What can I even say? She's right. We took that choice away from her. Her father manipulated me, and I let him, because I thought I was doing what was best for her. But all I've done is hurt her.

"You said you didn't love me anymore," Maliah whispers, her voice trembling as her gaze falls to the floor, her eyes glossing over with unshed tears. The crack in her voice is like a knife to the chest, cutting deeper than I thought possible.

"I never stopped loving you, Maliah," I whisper back, my heart breaking with every word. "I told you, you've always been the one for me."

She shakes her head slowly, the first tear slipping down her cheek. Then another. And another. "Do you know what it's like to hear the person you want to spend the rest of your life with say they don't love you anymore?" Her voice cracks, and she doesn't look at me, her pain too raw.

I feel like the worst kind of asshole, and I don't even care that her father is standing right there, watching all of this unfold. The guilt is so heavy it nearly crushes me. Without thinking, I take quick strides towards her, closing the distance between us in seconds. I wrap my arms around her shaking body, pulling her tightly against me, holding her like she might slip away if I let go.

"I'm so sorry, princess," I murmur into her hair, my voice barely holding steady. "I know that no matter how much I apologize, it will never make it okay, but I'm so fucking sorry. If I could take it all back, I would. I couldn't even face you after I said those words—my heart was breaking, too."

She trembles in my arms, her breathing hitching as she cries softly against my chest. The sound of her tears is like salt in an open wound, and I squeeze her tighter, wishing I could erase every ounce of pain I've caused her.

She pulls back just enough to look up at me, her tear-filled eyes searching mine. There's pain there, yes, but something else too—a deep, burning anger mixed with confusion. She wipes at her face quickly, like she's trying to pull herself together, and steps out of my embrace.

"Why didn't you tell me what was going on instead of just ending it?" Her eyes flicker to her father, who still stands frozen near the bar, his expression unreadable.

I open my mouth to answer, but the words don't come out right away. Because how do I explain that? How do I tell her that I thought leaving her was the only way to protect her from her father's disapproval? From the life we'd have had with his constant interference?

"I thought..." I take a deep breath, running a hand through

my hair. "I thought it was the right thing to do. I didn't want to drag you into something your dad was so against. You deserved more, Maliah. You deserved better than what I could give you. I—" My voice falters, and I clench my jaw. "I thought I was doing the right thing by walking away."

Her hands drop to her sides, fists clenching. "And you didn't think I could decide that for myself? That maybe I wanted you despite what anyone else thought? You didn't give me the choice, Koa. You let him—" she points at her father, her voice rising, "you let him dictate our relationship. And you think that's what I deserve? To be lied to and controlled?"

The words hit me like a freight train. I don't know what to say, because she's right. I did make that choice for her, and it was a coward's choice.

"I was trying to protect you," I say, but the words sound weak even to my own ears.

Maliah shakes her head. "You weren't protecting me. You were protecting yourself."

Her father clears his throat, breaking the heavy silence. "Maliah—"

"No." She turns on him, fire in her eyes now. "You don't get to speak. Not after what I just heard. You tried to keep Koa from me, tried to sabotage our relationship because you thought you knew better. But you don't." Her voice cracks again, but she presses on, standing taller, stronger. "I loved him. I still do. And you tried to ruin that because you can't stand the idea of someone you don't approve of being good enough for me. For you."

Her father looks stunned, as if she slapped him across the face, and for the first time, I see real shock flash in his eyes. She doesn't wait for a response. Her expression is hard as stone, and she turns her back on him without hesitation, heading for the door.

I swallow hard, feeling the weight of everything that just happened between us, but this isn't the time to dwell on it. She needs to get out of here before she crumbles. I need to get her out of here. "Let's go," I say quietly, following behind her as she storms out.

Just before we leave the room, Maliah stops abruptly and turns back to face her father one last time. Her voice drips with venom as she speaks, "And you...pretend like I left with your last wife, too. Never contact me again. I'm done playing your games. I hope you have a long, healthy life with your gold digger girlfriend."

The words hang in the air like a death sentence, and her father's face contorts in a mix of rage and disbelief as his eyes find mine. He opens his mouth, but nothing comes out.

Maliah doesn't wait for him to recover. She stomps out, her heels clicking sharply against the polished floors, passing the servers who have just arrived with dessert, Portuguese custard tarts, Maliah's favourite. It feels like a twisted irony, the fancy meal, the perfect setting, completely ruined by the truth that's been boiling underneath the surface for too long.

I snatch a tart off the server's platter and glance back at her father. He's still standing there, frozen, his hand gripping the back of a chair so hard his knuckles are white. His expression is seared into my mind—shock, anger, but most of all, defeat. It's a moment I'll never forget, seeing him like this. His eyes find mine and out of spite I take a bite of one of the tarts, winking at him before putting it back on the platter and turning around to leave. But it doesn't bring me any satisfaction. All I feel is the weight of everything that's come to light tonight.

I trail behind Maliah, my heart racing as I catch up to her. She's already outside, breathing in short, angry bursts as she stands by our rental car.

I unlock the door, and we both get in, the silence between

us heavy as I start the engine. I don't know what to say, but I know we need to get far away from here—away from him, away from all of it. So, I drive, the night swallowing us up as we leave her father's house behind.

WE PULL INTO THE DRIVEWAY, THE SOFT HUM OF THE ENGINE THE only sound as I shut it off. The house feels eerily quiet, especially now that Griffin and Eliana are gone. It's just the two of us, and Maliah hasn't said a single word since we left her father's. She's been crying, her quiet sobs breaking me apart as I drove.

She gets out of the car and heads toward the door, her shoulders slumped, and I can tell she's about to shut herself off for the night. The thought of going to bed like this, with everything left hanging in the air, makes my chest tighten. I can't stand it. Not after all the truth that's come out.

Before she can slip away into the bedroom, I gently grab her wrist, stopping her in her tracks. "Please talk to me, princess," I beg quietly, my voice sounding more broken than I expected.

For a second, I'm afraid she's going to pull away, but to my surprise her shoulders start to shake, and she bursts into sobs. Her whole body trembles as she breaks down in front of me.

"I'm so sorry," she chokes out, her voice thick with emotion. "I'm sorry for everything. For what my father said, for how he put you down. I should've fought for you, for us…I shouldn't have believed you when you said you didn't love me anymore. I should've known something wasn't right. And then…the way I treated you after, Koa, I've been horrible to you."

Her words are a mess of apologies, tumbling out between

sobs, and it's killing me to see her like this. I pull her trembling body into my arms, holding her tightly against me.

"Shh, none of that matters anymore," I whisper, rubbing her hair, my chin resting on top of her head. "You don't need to apologize, princess. None of it matters."

But she keeps crying, her tears soaking into my shirt as I hold her. I know she's carrying a lot of guilt, but none of it is on her. Not the breakup, not what her father said. It's on me. I should've told her the truth from the start, should've never let things get this far. But I hold her tighter now, trying to soothe her with every touch, every whispered word.

All I want is for her to know that we're in this together. No more lies, no more running.

Just us.

I pull back just enough to look at her, brushing the tears from her cheeks with my thumbs. Her eyes are red, face streaked with tears, but to me, she's still the most beautiful person in the world. I take a deep breath, my heart pounding as I gather the words I've been holding inside for so long.

"Maliah," I whisper, cupping her face, "I love you. I've always loved you. You're it for me, princess. There's no one else, no one I've ever wanted or will ever want the way I want you."

She looks at me, her lip trembling, like she's not sure whether to believe me after everything. But I keep going, needing her to know this, to feel it in every word.

"I'd go through it all again," I say, my voice shaking with the weight of the truth. "Every fight, the breakup, every moment of pain since then—if it means you'd come back to me in the end. I'd do it all, because you're worth it, Maliah. You've always been worth it."

Her tears start falling again, but this time there's something different in her eyes. She's looking at me like she's seeing me for the first time in a long time. I lean my forehead against hers, our breaths mingling as we stand there, so close, like the rest of the world doesn't exist anymore.

"You're my heart, princess. You always have been. I don't want anyone else. I don't need anyone else. Just you."

I kiss her then, soft and slow, pouring everything I have into that kiss. It's not about passion this time, not about desire—it's about love, about everything I feel for her, everything I've been holding back. And as her arms wrap around me, holding me as tightly as I'm holding her, I know she feels it too.

I lift her up into my arms, cradling her against my chest as I carry her to the bedroom. She rests her head against my shoulder, her fingers gripping the fabric of my shirt, and I feel like I'm holding my whole world in my arms. Gently, I lay her down on the bed, kneeling in front of her, my heart beating loudly in my chest as I begin to take off her heels. I press soft kisses from her ankle to her knee, my lips lingering on her skin, worshipping every inch of her.

She watches me, her breathing shallow, her eyes filled with something raw and vulnerable, but I can see the love there too. I help her take off her dress, sliding it down her body, and then her underwear, leaving her bare before me. The sight of her takes my breath away.

I feel her fingers working at my shirt, untucking it, and then she's unbuckling my belt, her touch so familiar yet so electrifying.

I stand naked before her, watching as her eyes travel over my body until her eyes find mine again, and it feels like the world stops spinning, and everything we've been through fades away. I gently lower her back to the bed, crawling over her and pressing my lips to hers, kissing her slowly. It's consuming, the kind of kiss that speaks every unsaid word between us. Her lips are soft and warm, moving against mine in perfect unison.

Every brush of her fingers across my skin feels like it carries the weight of every moment we've missed, every tear, every longing.

My hands slide down her sides, memorizing the familiar curves of her body. I can feel her trembling beneath my fingers, her breath hitching as I press kisses down her neck, over her collarbone, and across her chest.

She arches into me, her skin warm and inviting, and I take my time, worshipping every inch of her. I want her to feel it, how much I love her, how much I've always loved her.

Her hands roam my body, urgent but tender, pulling me closer like she can't get enough. Her touch is desperate, almost frantic, but I can feel the emotion behind it—the years of love, the months of hurt, all pouring out at once.

I press myself against her wet entrance until I slide in. She gasps softly, and I press my forehead to hers, lost in the way her body fits so perfectly against mine. Every movement is filled with intention, slow and deliberate, like we're making promises to each other with every thrust. Her moans are soft in my ear, and a shudder runs through me.

She's everything.

I never want this moment to end.

We move together, our breaths synchronized, building something more than just pleasure—it's healing, it's forgiveness, it's love.

We make love and it's different from before—better, because now there are no walls, no lies, no fear. Every movement feels like a vow to stay, to love, to never let go again. Her nails dig into my back as I press deeper, and I feel the shiver that runs through her body as we both reach the edge. She whispers my name and it sounds like salvation.

When we finally collapse, our bodies slick with sweat and our breaths still heavy, it feels like we've finally broken through something. Like we've found each other again, stronger than before. I pull her close, her head resting against my chest, her fingers tracing lazy patterns on my skin.

I kiss her forehead, then her cheek, and finally her lips.

Gentle, tender touches that feel like home.

"Maliah," I whisper, brushing her blonde hair away from her face, my thumb grazing her bottom lip, "we're not just starting over. We're starting better. Okay?"

Her eyes soften as she looks up at me, a small smile tugging at her lips. She nods, her hand resting on my chest.

This is where we belong, together.

TWENTY-EIGHT

MALIAH | OAHU, HAWAII

WE'RE FINALLY IN OAHU, the last stop on this whirlwind tour, and I can feel the energy in the air. This is Koa's home. I can see the pride in his eyes as we step onto the sands of Sunset Beach for the competition, a glint of something deeper—something more personal—every time he glances out at the ocean.

The heat of the sun, the salt on my skin, the cheers from the crowd, everything feels heightened today. We ride those waves like we're made for them, Koa and I in perfect sync with the ocean. Every turn, every drop feels right, like we've tapped into something primal, something that flows deeper than just skill. And when we finish, the scores flash on the screen—first place. It's a rush, but there's also this calm that washes over me as I turn to Koa, knowing we did it together. He grins at me with that boyish grin before starting to paddle back to shore.

As soon as we reach the sand, towels are thrown over our heads and our boards are taken before we're whisked to a small tent near the beach for interviews. I try my best to dry my hair and body with the towel as the cameras finish setting up, the reporters already buzzing around, eager for sound bites. Koa sits beside me, the ocean behind us, his arm draped casually over the back of my chair.

The cameras roll, and the interviewer jumps right in.

"First place at Sunset Beach, congratulations to both of you! How are you feeling, knowing Pipeline is just around the corner?"

My heart skips a beat at the mention of Pipeline so I glance at Koa, and he gives me a small nod, letting me take the first response.

"We're excited," I say with a smile, still catching my breath from the rush of it all. "I've heard that Pipeline is no joke, though. It's one of the most dangerous waves in the world."

Koa leans in slightly, his voice calm but serious. "The ocean here in Hawaii...she'll either give you everything or take it all away. You have to respect her, or she'll take it from you."

His words hang in the air, heavy with meaning. He knows the water better than anyone, and I can tell the weight of surfing Pipeline isn't lost on him.

The interviewer seems to catch onto the gravity of what he's saying, nodding thoughtfully before moving on to lighter topics. But I can feel it. Pipeline is looming, and while we've both surfed dangerous waves before, this one is different. It's not just the danger—it's the history, the stakes, and for Koa, it's personal.

I've heard stories of Pipeline almost my whole surfing career and it's always been the wave that haunts my dreams; the one that terrifies me in a way no other wave does. I can feel the nervous tremor in my leg, even as I try to keep it still.

Without a word, Koa's hand finds its way to my knee, his fingers pressing gently but firmly, grounding me in the moment. I don't look at him, but I breathe a little easier, grateful that he knows me well enough to sense my fear.

The interviewer shifts, leaning in. "And about the two of

you, there's been a lot of speculation. The chemistry on screen —let's just say it's noticeable. So, what's the story?"

I feel the question hit like a soft blow, the kind that leaves you momentarily stunned. For a second, I'm speechless, but then Koa's hand squeezes my knee, a reminder that I don't have to hide this anymore. I turn toward him, and he's already smiling at me, like he knew this was coming.

"Yeah," I finally say, my voice clear. "We're together. We're happy with what we have."

The words feel freeing, as if saying them out loud makes them real all over again. Koa grins at me, his eyes full of warmth, and I can't help but smile back.

The interviewer looks pleased, maybe even a little too pleased, but I don't care. The camera cuts, the lights dim slightly, and for a moment, it's just the two of us again. No cameras, no tour, no waves.

Just Koa and me.

After the interviewer wraps, the SurfFlix producers usher us off the set, sending the top five teams of remaining surfers back to the hotels to get ready for dinner, while the others have already been sent home. Cut from the tour—including Charles.

Dinner is supposed to be a big celebration after today's competition, the last chance to unwind with other surfers before we face the intensity of Pipeline next week.

Koa and I make our way back to our shared room, the silence between us comfortable, but the adrenaline from the day still buzzing in my veins. The moment we step inside, the atmosphere shifts, like we both know exactly what's coming next.

"I'm going to hop in the shower," I say, my voice a little lower, a little more suggestive.

Koa's eyes flicker with amusement. "I think I'll join you," he replies, his lips curving into that familiar grin. We barely make it into the bathroom before his hands are on me, peeling away at my sweat and sand-stained clothes from the day.

When the hot water hits us, Koa's lips crash against mine. The steam rises around us, his hands sliding down my body, slick with water. I moan softly into his mouth, the rush of the shower only making it feel more urgent, more necessary. We don't have time to be slow or gentle, but that's okay—we don't need to be.

His hands grip my hips as I press my back against the cool tile wall, gasping when he lifts me up effortlessly. I wrap my legs around him and feel him fill me completely, losing myself in the feeling.

It's quick, intense, our bodies moving together like we're racing the clock. His mouth finds my neck, kissing, biting softly as I arch into him, every nerve in my body alive with need. We both know we don't have much time, but that only makes it better, like we're stealing these moments before we're thrown back into the whirlwind of the tour.

We finally come together and it's like the last of the tension from the day melts away, replaced with something deeper, more grounding.

We stay like that for a moment, catching our breath, the water still pouring down over us. Then, Koa lets out a breathless chuckle, his forehead resting against mine. "Shower sex definitely beats a post-comp interview."

I laugh, my heart still racing, and kiss him once more before we pull ourselves apart to actually start getting ready for dinner.

WE MEET THE REST OF THE SURFERS IN THE HOTEL LOBBY, waiting for the bus that's taking us to dinner. The producers have set up this whole event—a traditional luau to honour Polynesian history, complete with Mauka warriors. Everyone seems excited, chatting easily, but my mind keeps drifting back to Pipeline, the wave that's been waiting for me.

Koa stands beside me, his hand firmly in mine. I can feel his thumb brush soothing circles on my skin, his way of grounding me, but my thoughts are still racing. I know he's trying to distract me, trying to keep me in the moment, but I'm struggling to shake the heaviness that's settled in my chest.

As we board the bus, the chatter around me blurs. My leg bounces anxiously against the floor, and I stare out the window at the fading sun, the ocean in the distance like a reminder of what's coming. Koa leans over, his voice soft as he whispers, "You okay?"

I nod quickly. "Yeah, just...thinking."

His eyes search mine, and I can see he knows I'm not fine, but he doesn't push it. Instead, he just pulls me closer, resting his arm around my shoulders, letting me lean into him. I close my eyes for a moment, focusing on the warmth of his body against mine, his steady breathing. But even with him right here, I can't stop the images flashing in my mind—of being swallowed by Pipeline, of making one wrong move and the ocean punishing me for it, of being dragged down below the barrel, watching the world above me fade away.

When we arrive at the luau, the night feels electric. The sound of drums fills the air, the crackle of fire from torches along the beach casting an orange glow over everything. The Mauka warriors are already starting their performance, their movements powerful, telling the story of their ancestors. Of Koa's ancestors. It's breathtaking, the energy palpable, and yet, I can't shake the unease that's settled in my stomach.

We sit down at a long wooden table, the others around us

laughing and chatting. Koa stays close, his hand slipping from my shoulder to rest on my thigh under the table, a silent way of letting me know he's here. I glance at him, and he gives me a small, reassuring smile.

"You're going to be fine, princess," he says softly, his voice low enough that only I can hear. "You've surfed tougher waves, trust me."

I want to believe him, but Pipeline isn't just another wave. It's massive. The kind of wave that can break bones—or worse. I've heard the stories, seen the wipeouts that end careers or take lives, and no amount of experience prepares you for something like that.

"I don't know," I whisper, biting my lip as I finally let the fear slip into my voice. "What if I can't do it, Koa? What if something goes wrong?"

He tightens his grip on my leg, his thumb brushing against my skin in slow, calming strokes. "You're one of the best surfers in the world, Maliah. You've earned your spot on this tour, and you can handle Pipeline. You're stronger than you think."

I shake my head, swallowing hard. The lump in my throat makes it hard to speak, the fear clawing at me.

"How about we head over to Pipeline over the next week, get you used to the waves in time for the competition. Do you think that would help?" he suggests, his expression softening.

I swallow, feeling the tightness in my chest expand. I want to believe in the strength he sees in me, but the fear won't let go. "Okay," I say quietly, my voice trembling just a little.

He leans in close, his eyes locking onto mine. "I'll be right there with you, every step of the way. Always."

He nudges me with his shoulder, giving me a playful smile as he looks back at the performers. "It's beautiful, right? Just focus on this tonight, okay? We'll worry about Pipeline tomorrow."

I nod, trying to let myself enjoy the moment. The food is

incredible, the dancers are mesmerizing, and the energy from the warriors feel electric. Koa's arm wraps around my waist, his thumb tracing a slow, comforting pattern on my side. He's doing everything he can to keep me present and I appreciate it more than he'll ever know.

TWENTY-NINE

KOA | OAHU, HAWAII

I WAKE UP EARLY, the soft glow of the Hawaiian sun filtering through the curtains, breathing life back into my soul. I've missed it here. Maliah is still asleep beside me, curled up under the blankets, her face peaceful despite the storm I know is raging inside her. I kiss her shoulder softly before slipping out of bed and pulling on my board shorts and a T-shirt. Today's a big day—it's time to take her out to Pipeline.

I know she's scared. Hell, I'd be worried if she wasn't. Pipeline is no joke, and the closer we get to the competition, the more that fear has been eating at her. But I also know that Maliah's stronger than she gives herself credit for. She's faced down some of the toughest waves in the world, but this one—it's different.

I grab a couple of boards and throw them in the back of the Jeep, making sure to pack some water and snacks for later. When I head back inside, Maliah is stirring, her eyes blinking open as she stretches. I lean down to kiss her forehead, and she smiles sleepily at me.

"Morning, princess. Are you ready to face the beast?" I ask, trying to keep my tone light.

She offers me a half-hearted smile, but I can see the worry flickering in her eyes. "I don't know if I'll ever be ready," she admits quietly, sitting up and hugging her knees.

I sit down on the edge of the bed, reaching out to tuck a strand of hair behind her ear. "That's okay. We'll take it one step at a time. First, we're just going to watch, study the waves, and talk to some locals. No pressure to do anything yet."

She nods but I can tell the idea of even going to Pipeline is weighing on her. I don't push her any further, knowing she needs time to warm up to the wave on her own. "Come on," I say gently. "Let's get some breakfast, and then we'll head out."

AFTER BREAKFAST, WE DRIVE OUT TO PIPELINE. IT'S STILL EARLY, but the surf is already picking up, and a few locals are out there carving through the waves like it's just another day. I park the Jeep and walk down to the beach with Maliah beside me. The sight of Pipeline, even from here, sends a shiver down my spine. The waves are massive, hollow tubes crashing with a demanding force. It's beautiful, but it's brutal.

Maliah's quiet as we sit on the sand, her eyes fixed on the water. I know what's going through her head because it's the same thing I went through the first time I faced Pipeline. You look at those waves, and all you can think about is how easily they can take you from this world.

We sit in silence for a while, just watching, studying. The locals out there make it look effortless, but I know better. They've spent years mastering this wave, learning every nuance, every ripple in the water. It's not just about skill—it's about understanding Pipeline.

After a while, a couple of local surfers come up the beach,

one of them I recognize—Kelani, a guy I grew up with, who's been surfing this break since we were kids.

"Koa Foster," he says with a chuckle and big grin.

I stand up and we clap hands, pulling each other in for a hug. "Kelani Makana, it's been a while," I say, pulling back to smile at him.

"Too long, my friend," he replies before glancing down at Maliah. "You brought her to the lion's den, huh?" Kelani says with a grin, his voice thick with the local Pidgin accent.

Maliah tenses beside me, and I can tell his words are hitting her harder than they should. I shoot him a look. "We're just here to study the waves," I say firmly. "No need to scare her off before she even gets in the water."

Kelani chuckles, but his face turns serious as he looks back at Pipeline. "Nah, I'm not trying to scare her. But she needs to know. Pipeline ain't like the others, braddah. She'll take you out if you don't give her respect. We've seen it too many times—guys think they've got it, and then boom, one bad wipeout and it's over."

Maliah's eyes widen, and I can see the fear creeping back in. I squeeze her hand, trying to ground her. "Kelani, maybe ease up a little," I say, my tone tight.

He shrugs. "I'm just saying what everyone knows. Pipeline's killed more surfers than any other wave out here. The reef is sharp, and if you fall wrong, it's not just a wipeout. It's your life."

Maliah's hand goes cold in mine, and I can feel the tension radiating from her. This is exactly what I didn't want to happen. Her hearing all the horror stories before she's even had a chance to get her head straight.

I turn to her, placing a hand on her cheek. "Hey, you don't have to listen to that, okay? I know it's scary, but you've got this. We'll take it slow. No one's rushing you."

She nods, but I can tell she's rattled. I shoot Kelani another look, and he raises his hands in mock surrender. "Alright, alright. I'll shut up. But if she wants some tips, we can help. You've been here before, Koa, you know what it takes."

I nod, grateful that he's willing to share his experience, but annoyed that he's made it worse for Maliah. "Thanks, man. We'll catch up later."

"Are you visiting your mom soon? You're all she's been talking about since she found out you made it on the tour."

I nod. "Yeah, we're heading over to hers in a couple days for Christmas. See you there?"

Kelani nods before him and his friend head off down the beach, leaving us alone again. Maliah's still staring at the water, her face pale. I pull her into my arms, holding her close. "I know that was a lot to hear, but you're not alone in this, okay? I'm right here with you."

She closes her eyes and nods, her breathing shallow. We sit like that for a while, her body pressed against mine, the sound of the crashing waves filling the silence between us. I can tell she's still scared, and I hate seeing her like this, so unsure of herself, so unlike the fierce woman I know she is. She's quiet, lost in thought, and I know I need to do something to ease her mind before it eats her alive.

I pull out my phone and scroll through my contacts until I land on Gabriel's name. If there's anyone who can help snap her out of this, it's him. He's tough, but he's always known how to push us in the right ways.

I click video call and watch as Maliah and I pop up on the screen, waiting for him to answer.

"Yea, what's up, Koa?"

He looks exhausted, as if he hasn't slept all night. I can see Zalea asleep on the couch behind him.

"Hey, Coach. I'm out at Pipeline with Maliah, trying to get a feel for the wave before next week's competition. Any pointers?"

Gabriel pauses, his eyes narrowing as he studies the two of us through the screen. I can see the wheels turning in his head, like he's reading more than just the situation at Pipeline.

"You're asking for tips?" he finally says, raising an eyebrow. "Koa, you've surfed Pipeline before. So, what's really going on?"

I glance at Maliah, her arms wrapped around her knees as she stares out at the ocean. I hesitate for a moment before answering, "She's spooked, Gabriel. The wave...it's in her head."

Gabriel doesn't react right away, but I can tell he's thinking, his expression softening as he leans closer to the camera. "Put her on."

I nudge Maliah gently, holding the phone out toward her. "Gabriel wants to talk to you."

She hesitates, like she doesn't want to face him, but eventually she takes the phone from me, holding it up in front of her. "Hey, Coach," she says, her voice barely above a whisper.

"Maliah." His tone is firm but not unkind. "What's going on? You've surfed bigger waves than Pipeline. Why is this one getting to you?"

She swallows hard, looking down for a second before meeting his gaze on the screen. "I don't know," she admits. "It's just...everything I've heard about it, the wipeouts, the reef, the injuries. I can't stop thinking about all the ways it could go wrong."

Gabriel nods slowly, his eyes never leaving hers. "That fear you're feeling? It's natural. Hell, every surfer has felt it at some point. But you can't let it control you. Fear's only useful if you know how to channel it."

Maliah's eyes are locked on the screen, hanging on his every word.

"Listen," Gabriel continues, "you've been training for this your whole life. You've faced insane conditions, more than most people could handle. This isn't about being fearless, it's about being smart. Learn the waves patterns, and you surf it like you know how. You've got everything you need right here," he says, tapping his temple. "Trust yourself."

Maliah nods slowly, and I can see the tension in her shoulders easing just a bit.

"Thanks, Coach," she whispers.

She hands the phone back to me, looking a little more grounded now. I end the call and look back at her, still sitting quietly beside me. I wrap an arm around her and pull her close, pressing a kiss to the top of her head, and she leans into me, her body relaxing a little more.

"What is scaring you the most about the wave?" I ask softly. "The real reason."

She takes a deep breath. "Getting sucked below the barrel."

"What about it, the risk of hitting the reef?"

She shakes her head. "Just being below it, watching the world fade away above me."

I frown as I look at her. "If you were sucked below the water's surface, watching the barrel crashing above you, I'd be by your side in seconds, bringing you back to the top. You wouldn't just fade away under there. I promise."

Her eyes search mine and she swallows hard, brows furrowing. "It's just...it's so unpredictable."

"Life is unpredictable. This is just another challenge. We can learn the rhythm of Pipeline together."

She bites her lip, contemplating my words. "What if I freeze up? The way I did in Teahupo'o?"

"Then you remind yourself of who you are. You're a fighter, Mal. You don't back down from challenges. Remember when you caught a wave at Saquarema? How alive you felt?"

She nods slowly, her breath hitching. "That was different. I was just—"

"No," I interrupt, holding her gaze. "You were brave. And

you *are* brave. This is just another opportunity to show the world what I already know."

Her shoulders drop slightly, the tension easing, and I can see her considering my words. "Okay," she finally says, a glimmer of determination sparking in her eyes. "Let's go check it out."

"That's my girl," I reply, feeling a surge of pride. I stand up and extend my hand to her, but she just stares at me, face completely flushed.

"Don't say that again, not right before we go surfing," she says, her voice breathy.

I blink before I give her a half smirk. "Why?" I ask in a low voice. "Did me calling you *my* girl turn you on?"

She grabs a fistful of sand and throws it at me. I burst out into laughter as I watch her face turn crimson. "Shut up," she hisses before rising to her feet.

I grin at her before my eyes travel to Kelani in the background, further down the beach with his friend. "Let's go talk to Kelani and see if he has any experience with being swallowed up by barrels out here."

She nods, her determination solidifying. "Yeah, that sounds good."

We move along the beach until we're closer to him. "Hey!" I call out. "Has a barrel ever pulled you under out here?"

They exchange glances, then his friend, a tall guy with sun-kissed skin and a wide grin, steps forward. "Yeah, just yesterday."

Maliah's eyes go wide as she stares at him, living proof that she won't just fade away. "What's it like?" she asks him.

His expression turns serious. "It's intense. You have to stay calm and remember to look for the surface. If you panic, that's when things could get messy," he says, eyeing her. "But it's not all bad. Once you're back up, you realize how beautiful it is. The thrill is worth the fear."

She glances at me, and I can see the mix of fear and excitement swirling in her eyes. I lean in closer, whispering, "See? You've got this."

We stand and talk with Kelani and his friend, Makoa, for a while, listening as they offer more tips and sharing their experiences. I watch as Maliah's expression shifts, the fear beginning to fade.

"You ready to tackle this?" I ask, looking down at her.

She meets my gaze, her eyes shining with confidence. "Yeah, let's do it."

WE PADDLE IN FROM THE OCEAN AND AS I GLANCE AT MALIAH, there's a glow about her—something radiant and alive that wasn't there before. The way her smile lights up her face as she glides over the warm ocean water is infectious. She almost looks like she could stay out here forever, and I can't blame her.

As we reach the shore, I see her hesitate, glancing back at the waves as if they're calling to her. "Princess," I say, giving her a playful nudge with my elbow. "You've got to save some energy for the competition."

She bites her lip, a mix of reluctance and excitement in her gaze. "I just feel so alive out there."

"I get it, believe me," I reply, brushing a hand through my hair as I scan the waves behind us. "But the ocean isn't going anywhere, we'll be back soon."

She takes a deep breath, looking back one last time at the surf before turning toward me. "Okay, you're right."

We walk up the beach, and once we reach the car, I load our boards in and slide into the driver's seat while she hops in next

to me. She turns on the music as we start driving off and immediately begins to hum along, her voice light and carefree.

This is the Maliah I've missed.

The one that can just be herself around me.

The one I can't ever let slip through my fingers again.

THIRTY

MALIAH | OAHU, HAWAII

THE DRIVE to Koa's childhood home feels like something out of a movie. The sun is high in the sky, and the lush, tropical greenery surrounds the winding road as we head further inland. The ocean sparkles on the horizon, but we're moving away from beaches and into the heart of Oahu. I can feel the warmth of the island even with the windows rolled down, the breeze carrying the scent of saltwater and hibiscus.

Koa's hand rests on my knee, his excitement radiating off him like heat waves. He hasn't stopped smiling the whole drive, and it's infectious. But underneath my own smile is a layer of nerves I can't seem to shake. I've never met a boyfriend's parents before. What if his mom doesn't like me? What if I don't fit in?

I try to push the thoughts aside, but they linger as we continue driving. The scenery is breathtaking, yet my focus is consumed by the knot in my stomach. The closer we get, the tighter it becomes.

Finally, we turn down a dirt road lined with towering palm trees, and I see it—his childhood home. It's nestled on a large plot of land, a cozy, inviting house with wooden beams and a wide porch that wraps around the front. The whole place feels like it was built with love, and it has this charm that makes me feel a little more at ease.

"This is your home?" I ask, my voice full of surprise as I take in the size of it.

Koa laughs, squeezing my knee. "It was. What, were you expecting a little shack?"

I feel guilty for thinking it, but I definitely wasn't expecting a house that looked like it could rival the Saltwater Shredders' house back home. It's bigger than I imagined, yet somehow still feels intimate.

"My dad built this house from the ground up with his brothers," Koa says, his pride evident as he climbs out of the car. "After our first comp win, I sent all my earnings back home and they were able to renovate and make it bigger."

I follow him, taking in the wide-open space around us, the rolling green hills, and the distant sounds of animals in the background. Before I can process much more, I hear a high-pitched screech and look up to see a group of people rushing towards us from the porch.

A woman—who can only be Koa's mom—reaches him first, tears already in her eyes as she throws her arms around him. A few girls around our age follow close behind, and a couple of guys, including Kelani, join the group.

Koa's mom holds him tight, sobbing as she presses her face against his chest. He hugs her back just as fiercely, his eyes closing as the biggest smile spreads across his face.

"Hey, Mama," he says gently, his voice full of warmth and love.

As Koa's mom clings to him, I stand back, feeling like an outsider to this emotional reunion. My heart swells seeing how much she loves him, but it also intensifies the nerves I've been trying to push down. I try to take a deep breath and calm myself, reminding myself that this moment is about Koa. He hasn't been home in so long, and I know this means everything to him.

The rest of his family circles around, laughing and chatting as they greet him with hugs and pats on the back. Kelani grins and gives Koa a playful shove, and the girls are all beaming with excitement, peppering him with questions about the tour.

For a moment, I just watch them, unsure of where I fit into this scene. Koa finally pulls back from his mom, still holding her hand, and turns to look at me, his eyes searching for mine. He steps towards me, wrapping an arm around my waist, pulling me in close to his side.

"Everyone, this is Maliah," he says, his voice full of pride. "My girlfriend."

I try to smile through my nerves, feeling the weight of all their eyes on me. Koa's mom, who had been crying just seconds ago, turns her attention to me. She wipes her tears and steps forward, giving me the same warm, loving look she gave Koa.

"Maliah," she says softly, reaching out to take my hand in hers. "We've heard so much about you."

I blink, taken aback. "You have?"

She nods, squeezing my hand. "Ever since Koa left home to join the team, you're all he speaks about. We barely know how surfing is going because it's always Maliah this and Maliah that." She winks playfully. "I'm so happy to finally meet the girl who's made my son so happy."

Her words wash over me, soothing some of the tension in my chest. I glance at Koa over her shoulder and he's beat red, pulling a genuine smile out of me as I feel the weight of my worries lift. "It's so nice to meet you, too."

Koa's mom pulls me into a hug, surprising me with how tight it is. She smells like coconut and something sweet, and I can feel the genuine affection in the way she holds me. When she pulls back, she's smiling warmly.

"You're family now," she says, and I can tell she means it.

One by one, the rest of Koa's family greets me. Kelani gives me a lopsided grin and a hug that's more of a bear trap, while the girls, Koa's cousins, bombard me with questions about surfing and what it's like traveling around the world. It's overwhelming, but their excitement is contagious.

We're eventually ushered inside the house, where the warmth of family life is everywhere. The smell of food hits me instantly, and I can hear laughter coming from the kitchen. The house feels like it's alive, full of memories, love, and history.

Koa grabs my hand again, guiding me through the front door. "You good?" he asks, his voice low, meant just for me.

I nod, squeezing his hand. "Yeah. They're really great."

"They are," he agrees, looking around with fondness I've rarely seen. "And they're going to love you. I promise."

The living room is warm and filled with the scent of pine, cinnamon, and the sound of laughter as we all sit around the bare Christmas tree. Koa's mom wouldn't let anyone start decorating it until Koa and I arrived.

"Alright, now that we're all here, we can finally get started," Koa's mom says with a beaming smile. She passes out bowls of popcorn, and we all begin to string it together, weaving it through the branches of the tree. Koa and I work in sync, our hands brushing occasionally as we drape the strings around the branches, and every touch sends a small thrill through me.

As we decorate, Koa's mom hands us small, sentimental ornaments—pieces of Koa's life wrapped in memories. A tiny surfboard with his name etched in the wood, a glass ball painted with Hawaiian flowers, and an ornament with a picture of Koa as a baby inside. Each piece feels like a window into his past, and I feel honoured to be part of this moment, placing his family's history on display.

We take our time, laughing and telling stories, and when the last of the popcorn garlands are hung and the ornaments perfectly placed, Koa stands back, looking at the tree with a content smile.

"All that's left is the star," he says quietly, his voice filled with a touch of nostalgia. His eyes linger on the empty space at the top of the tree. "That was always my dad's job."

I feel a lump form in my throat as I glance at him. There's a weight in his voice, and I realize in this moment how important this tradition is. "What happened to him?" I ask softly, expecting to hear the kind of story that breaks my heart.

But before Koa can answer, I hear a voice behind me, warm and full of life. "Nothing crazy, just can't reach the top anymore."

I turn around to see a man that looks so much like Koa—but older, with deep lines of experience etched into his tanned face. He's sitting in a wheelchair, and the resemblance between them is undeniable.

"Dad," Koa says with a chuckle, walking over to him. He bends down and hugs his father tightly, the warmth between them palpable.

Koa's mom emerges from the kitchen, wiping her hands on a towel before gently rubbing her husband's shoulders. She smiles at him with so much love, it makes my chest ache a little.

"I was just about to call you," she says softly.

He reaches up and takes one of her hands, kissing the back of it before turning his attention to me with a friendly grin. "And you must be Maliah."

I take a step forward, holding out my hand nervously. "It's nice to meet you."

His grip is firm, but he pulls me into a quick hug instead of just a handshake. "C'mere, give me a real hug."

I laugh, hugging him back, surprised by the affection but grateful for the warmth of it. He squeezes me tight but quick, then pulls away with a smile. "We've been waiting to meet you for years. I was hoping I'd meet you standing on my own two feet, but life had other plans. Wheels will have to do."

There's no bitterness in his voice, just acceptance and a lightness that puts me at ease. I smile, touched by how easy-going he is. "It's a pleasure to finally meet you, wheels or not."

Koa steps back to the tree and picks up the star from the box of decorations. He walks back to his father, kneeling beside him. "Ready for the finishing touch, Dad?"

His father's eyes light up. "Go for it, son."

With a soft smile, Koa reaches up and places the star at the top of the tree, carefully adjusting it so it sits perfectly. When he steps back, the whole tree seems to glow even brighter. His dad watches with pride, his smile full of emotion, while Koa's mom gives his shoulders another gentle squeeze.

"Perfect," Koa's dad says softly.

And it really is.

"Koa tells me you like to bake! How about we head into the kitchen and whip up dessert together and leave these guys to catch up?" Koa's mom asks, her eyes sparkling with warmth.

My eyes light up at the invitation, a little thrill running through me at the thought of spending time with her doing something I love. "I'd love that," I reply, following her into the kitchen.

As soon as we step inside, I'm in awe. The kitchen is spacious, with warm wooden cabinets lining the walls and a large island in the centre. The countertops are polished granite, and the air smells faintly of coffee and coconut. A set of open windows lets in a soft breeze, carrying the scent of the ocean and the distant hum of waves. It's cozy and homey, with a lived-in feel that immediately puts me at ease.

"What were you thinking of making for dessert?" I ask, excitement bubbling up inside me.

She taps her chin thoughtfully, a playful glint in her eye. "Hmm, what's your favourite Christmas dessert?"

I think for a moment, recalling the recipes I used to make during the holidays. "I haven't made them in a while, but I used to love making chocolate cupcakes with peppermint frosting," I offer, almost shyly.

Her face lights up as if I've just suggested something extravagant. "That sounds absolutely delicious! Let's make that."

Her enthusiasm makes me grin, and soon enough we're pulling out ingredients from the cabinets, setting everything up on the island. The kitchen fills with the sounds of mixing bowls and laughter as we chat and work side by side, quickly falling into an easy rhythm.

We spend the next thirty minutes prepping the dessert together, carefully measuring out cocoa powder, sugar, and flour, whisking it all into a rich batter, Koa's mom stirs the chocolate mixture with graceful familiarity.

"You know, Koa was always so passionate about surfing," she says, her voice softening with nostalgia. "From the moment he could walk, that boy was drawn to the ocean. It became his whole world. I swear, he spent more time in the water than on land. It was clear early on that it wasn't just a hobby for him—it was everything."

I smile at the thought, imagining a young Koa with that same determined glint in his eye, probably the tiniest surfboard tucked under his arm. "I wish I could see what he looked like back then."

"I'll sneak you some pictures when he's not looking." She laughs as she wipes her hands on a towel. "Sending him off to The Saltwater Shredders was one of the hardest things I've ever done. We're such a tight-knit family. My sisters, their kids, they come by almost every day. It almost feels like we all live here together in this house. And the idea of not having Koa around, not seeing him at the dinner table every night, it broke me."

I glance over at her, seeing the quiet pain in her expression as she remembers those days. I feel a wave of guilt knowing that his time with The Shredders is what kept him away from her. From here.

"But," she continues, her voice lifting with a smile, "when I heard how much he was loving it there...because of you, Maliah...I knew I made the right decision for him. He speaks about you a lot, you know. I can hear how happy he is in his voice."

My heart skips at her words. I never thought Koa had talked about me with his mom, and hearing it now sends a warm rush through my chest. "He does?" I ask quietly, almost not believing it.

"Oh, he does," she says with a knowing smile, setting the cupcakes into the oven. "He always said you kept him grounded, kept him focused on what really mattered. It was like he'd found someone who finally understood him, in a way none of us ever could."

I swallow the lump forming in my throat, overwhelmed by the unexpected compliment. "I didn't know he felt that way," I say, my voice thick with emotion.

Koa's mom smiles warmly at me, reaching over to give my hand a gentle squeeze. "He always has, and he still does."

Koa walks into the kitchen, leaning against the doorframe with a soft smile. "Hey, do you mind if I steal Maliah for a bit?" His voice is casual, but there's something in the way he looks at his mom that catches my attention.

His mom shares a quick, almost secretive glance with him, but it's gone as quickly as it came, and I try not to overthink it.

"I can't," I argue lightly, pointing at the oven. "I still have to pipe the frosting onto these when they're out of the oven."

"Oh, it's alright, sweetheart," his mom says with a warm smile, waving her hand dismissively. "The cupcakes will need some time to cool before we can do that. You two go on, enjoy yourselves for a bit. I'll finish up dinner, and once they're ready to frost, we can come back and do it together."

I hesitate, glancing at Koa, who's now grinning at me like he knows something I don't. His mom gently ushers me out of the kitchen, her hand resting on my back, as if silently encouraging me to go. "Go, have some fun," she says softly, her tone full of kindness.

I nod, feeling a mix of curiosity and excitement bubbling up inside me as Koa leads me out of the kitchen and down the hall. "Where are we going?" I ask, glancing up at him.

"You'll see," he says, that mischievous smile still lingering on his lips as we head outside.

THIRTY-ONE

KOA | OAHU, HAWAII

IT'S SUNSET, the sky a mix of warm oranges and pinks that blend with the blue horizon, and I've finally managed to get Maliah out of the house without giving her too many hints about where we're headed. She's been asking questions the whole way, but I've just kept smiling, telling her to be patient. I lead her out back, and we follow a small, hidden pathway from my family's house up the hill. The smell of tropical flowers fills the air, and the evening breeze is soft and warm against our skin.

As we reach the top of the hill, the view opens up in front of us—the whole of Oahu spreads out below, the vibrant greens of the land meeting the deep blue ocean beyond. The sun dips low, casting a golden glow over everything. Maliah gasps, releasing my hand as she takes a step closer to the edge of the overlook.

"This is amazing," she breathes, completely awestruck.

I can't stop staring at her. The way the sunlight touches her face, making her blonde hair shimmer like gold, and the soft, peaceful expression settling on her features—it's as if she's part of the view itself. Her eyes are wide, sparkling with the fading light of the day, and her lips part slightly in awe. She's beautiful —no, stunning—beyond words, and I feel my chest tighten with the sheer force of how much I love her.

I take a deep breath, feeling the weight of the small box in my pocket. My heart races as I pull it out, the velvet edges familiar under my fingers. My hands tremble slightly as I drop down to one knee behind her, waiting for her to turn around.

"Maliah," I call out softly, just enough for her to hear.

She turns slowly, and the moment she sees me kneeling, her eyes widen and a gasp escapes from her lips. Tears fill her eyes instantly, and she presses her hand to her mouth, completely speechless.

I smile up at her, my heart full. "I've been waiting for the right moment to do this...and standing here with you, in this place, it feels right."

Her tears spill over, and she wipes at them, still staring at me in disbelief.

"Maliah, you've changed my life. You've been my light, my best friend, and the love I didn't even know I needed. And I'm so grateful that you're here, with me, sharing the things we love, doing this crazy life together."

I glance down at the ring in my hand—a pearl and a diamond sharing a white gold band. It glimmers in the light, as perfect as she is. "I had this ring made for you a couple of years ago, when I realized I couldn't imagine my life without you in it. I know it's not much, but it's a piece of me, of us, and I hope...I hope you'll accept it, and me. Maliah Cooper, will you marry me?"

Her breath hitches as she starts to sob, nodding rapidly before I even finish my sentence. She holds out her hand, her fingers trembling.

"Yes," she whispers, her voice barely there through the emotion.

I can barely believe it as I slide the ring onto her finger, and it's a perfect fit. My heart feels like it's going to explode, a mix of elation, relief, and pure love. I rise to my feet, pulling her into my arms as she continues to cry, burying her face in my chest. I hold her tight, pressing my lips to her hair, feeling like the luckiest guy on the planet.

She's mine. She's finally mine. And I'll spend the rest of my life making sure she knows just how much she means to me.

Maliah is surrounded by my cousins, aunts, and parents, all of them gathered around her, admiring the ring on her finger. She's glowing, her face lit up with happiness as she holds her hand out, showing it off. Her laughter fills the room, blending with the excited voices of my family, and I can't help but smile. Seeing her like this, so accepted, so loved—It's everything I wanted.

My dad pats my arm from where he's sitting in his wheelchair beside me. "You did good, son," he says with a proud smile.

I nod, feeling a wave of emotion that I can't quite put into words. "Thanks, Dad."

My mom, tears in her eyes, steps forward to embrace Maliah, pulling her into a warm hug. "Welcome to the family, Maliah," she says, her voice thick with emotion. "And if you need any help at all with the wedding or dress shopping...I'd be ecstatic to help you plan. Anything you need."

Maliah smiles, her eyes shining with tears of her own. "Thank you," she whispers, looking so touched.

Dinner is lively, everyone around the table talking, laughing, and eating like there's no tomorrow. The scent of roasted turkey, glazed ham, and all the side dishes fills the air. I watch

Maliah throughout, the way she fits right in, talking with my cousins, laughing with my aunts, and sneaking glances at me from across the table.

After dinner, Maliah and my mom sneak off to the kitchen to finish icing the cupcakes. I know they're probably sharing stories again and getting to know each other better, and it makes me feel so damn lucky that the two most important women in my life get along so well.

A little while later, Maliah comes back into the living room, holding a tray of cupcakes in her hands. She's beaming as she sets them down on the coffee table, and everyone grabs one while we start opening presents. The tree is glowing with lights, the room filled with wrapping paper, gifts being passed around, and the sound of laughter as my cousins open their presents.

Maliah suddenly walks over to me, a small box in her hands. She gives me a sheepish smile. "I know we said no gifts because there's not much space left in our luggage, but this is something you won't have to pack."

Curious, I take the box from her, pulling off the ribbon and lifting the lid. Inside is a handmade bracelet, black beads with a couple of white ones spelling out M and K. I glance at her, confused for a second, until she holds out her wrist, showing me she's wearing a matching bracelet, except hers is pink instead of black.

"M and K?" I ask, feeling my heart swell.

"Maliah and Koa," she says softly, her voice filled with so much love. "Just, Maliah and Koa."

A huge smile spreads across my face, and I know this is the best gift I've ever gotten in my life. I slide the bracelet onto my wrist, feeling the weight of it, not just physically but emotionally too. I pull her into my arms, pressing a kiss to her lips, and of course my younger cousins immediately start making gagging sounds.

"Ewww," one of them says loudly, earning a smack in the

back of the head by Kelani, which only makes Maliah laugh as she kisses me again, softer this time.

This is perfect. This moment, this night—it's everything.

THIRTY-TWO

MALIAH | OAHU, HAWAII

THE WAVES at Pipeline are massive today, bigger than I've ever seen. Each one is a towering wall of water, crashing down with the power that makes the ground tremble beneath my feet. Even Koa, who usually looks calm and collected no matter what, has a hint of worry in his eyes. I glance over at him as he preps his board, watching him steady his breath. He gives me a small, encouraging smile.

He goes first, paddling out with smooth, powerful strokes. My heart is pounding as I watch him navigate the monster waves, catching a perfect one and riding it with the kind of grace and skill that only Koa has. He maneuvers through the barrel, coming out the other side as the crowd roars with excitement. He scores enough points to put us in pending first place, but it's not over yet.

It's my turn now, and everything is on me. If I nail this, we'll lock in first place. If I mess up...we could lose it all.

I take a deep breath, reminding myself that I've worked too hard for this, for *us*. I can't let fear win. I think back to all the encouragement Koa has given me over the past few months, the way he pushed me to be better, to trust myself. Gabriel too, with his tough love and no-nonsense attitude, always knowing just what to say to get me fired up.

And now...Koa's family is here, on the beach, watching. Cheering me on. His mom, his dad, even his cousins. I can hear Kelani's voice in my head, telling me how he surfed Pipeline, how he owned it, and Makoa's words of advice on how to handle these massive waves. I think about how it felt when I first surfed here, the thrill, the fear, and how I overcame it.

I'm ready.

I grab my board and start paddling out, my muscles burning with each stroke, but I push through it. The ocean feels different today—angrier, more chaotic. But I focus on my breathing, staying calm, remembering everything I've learned.

As I sit out there, waiting for the right wave, I can feel the energy in the water. The power of the ocean, the roar of the crowd, the pressure of the competition—it's all crashing into me at once. But then, I see it. The perfect wave. It's massive, and it's coming right for me.

That's it.

I start paddling with everything I've got, my heart racing as I feel the pull of the wave behind me. And then I'm up. I'm on the wave, riding it, feeling the board under me feels like an extension of myself. I drop down the face of it, speeding through the water, the wind whipping through my hair.

The wave barrels, and I crouch low, tucking into it. The water curls over me, and for a second, everything goes silent. It's just me and the wave, the world fading away, and I'm completely in the moment. I can hear Koa's voice in my head, telling me I've got this, and I hold on tight as I shoot out of the barrel, the wave crashing behind me.

The roar of the crowd hits me like a wall, but all I can feel is the rush of adrenaline, the sheer joy of knowing I did it. I ride the wave all the way in, my heart pounding in my chest, and when I finally reach the shore, I'm grinning like crazy.

I turn back to Koa on the beach, and he's standing there, arms raised in triumph, the biggest smile on his face.

I did it.

We did it.

We're first.

THE TENSION IN THE AIR IS THICK, ELECTRIC EVEN, AS WE stand side by side, our hands locked together. My heart feels like it's about to leap out of my chest, and I know Koa must feel the same. We're both waiting, praying, for our names to be called. The crowd's energy is buzzing all around us, but I can barely hear it over the pounding of my own heartbeat.

I glance at Koa, and he's watching the stage, his jaw set in determination, though I can see that excitement in his eyes. Time seems to slow as the announcer builds the suspense, stretching out each second, making my nerves ricochet with every drawn-out pause.

Breathe, Maliah. Breathe.

"Our 2024 World Champions...Koa and Maliah!"

The sound of the crowd explodes, but it feels like the world narrows in on just us.

We did it.

I can't even react at first. The title we've dreamed of, worked so hard for—it's ours. Koa squeezes my hand, pulling me back to reality, and suddenly I'm laughing, tears welling up in my eyes. I can't stop smiling.

We actually did it.

As the noise swells around us, the next announcement hits like a shockwave.

"Along with the title, a prize of two-hundred thousand, to be split between the two."

My jaw drops. I stare at Koa, wide-eyed. Two hundred thousand dollars is enough to change everything. I knew there would be a cash prize, but I never expected it to be that much.

Koa, in his excitement, bends down and picks me up, throwing me over his shoulder as he holds the back of my thighs. I twist my body so I can see him as he grins at me with that infectious energy he always has.

"Hey, princess," he says softly, the warmth in his eyes making my heart flutter. "When the house is fixed up...will you move in with me?"

A giggle escapes me, shaking my head as a playful grin spreads across my face. "What makes you think *you're* getting that house? I have a bakery to open," I tease, my heart light.

Koa grins back, his eyes sparkling in that way that always makes me weak in the knees. "I guess we're still going to have that bidding war then, huh?"

I laugh, the sound coming out brighter than I expect, and shake my head. "How about...we just buy it together?"

There's a pause, but then that grin softens into something deeper, something more tender. He nods, giving my thighs a gentle squeeze.

"Together," he says, his voice low and full of promise before he parades me towards his family who have been cheering us on this whole time.

It feels like everything has come full circle.

For so long, it felt like I was below the barrel of life, sinking further into the weight of everything I had lost when Koa and I fell apart. I wasn't just heartbroken; I was fading. Fading into this nothingness that swallowed me whole.

It was like I'd forgotten how to breathe without him, without the love and fire we shared. Every day without him chipped away at me, leaving me feeling like a shell of who I used to be and just angry all the time.

But somehow, we found our way back to each other. It wasn't easy, not the fairytale story I had always planned for myself. It was messy and hard, with moments I thought I'd never recover from. Yet, coming back to him felt like breaking through the surface of drowning for so long. The world doesn't feel dark anymore—it's alive, vibrant, and more beautiful than I remember. And I can finally *feel* again.

Maybe that's why I was so scared of Pipeline; to experience that drowning feeling again.

I look down at the beautiful ring on my finger and I can't help but smile. I'm not just excited for what's ahead, I'm ready for it. For every sunrise we'll share in our new home, for every wave we'll ride, for every moment that makes us laugh or cry.

Whatever comes next, we'll face it together. And that, right there, is everything I've ever wanted. Everything I've ever needed.

Just us.

Just Koa and Maliah.

The End.

EPILOGUE

KOA | SALTWATER SPRINGS

MY HAMMER HITS the final nail in place. I step down the ladder, and watch Maliah's reaction as she stares at the wooden sign I just finished hanging over the front door of our newly renovated house: *Salty Sweets Bakery.* The letters curve softly, carved and painted in a way that makes them stand out, familiar yet new. She traces the edges with her eyes, her lips parting in a silent gasp, and when she turns to me, her eyes are glistening.

"Thank you," she says softly, her voice full of awe, and I feel her hands slide up to rest on my chest as she leans in and kisses me softly.

When she pulls back, she takes a deep breath, and looks around with a mixture of excitement and anxiety.

"Are you sure you're ready for this?" I ask her, genuinely wanting to make sure this is what she wants. "It's a big step, taking a break from The Saltwater Shredders."

Part of me can't help but worry that she's stepping away from the team just because I did, but I need to know this decision is hers.

She gives me a reassuring smile. "Surfing...it was always my father's dream for me. I used to think it was mine too, but maybe it's time I find out what my own dream looks like," she says, her gaze drifting back to the sign. "I want to try something new and see how it feels after a few months."

Her words are steady, but I can see the nervousness playing on her face. It means even more that she wants me here with her as her partner—not just in life, but in this new business venture, too.

I pause, glancing down, feeling a need to ask something else. "Have you heard from him?"

She shakes her head slowly. "No," she says. "And it's better this way, at least for now. There's a part of me that...that hates him for what he did."

I pull her close, rubbing her back as we stand together. "He'll come around."

As much as I dislike her father, I don't think he's a complete asshole. He'll realize what he did was wrong, and I know it's only a matter of time before he shows up, showering her with apology gifts.

We head inside together, grabbing the trays of Maliah's baked goods off the kitchen counter and making our way to the living room to settle on the couch, our sides pressed close. Tomorrow is the grand opening of her bakery, and she's planned a whole night of taste testing her menu while we binge SurfFlix episodes together.

She hits a button on the remote and the episode starts. I try to focus on it, but my eyes keep drifting to her, watching her laugh and cringe. She reaches for the remote and pauses the screen, freezing a shot of her talking to Charles with me in the background glaring at them.

"You looked so jealous whenever I was talking to him," she teases, her eyes glinting mischievously.

I grunt, remembering those moments too clearly. "Yeah, well, I should've punched him harder."

I shift, glancing down at her. This has been on my mind for a while now. "About that night he touched you," I start slowly, searching her face. "I know you didn't want to risk us getting kicked off by saying anything then, but now that the tour's done, are you sure you don't want to press charges?"

She shakes her head, sighing, her expression going soft but resolute. "I don't want to go there, Koa. He'll get what's coming to him one day."

I nod, respecting her choice. If she wants to move past it, then I'll make sure that's what happens. I brush her cheek with my thumb before I pick up a pastry she made earlier today, some kind of rich chocolate tart.

"This one's dangerous," I say as I take a big bite and groan in exaggerated bliss. "Pretty sure people will keep coming back for these."

She laughs before picking up something that looks like a mini pie and taking a bite, closing her eyes on a sigh as she chews away. There's a bit of whipped cream on her lip and I can't help but lean forward and lick it off. I watch her cheeks instantly redden and her eyes open wide.

"I love that I can still get these reactions out of you," I say in a low voice, feeling my pants tighten. "I really love it."

She smiles shyly before shoving the rest of the pie in my mouth and hitting play on the TV again. By the time we finish the tray of pastries and reach the last episode, Maliah's groaned at every dark outfit I've worn on screen, which is pretty much every single episode.

"We're fixing your wardrobe as soon as the grand opening is over tomorrow," she declares, shooting me a look.

I laugh, pulling her closer to me and pressing a kiss to her forehead. "That's fine with me. I have no reason to wear black anymore."

She grins up at me, and I take her lips in a kiss, feeling that same spark we've always had. It deepens, growing more intense, until nothing else exists except her. I lower her onto the couch, hovering above her as I slowly pull down her shorts while she unbuttons mine. I slide her thong down her smooth legs and burry myself inside of her for the fourth time today.

TODAY IS THE GRAND OPENING OF THE BAKERY. ALMOST EVERYONE in Saltwater Springs has shown up, thanks to Eliana's relentless social media blitz. There's a line leading up to the pickup window and Maliah is behind it, handing out orders with the happiest smile I've ever seen on her face. This is her dream come true.

Out of the corner of my eye, I spot Griffin making his way towards me. I feel the tension in the air as he comes to stop next to me; things have been weird ever since Maliah and I decided to take a break from the team. He didn't take the news too well, especially with Gabriel, Zalea, and Zale off the radar lately.

"Any news?" I ask him as he crosses his arms and watches the crowd.

Griffin nods. "Yeah, all three flew to Hawaii last night but Zale should be back in two weeks."

"What about Gabriel?"

Griffin hesitates before turning to look at me. "Gabriel wants me to step up and lead the team until he returns. He asked me to pretty much rebuild it from scratch."

I nod, feeling a strange mix of pride and sadness for the team we built. The Shredders are in good hands with Fin, that's for sure, but it feels like the end of an era.

"If anyone can do it, Fin, it's you."

He sighs before turning his attention to Eliana. "I sure hope so."

As we watch Colton work the crowd alongside Eliana, and Kairi heads inside to help Maliah, a few fans approach, holding out their phones and asking for pictures. I'm used to it by now. It was definitely a shock at first, normally fans only want pictures with Griffin but ever since SurfFlix aired, I've had my fair share of obsessed fangirls.

I look over their heads toward Maliah and notice that she's watching me with an expression I can only describe as jealous amusement. She tries to hide it, but I catch that little flash in her eyes. I chuckle to myself and pose for a few quick photos, making a mental note to tease her about it later the way she'd teased me about Charles.

Once the fans move on, Griffin rejoins me, a warm smile on his face. "So, any progress on the wedding planning?"

"Yeah," I tell him. "We're heading to Hawaii at the end of the month. We're going to start planning it with my family—should be an experience, to say the least."

He laughs, nodding knowingly. "Same here. Eliana's got everything scheduled down to the hour for next year." He grins. "Invitations are going out soon, so you two better keep your calendar open."

"Wouldn't miss it," I reply.

Griffin claps me on the shoulder, his gaze steady. "I'm really happy you two worked out all the bullshit. It better stay that way," he says with a smirk. Then he adds, "And hey, if you both ever decide you want back on the team, there will always be a spot for you. No questions asked."

I nod, appreciating his words more than I can say. We share a quick handshake before he heads off to help the others. I glance over to see Maliah walking toward me, slipping her hand into mine as she watches the crowd and the bustling bakery. Her eyes sparkle, full of excitement and warmth as she leans into me.

I take a deep breath, feeling gratitude settle over me. Not

too long ago, it felt like I'd lost her for good, like everything I'd wanted was slipping right through my hands. But now? Now I've been given this second chance. She's here, we're here, together, and I know in my bones I'm never letting anything, or anyone come between us again.

This is our beginning, and I wouldn't trade it for the world.

AUTHOR'S NOTE

Hi there, lovely reader!

Thank you so much for diving into Koa and Maliah's story. It means the world to me that you're here, and if you enjoyed the journey, it would mean even more if you could leave a quick review or rating online.

This story is personal to me, sharing that intense, messy, young love—the kind where you sometimes have to hurt yourself to protect someone else (or yourself). But it's also about the incredible beauty of second chances and how love can come back stronger and wiser.

Second chances aren't easy, but wow, when things finally go right, it's like magic.

Thank you to my husband for being my muse for every sweet, falling-in-love scene in this book. I can't wait for our next zipline adventure—I promise to scream even louder this time. ;]

Huge thanks to Chelsea for tackling the first draft with such enthusiasm and eye-opening feedback. Your support blows my mind and keeps me going!

And a shoutout to my editor, Ramona Mihai, who jumped

through hoops to help bring this book to life, even with such a tight schedule. Your encouragement means everything.

Lastly, to all my readers—thank you for sharing your excitement on social media, in my DMs, and through your reviews. You make this all so worth it!

ALSO BY TANISHA HEADLEY

Saltwater Springs Series

Beyond the Break (Griffin and Eliana)

Below the Barrel (Koa and Maliah)

ABOUT THE AUTHOR

Tanisha Headley is a Canadian author, and a fresh voice in the world of romance fiction. Tanisha brings to life relatable and flawed characters, heartfelt angst, and laugh-out-loud banter while exploring the steamy corners of romance.

Residing in the beautiful landscapes of Alberta, Canada, Tanisha shares her life with her husband, son, and a four-legged adventure buddy. When she's not immersed in writing swoon-worthy stories, you can find her exploring the scenic mountains and charming small towns with her family, seeking inspiration in the beauty of her surroundings. An expert of the perfect chai tea latte, Tanisha is always on the lookout for new and delightful coffee shops.

Connect with Tanisha on social media **@authortanisha-headley** for updates, behind-the-scenes glimpses, and more. For a complete list of her books and more, visit **tanisha-headley.com.**